CRITICAL ACCLAIM
FOR

A Fragile Peace

"This powerful novel about alcoholism makes the finest wine taste bitter. Jonellen Heckler says she wrote from firsthand experience as the daughter of an alcoholic. But she adds, 'What I wrote was not my story, but a universal story.' "

—*United Press International*

"*A FRAGILE PEACE* is as current as the headlines, but Jonellen Heckler brings these characters to life in a way that no news story can . . ."

—*Newsday*

"Searing . . . It is impossible not to be moved by the pathetic, all-too-real story that Heckler relates."

—*Publishers Weekly*

"Heckler describes the Stockton household with insight and sympathy . . . *A FRAGILE PEACE* is a realistic account of a family illness . . ."

—*San Diego Union*

"Astonishing . . . A deceptively simple story that actually is a *tour de force* . . ."

—*Grand Rapids Press*

A Fragile Peace

Jonellen Heckler

PUBLISHED BY POCKET BOOKS NEW YORK

POCKET BOOKS, a division of Simon & Schuster, Inc.
1230 Avenue of the Americas, New York, N.Y. 10020

Copyright © 1986 by Jonellen Heckler
Cover photograph copyright © 1987 Mort Engel Studio

Published by arrangement with G. P. Putnam's Sons,
a division of The Putnam Publishing Group
Library of Congress Catalog Card Number: 85-19181

ISBN: 0-671-63389-9

First Pocket Books printing July 1987

10 9 8 7 6 5 4 3 2 1

POCKET and colophon are registered trademarks
of Simon & Schuster, Inc.

Printed in the U.S.A.

For
the children of
alcoholics

I hear my father; I need never fear.

I hear my mother; I shall never be lonely, or want for love.

When I am hungry it is they who provide for me; when I am in dismay, it is they who fill me with comfort.

When I am astonished or bewildered, it is they who make the weak ground firm beneath my soul: it is in them that I put my trust.

When I am sick it is they who send for the doctor; when I am well and happy, it is in their eyes that I know best that I am loved; and it is towards the shining of their smiles that I lift up my heart and in their laughter that I know my best delight.

I hear my father and my mother and they are my giants, my king and my queen, beside whom there are no others so wise or worthy or honorable or brave or beautiful in this world.

I need never fear: nor ever shall I lack for loving kindness.

—*James Agee*

A Fragile Peace

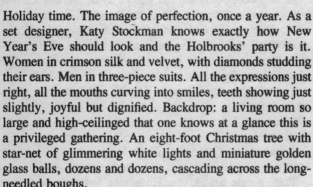

1

Holiday time. The image of perfection, once a year. As a set designer, Katy Stockman knows exactly how New Year's Eve should look and the Holbrooks' party is it. Women in crimson silk and velvet, with diamonds studding their ears. Men in three-piece suits. All the expressions just right, all the mouths curving into smiles, teeth showing just slightly, joyful but dignified. Backdrop: a living room so large and high-ceilinged that one knows at a glance this is a privileged gathering. An eight-foot Christmas tree with star-net of glimmering white lights and miniature golden glass balls, dozens and dozens, cascading across the long-needled boughs.

She scans faces, pausing three times, once for her husband and once for each of her children. An elegant illusion, models for a Vogue photograph: Mike of the copious hair and tennis build; Lee resplendent in white satin, the V neckline flattering to her budding figure; her son Rick, for once stuffed into a neatly pressed suit.

She has always loved things that are pleasing to the eye, delighted in her ability to create an artistically unified scene: set, costume and prop. She remembers the absorbing satisfaction of paper dolls, a childhood spent clipping wardrobes and planning make-believe events: horseback riding, trips to France. But then she could play all the parts, decide what each doll would wear and say. She has no control now. She can dress them up, but she cannot make them do what she wants.

Tina Holbrook floats through the din to hand Katy a glass of champagne and plunk down beside her in a puff of pink taffeta. "Happy New Year!"

Katy pecks her on the cheek. "Your party is fabulous."

"Oh, it was nothing," Tina says, crossing her eyes.

"Just a little something you whipped up?"

"Right."

In the two months she has known Tina, she has learned how to laugh. Tina is a public princess and a private cartoon, flipping her tablecloth to the clean side for a few more days' wear, tearing page after page out of a paperback book as she reads it, advocating nylon panties as the ideal shower cap.

Tina tilts her head close to Katy's. "Want to hear some juicy gossip?"

"You bet."

"I'm pregnant."

A miracle. Katy touches Tina's hand.

"Can you believe it, after nine years?"

They glance toward the Holbrooks' adopted one-year-old, Nathan, who is kneeling beside the Christmas tree, pounding on a toy xylophone. An angel. Porcelain skin and russet feather-down hair.

"When are you due?"

"August."

In her peripheral vision, Katy catches the motion of her husband turning to stare at the tree. He has been standing on the other side of it, sipping a drink and talking with two men. Now he steps back from it, his eyes registering disbelief. His chin tips sharply upward; his drink begins to spill onto the white carpet. She strains to see what he is watching, but there is nothing in front of him except the winking lights and glittering glass.

Damn. What the—? Mike can feel icy liquid on his fingers as the tree lurches toward him. Can't be. No way. Shit! It *is*, the whole thing is coming down on him. He blocks it with his forearm, shattering several ornaments, feeling pine needles gouge his face. Lights sear his hands and neck as he struggles with its shifting weight. Why isn't someone helping him?

What is he doing? Katy jolts to her feet. He has flung himself at the tree, its metal base springing suddenly from beneath a spangled sheet, turning over the animals and figures of a wooden crèche. She silently wills him to stop, but he and the tree are slamming sideways, raining ornaments down on Nathan. The little boy peers up, astonished, as a fog of gilded fragments begins to slice his flesh and groaning branches engulf him.

Katy collides with Evan Holbrook; the room is alive with cries. Evan jerks Mike from his half-leaning, half-kneeling position and rolls him onto the floor; she can see that he is all right. Breathless, she pulls at sticky twigs, vines of wires. The tree settles, moving under her like an ocean wave. As many hands lift it, Nathan's screams assault her with the force of physical blows. His head! A mass of cuts, blood running into his eyes. Or *from* his eyes?

Tina snatches him up. "Get my purse!"

Katy reaches out for Tina. "Let me drive. I'll take you."

Tina looks at her with chilling resentment. "No."

"Come on!" Evan's mother emerges from the bedroom, carrying car keys and a blanket.

"Let me go with you," Katy begs.

"No, no!"

Evan takes the child from Tina, wrapping him in the blanket. Her cheeks and pale pink blouse are caked with blood. She turns away from Katy.

"I can't understand why they didn't want us to go with them," Mike whispers in the darkness.

Katy keeps her eyes on the road, concentrating on mechanical things, trying not to feel. She aims the headlights between the yellow lines, slows and turns with precision, holds the car at an even 30 mph as she guides it along the palm-lined street.

"I didn't know he was there," Mike says, his voice cracking. "The tree was coming down on me. It was a reflex."

In the rearview mirror, she can see the silhouettes of her children as they gaze out the windows. Shadows hide their faces.

Mike bends forward, resting his head against the dash, his fingers covering his eyes. She wheels the car gingerly into the circular driveway of their home and sets the emergency brake.

"I feel sick." Mike opens his door; the ceiling light blinks on.

Now she can see clearly. Rick's face is a mask of disgust. "Come and help your dad," she says, speaking into the mirror.

Rick does not move.

"Rick."

He leaves the car and goes to Mike. "Here," he says as he closes his arm around his father's waist.

Katy and Lee walk ahead of them, unlocking the dead bolt, propping the door open, putting on lamps.

4

"I just want to lie on the sofa," Mike protests as Rick tries to steer him toward the bedroom.

Katy blocks the way. "No. Rick, take him in there."

She follows them, pulls back the covers on the king-size bed and helps to lower Mike onto the white-eyelet-trimmed sheets. He seems to be asleep before she lifts his feet.

Rick's unchanging expression angers her. Seventeen, and no empathy. Contempt, barely disguised, resides like a stone in him. Every day.

So the man drinks too much. Sometimes. So what? So do a lot of people who are plagued to death by circumstances. Grow up.

"We need to get his shoes off," she directs. "Lord, he's in his best suit, too." She considers the financial consequence of leaving him in it.

Rick crosses his arms, waiting. He will do only what she tells him and no more. Lee picks at the laces, gently slides the shoes from her father's feet. They strip Mike to his underwear, Lee on one side of her, Rick on the other. As her children work, Katy perceives their auras almost as degrees of temperature. That measurable. Or hues: Lee's a comforting deep purple; Rick's white, nearly transparent.

She pulls the blanket up across Mike's chest, places her fingertips lightly on his forehead.

"It wasn't falling over," Rick says.

"Be quiet," she snaps.

The moon is a milky eye, hunting for them through the tight weave of the drapery. Katy puts a protective arm across Mike's waist. He is sleeping on his back, head far to one side, arms outstretched in a pose of abandon, as though someone had thrown him there. She is congested from crying, the tears dried into tight grainy patches at her temples.

It cannot *all* be his fault. Can any of it be his fault? A

good and loyal man. A man besieged by childhood haunt-
ings and by corporate struggles. If he is weak now, she
must be strong, fighting for him as he would do for her,
their marriage of eighteen years a strong roof over them.

Images of him come to her. They are more than visual;
they have voices and hands. *She and Mike, lying on a hot
Atlantic beach, enchanted by the newness of their love. A
high cloud, spun like gray lace, drifts across them, dragging with it ominous chill. The bright mosaic of bikinis and
hairy chests, umbrellas, blankets, coolers, lawn chairs,
plastic buckets and Frisbees unglues itself, the pieces sliding away from the center: the old climbing-rose bedspread
on which she and Mike float. They are alone. Hail begins,
a deluge of heavy stones, pelting their legs and backs. They
pull the flowers up over them, a fabric trellis through which
chill rain begins to leak and then flow as the tumult increases. They are immensely pleasured. They open their
mouths and drink.*

Canopied spaces . . . quiet secret sharing . . .

*Mike with Rick—a winsome three-year-old. They are
snoring in a sheet-and-card-table tent on the living room
rug, Mike's feet sticking out. How did he ever last the
night? She stretches onto her stomach to have a look. Inside, Rick is curled against Mike's ribs, the peach dawn-
glow of the sheet illuminating their contented faces. There
is a vague, untraceable scent of clover.*

She moves close to Mike in the moonlight, seeking his
curves with her own. She, with patience, can soothe the
trouble away. Patience. And shelter. A trellis of roses. She
will nurture him back to the man he used to be.

2

Tina answers Katy's knock, carrying Nathan. His bandages startle, sicken Katy: yards and yards of gauze, cocoonlike, around his head and veiling one eye. Tina's hair is tousled, the skin of her face drawn into austere vertical lines. She waits for Katy to speak.

"I've been trying to call you most of the night. You must have had your phone off the hook. How is he?"

Tina noticeably bristles. "We're not sure about one of his eyes."

God. "I'm really, really sorry. Is there anything I can do?"

"No."

The morning sun begins to burn her skin as though trained on her through a magnifying glass. She is suddenly aware of not being invited inside. The end. She has seen it before, many times. "Tina, Mike and I both feel so bad about this. He just couldn't come. He's a wreck."

"Yes, he is."

She stiffens. "What can I do?"

"Nothing."

"We'll pay all the bills. Of course."

"We have insurance."

7

Impassive, resolute. Katy will never forget this face.

"Do you want to sue us? Is that what you're thinking?"

"No."

"But you don't want to . . . continue. Right?"

Tina remains silent. She studies Katy sadly, then steps behind the door and gently closes it.

Mike awakens to the sound of ice cubes being dropped into soda water, one at a time, a long interval between each splash, the usual fear clawing the back of his throat, eating at the front of his brain. He believes it is the fear that brings him to consciousness every morning—a chemical thing, shooting through him when it reaches overflow. He cannot remember waking up any other way.

He pushes the covers back, rolls himself to a sitting position, legs over the side of the bed. His underwear is soaked with perspiration. He listens. The sound is coming from the swimming pool at the rear of the house. The fear subsides a little, rippling through him like a mild electric shock.

He can beat it.

He walks purposefully into the bathroom, stripping off his underclothes and stuffing them into the wicker hamper. In the shower, he runs water over his throbbing head; at six feet plus, he can stand under the shower nozzle and feel the hot beads directly massage his scalp.

Two puzzling reddish marks on his hands sting in the spray; he imagines he can feel the same tender spots along his jaw. He lathers, rinses, stops the water to towel off.

His bathing suit is hanging at the back of the bathroom door. He puts it on before the steamy mirror.

Now he can see: there is another mark on the side of his neck. He stares at it, avoiding his own eyes.

* * *

"Lee!"

She hears her father call to her as she makes her descent, parting the cool aqua water with her outstretched hands. Bubbles drift from her mouth, her fingertips brush the bottom of the pool. She will wait as long as she can before coming up. It is safe here: soundless, solitary. She has been practicing her backflip for forty minutes, teaching herself exact alignment of spine and toes, dizzying herself with the pleasure of her own motion. The hum of water in her ears moves to increasingly higher pitches as she floats slowly upward.

Her first glimpse of him tells her everything. Trouble. He is disoriented, agitated; she will have to be careful.

"Lee," he says solemnly, "did you know that your head is only missing the board by an inch or so?"

Wrong. She knows distance. But something in him perpetually sees her in danger. She is always too close to the curb or the bonfire, or the edge of the diving board.

She climbs out and takes the fresh towel he offers; they go to sit at a small wrought-iron table. She begins to dry her hair in short, swift strokes.

"Did you know that, honey?"

"No."

"A boy in our high school got paralyzed that way."

She can see the memory moving behind his eyes, scaring him. Whatever can happen to change a person's life or end it, he has known one of each. A girl who got killed on a bike. A boy who died from a baseball hitting the back of his ear as he rounded third.

"You shouldn't be swimming by yourself anyway." His mouth is an O, a silent cry.

"All right." The intensity of his fear never fails to affect her; his very presence floods her with anxiety.

"Where's mother?" he asks.

She regards him closely, the sunny, graying hair, the inexplicably darker hairs of his chest, sprinkled with silver.

9

In this light, at this time of day, he appears earnest—almost boyish. His cheeks are scrubbed shiny; his blue eyes, wide, intent, wait for her answer.

She cannot figure out what he remembers and what he doesn't remember. He asks her the obvious and the obscure in the same tone. Is he constantly testing her?

"Lee?"

"She'll be back in a few minutes." *He couldn't have forgotten about Nathan.* She has spent much of the night reliving the blurred descent of the tree amid flying shards, the jagged ripping of the baby's scalp.

He should stop. Stop drinking. Surely he will now. Her father's pretense at normalcy the morning after an incident puzzles and insults her. Still, it would be worse to speak of such things; the emotional upheaval is impossible to contemplate.

She shifts, studying the brown mountains that tower behind a veil of haze. She hadn't understood at first that it was smog, the reason her lungs hurt when she took a deep breath. A strange place, Los Angeles, desolate in its vastness. She longs for the year to be over so they can go on to the next city.

"I'm going to take you out to lunch for your birthday, okay? Fourteen's special."

A game: *Don't talk about anything meaningful. Play along.* She nods.

He smiles at last.

She should feed him, make him eat. His appearance disturbs her: the whites of the eyes a pale yellow, slashes of yellow under the lower lids. "I baked a coffee cake. Want a piece?"

"No, thanks."

She is afraid to let him go. He will begin the day's drinking. Or has he already begun? "Come swim with me, Dad."

He stares at the glinting pool, then at her. "I'm too tired," he says. Hauling himself up from the chair, he walks inside.

She clenches her eyelids against the fiery glare, a toddler who has sleepily wandered from the blackness of her room out into the crashing conversation and harsh electric light of a party. She cannot find her parents in the forest of trousers and skirts, but she knows they will find her. Twitters of delight stir in her path; a man stoops down with cheese on a cracker, a woman's long, hard fingernails stroke her hair. She waits, groggy but certain. Her father slips his thumbs under her arms and lifts her up, up. She settles against his neck, already half asleep again. She does not need to look; she knows the shape of his bones, the contour of the hammock he makes with his hands. He is hers. Solid as earth. Father. He belongs to her. And now she is aware of music because he begins to dance. Slowly, slowly. A happy motion. The great heart of him is happy. She rests against that happiness, lulled, her cheek sliding to and fro on the slope of his shoulder.

He leaves Joey Dillon's house on his bike, stupid bike. Seventeen and no driver's license. How far can he go? But that's the point, isn't it? Keep tabs on this boy, cut his radius. He wonders just how far he could get before dark; the thought makes him pedal faster.

Joey and his dad come by, tooting, on their way to the Rose Bowl, Joey driving the tan Audi. *Have fun, damn you.*

The day stretches out in front of him, each hour empty and wide.

Legs aching, he takes a more rhythmic pace, peering at windows. Southern California: a movie set, unreal. Boxy pastel stucco houses jammed against blue-blue sky and mock Astroturf—the cloverlike dichondra that never fades and obligingly stops growing in winter. Lampposts like he used to have with his electric train set. Fairy-tale trees sagging with fat lemons and oranges. Brilliant colors, precise greenery. He has not seen this before. Not in Kansas City, not in Chicago, not in St. Louis. Everything manicured. *Put the camellias right there, and here. And here. Turn the blossoms streetward.* Some producer has arranged it, measured the distance between shrubs. He gets the eerie feeling that the houses are three-sided fronts with no people in them. Night is better. He can watch the mothers moving behind the sheers, setting food on the table for children clustered at flickering televisions.

So, what to do? Holidays are the pits. Nobody wants to see him. The grandmothers and grandfathers are visiting, their sleek cars hogging the driveways, everybody looking so cheerful. Busy. They pause when they come to the front screen. *Why isn't he home?* It is written on their foreheads. *A holiday, for heaven's sake.* They offer him a drink and a cookie, wait for him to go. They are saving their jokes for family. He bumps along the uncomfortable wall of their silence, trying to find his way out. Thanks for the Pepsi, have a nice day.

Little fingers of hunger press at his stomach. Noon sun sends trickles of perspiration through his hair. He rides.

Mike lies on his son's bed, staring at the popcorn ceiling.

The kid never comes home. Why is that? A nice room like this and he only sleeps in it.

He scans the bare walls for signs of life. Does he live here or not? You'd think he'd have a poster or a photograph of somebody or a ribbon or medal. But he never wins anything—not like Lee who has more awards than wall space. This guy is so closed down he doesn't leave anything on the dresser top.

12

And pretty soon he'll go away, and where are the memories then?

His little boy.

He wasn't one of those fathers who wouldn't rock a boy. No, they'd rock. Why not? For hours. Toast fireplace marshmallows soggy on sticks. Play hide-and-seek; he made himself into a hulk of a fool, stuffing himself behind curtains and into dusty closets, all for a child's laughter. Precious, precious. Where did he go, that boy?

Sons are supposed to be baseball and man-to-man chats. Building things together. Sons are camping trips, and a slap on the shoulder. Not this one, his child but not a son. He brings nothing to share. No sports, no academic triumphs. He does nothing. He is just there.

What does he think about? Does he rattle around in the space of his life? Or are there all kinds of things jammed into a secret drawer? Even his words are sparse. He neither laughs nor cries. Gifts are opened with a curt thank-you, bad news received with visible detachment.

I work my ass off and it's all the same bowl of oatmeal to him, something to choke down. Mike stands up slowly. *Does he think he's better than the rest of us? Is that it? What's wrong with a damned two-hundred-thousand-dollar house and a swimming pool?* He is shaking now, seized with the urge to grip his son's shoulder, back him into a chair. Rick is one big reason Why.

Dread begins to inch its way along the gray-red line of his fury. Vague. He senses that it is coming at him from the marks on his hand; he covers them with his other palm.

His wife's face is stern as she comes in from the garage. He has been waiting for her, sitting at the low counter in the kitchen. She places her purse on the telephone stand. The sorrow in her eyes frightens him. What has he done now? Jesus.

13

She fumbles in the cabinet for a glass, filling it with water from the tap and gulping it. "They don't know about one of his eyes. She doesn't want to be friends anymore."

He nods, somberly.

"What do you think we should do?" She puts the glass in the dishwasher. "I told her we'd pay the bills. I told her I was sorry. It didn't make any difference." He sees tears overtaking her. "You wouldn't hurt that baby for anything."

Baby. He runs through mental photographs of children they know. *What the hell happened?* His blood vessels are all dry. He is a leaf, brown and cracked, motionless.

How could he ever say it to her? *What did I do? I can't remember. Katy, help me. For God's sake. I feel crazy. Am I crazy?* She'd just get on him about the liquor, and it isn't that. It's not that at all.

She comes around the counter suddenly, throwing herself toward his chest, kneeling beside his chair. "I love you." The tone of her words is fierce.

Her hair smells of lilac. Putting his arms around her brings an avalanche of memories. But not the one he needs.

The master bathroom door locked, he lifts the top from the toilet tank. The bottle is still there, submerged. *Hello.* He forms the word silently like a prayer and sets the commode top on the carpet.

Lifting the dripping bottle, he examines the level of liquid. Less than half. He unscrews the lid and touches the opening to his lips, quickly tipping the bottle up, letting the whiskey fill his mouth. It burns sliding down, a river of fire.

He drinks as much as he dares. Just enough. He's not asking for indulgence. Some people get mind-bending drunk. He has more sense than that, than to get hooked. Mike Stockman, Phi Beta Kappa, M.A. in Public Relations, clothes by I. Magnin and Saks Fifth Avenue, knows better than to be a dumb-butt park-bench has-been.

The warmth snakes through him. He can picture it gliding from cell to cell, *wake up, shake loose*. Lord, how does anybody get moving without a little nudge? He recaps the bottle and slips it back into the tank; hefts the top and seats it squarely.

Whoops—breath. He searches through the medicine cabinet and under the vanity for mouthwash. There is none. He surveys the lineup of cosmetics, finally takes a swig of perfume and spits it into the sink.

Today is a beginning. New Year's resolutions, right? He'll start with hamburgers on the grill, everybody together. And no fatherly advice. He'll zip his lips when the kids talk. That's the best way in. Be a good listener.

He picks up his toothbrush and, squeezing paste onto it, begins a slow massage of his tongue. Strength is the seed in him now, ready to burst.

Nathan Holbrook.

What? He grips the edges of the sink, staring down into the limitless tunnel of the drain. A trembling begins in his ankles. He wipes his mouth with the hand towel and goes to sit on the commode lid, pressing the cloth hard against his teeth, trying to hold back the memory.

The scene whips toward him; he turns his face away from the evil tree, closing his eyes. He has the sensation of plunging backward through a bottomless shaft of air, a relentless hissing in his ears.

When it subsides, he sits for a long time watching a pattern of sunlight rearrange itself along the bathroom floor. Then, he stands with determination and lifts the top of the toilet tank again.

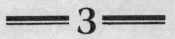

3

Lee checks the hue of Katy's skin with the cautious gaze of a physician. Is she getting too much sun? Her mother lies sleeping on a plastic lounge chair by the pool, dabs of pink beginning to bloom around her eyes, particularly just above her brow. Dragging the umbrella table over to create shade would make too much noise. Perhaps she could rig a beach towel between two chairs.

Her mother's face is unperturbed, serene as she dozes; her complexion has let go of all lines, the haven of sleep has filled them in with youthful smoothness. This is not her mother but someone younger, more carefree, a wax museum doll of her mother as a teenager: the coppery vital hair, the petal eyelids of palest plum, the pearly luminescent skin of the upper cheeks. Her lashes are tipped with gold. Beautiful.

Lee cannot decide to leave her. Or to disturb her. She knows her mother is exhausted from the accident. She stands strategically blocking the sun, casting a gray shadow across Katy's head and shoulders. Love has made Lee responsible for every outcome. Even a sunburn. At night before she goes to sleep, in the well of her tiredness, it seems to her that she is responsible for everyone. Sometimes she dreams of brackish water, of a dim scrub-grass swamp from which she retrieves her helpless family one by one, carrying them on her back. They slip heavily from her and she lifts them over and over, as she crawls toward morning.

A figure standing in the middle of the family room pulls her attention. She squints at the profile. Rick.

She moves toward him quietly; he waits without the slightest motion. Entering the shade, she sees the question in his gaze. *Where is Dad?* She indicates the closed door to the master bedroom. Rick's hair lies in wet dark curls that stream with perspiration, the droplets running freely down his neck and under his collar. He is ablaze with sun, silent and red-eyed. He has the bearing of a man who has been held under water.

They walk together into the kitchen and pull the pocket doors closed. She pours him a glass of milk and sets next to it the plastic-encased turkey sandwich she made for him earlier in the day; he peels it and hungrily eats. She watches him lean over the sink, chewing quickly, his eyes focused on the splash-board tile. Like a fugitive, she thinks. Restless, always ready to go. She cannot remember the last time he sat in an easy chair to read a book or lay on the living room couch.

His shirts are the right size but look too big. He slouches; the collar stands away from his neck, his chest caves in. He is hiding, down inside his clothes.

What flaw does her father see in Rick? Just that he won't try anymore? What a funny boy he was, rigging a quilt curtain across her bedroom door when she had the chicken pox and presenting a showtime of Rod Stewart impressions; furtively taking the mantel clock apart for her amazement, then putting it all back together perfectly; learning to juggle with onions. He had been a collector— of buttons and canceled stamps, of pop-tops and baseball cards. Until she began finding shoeboxes of his hobbies in the wastebaskets.

He could hate her. The contrast in their achievements is an anguish. But they are partners, sealed behind the same piece of glass.

A little rabbity thing, this sister. Shy, alert. She has the sixth sense of a wild creature; she knows what is in the wind. Rabbit pale: the long wispy hair and narrow face. Rabbit delicate: the tender fleshless bones that poke her clothing. She is gentle, friendly, increasingly mute. Their conspiracy used to have words. Now it is an instinctive charade.

He cannot look at her without thinking of Saturdays locked in the car: the two of them on rumbly streets or in secluded parking lots. They were allowed to keep the windows cracked just a little while their father went to the store; they would stick their noses up into the slit of breeze. Playing with her was hard. She couldn't add or subtract yet; he had to keep it all so simple, like bouncing her on his knees or telling stories or making up guessing games. She got tired sooner than he did and would cry or fall asleep. People went by, leaning down to stare with grave eyes, or waving and smiling. When people put their hands on the car, he became anxious. His father had warned him that some people intended bad things, and some people did not intend bad things but let them happen anyway. Rick would roll the windows up tight then, until the touchers went away. There was no clock, but he would count how many cars parked and drove away from a single spot. Or he would watch the building shadows slide along the sidewalk. Or he would keep track of people on a mission: boys who danced toward a park, dribbling basketballs, and returned with sweat-stained shirts. He became drowsy, but did not give in to it. What if, on waking, his sister was gone? He pressed the buttons on the radio, pretending to play it, imagining what he would be hearing on each of the stations. He knelt in the driver's seat, taking a make-believe tour of Canada. And then his father was back, startling him with the click of the lock. He'd have groceries—one bag—and complain how long it took him in the crowded line at the store. There would suddenly be a rank smell in the car like the damp spot that never dried on his back porch, up next to the brick of the house, a channel of greenish slipperiness that he did not go near.

He opens the fridge for more milk and finds Lee's handiwork: a platter of perfectly formed hamburger patties, a clay bowl heaped with potato salad and ringed with parsley. She reaches past him, into the hydrator, and extracts a bag of celery.

"I need to make a salad."

He helps her bring out and line up two slightly mushy tomatoes, a misshapen sweet pepper, carrots, a head of lettuce. "Do what?" he says.

"The carrots."

He roots through an overstuffed drawer past spoons and spatulas until he finds the peeler.

She is wrestling with the lettuce, digging her thumbs in, trying to part it into sections. Finally, she settles for unwrapping it leaf by leaf.

"I know an easy way," he offers. "I saw it on TV."

She hands the lettuce to him with a skeptical wrinkle of her nose.

"Have faith." He has seen the obese network gourmet neatly dissect a head of lettuce by striking its bottom firmly on a wooden board. He takes aim and gives it a good thump. Turning it over, he tries to twist the core.

"I like this. It's so much faster," she teases.

He lifts the lettuce chest high and closes one eye as he concentrates on the counter's edge.

"Don't . . ."

He slams the core decisively into its target; with a watery, ragged sound the head explodes, greenery flying in all directions. He is left holding air.

His sister reels backward against the refrigerator. He sputters, trying to get control over the hoot that is coming. He jams his hand against his mouth and laughs until he has to sit down on the floor. She shivers with muffled giggles, squatting beside him, gasping.

Thank God for a man's family! Mike looks around the dinner table at each of the three faces. His gaze rests on Lee, who is daintily picking at her potato salad, eyes downcast. She eats but never gains. He worries about that. Where does it go? Does her body use every calorie for her frantic tennis game? She is the school standout, gliding easily across the court, blocking some astonishing shots. It is her secret weapon, this dogged ability to keep volleys from going by—her racket always in the right spot, as though she would rather die than miss. Her serve and placement are nothing compared to her grinding defense.

"Here, star." He moves the potato salad bowl closer to her.

"No, thanks."

"Come on. We need to fatten you up."

"I'm full."

He stares down at his own plate of untouched food. Things haven't tasted right to him for months. He feels a lethargy slowly uncurl in him. No—not sleepy again. He's already had a nap. But no matter how much he sleeps, he feels tired. Bastards. Send him out here to the West Coast to jerk the office into shape and then roll a lot of barrels in his path. He sighs, contemplating the cold hamburger and warm potato salad. It will only upset his stomach to eat now.

Why isn't there any conversation around this table? They might as well not be together. Isn't this supposed to be a time of sharing? His wife seems so far away, sampling baked beans at the other end of the table. The table's too long anyway. He can barely see her. Her eyes are bright, feverish-looking, her forehead tinged with scarlet.

"What's the matter with your face, Katy?"

"I fell asleep on the patio."

"For how long?"

"A couple of hours, I guess."

A surge of anger surprises him, sending him off balance, stealing his breath. "Where the heck were the rest of you? Didn't you see your mother lying out there?"

Loud. Too loud. He knows that, but heat is splashing through him in bursts.

Lee glances up guiltily.

"What about it, girl?"

"I thought she was all right."

"All right? *Look* at her."

"I'm sorry."

"There's nothing to it," says Katy. "It doesn't even hurt."

He turns to Rick. "And where were you?"

"Riding my bike."

"I know that, but where? I thought you and I were going to watch the ball game."

"It was a nice day. I wanted to be out." Rick sets his fork beside his plate with a clunk. "Where were *you?*"

"Right here!" He straightens in his chair, suddenly fogged. Something begins to worm its way between his ears, a fuzzy ache with a static whisper to it.

Katy's food has taken on a square, indigestible shape in her stomach. Dinnertime seems to be the showdown of the day. Unless she can prevent it. She rises from her chair. "Chocolate pudding for dessert. How about it?"

"I want to know where this kid's been."

She sees the fury in Rick bubbling to the surface. Any minute it will be open warfare. "How many orders for chocolate pudding?"

"When I get an answer."

"I told you . . ."

"Where?"

"Part of the time I was at Joey Dillon's house."

"Why doesn't he come over here?"

If they would all jump up now . . . if they could just lay hands on Mike, pumping him through and through with their love like a faith healing . . . If. In her mind's eye she can see it, the benevolent radiance of their faces as they surround him, the stabbing joy of recognition as he receives them. He would fall down, straight back like they do at revival meetings, caught by strong arms and lowered to the ground. It would be the catharsis, the metamorphosis.

Love was the miracle. If only she could get them to heap it on him in large enough doses, it would remove the center of his doubt. He would be healed.

"I'll take some pudding," Lee says, touching her father's arm. "What about you?"

"I don't eat dessert," Mike answers.

"Rick?" Katy tries to give him visible encouragement, nodding.

"I don't think so."

"He'll have some," Mike says.

"No, thank you."

Mike's eyebrows lift to his hairline. "Your mother made it. You can damned well be polite enough to try it."

"Oh, gee . . ." Katy begins. "No one has to . . ."

"Are you contradicting me?" He swings the floodlight

22

of his attention to her, daring her, glowering. His mannerisms are so exaggerated at times like these that she does not recognize him: the demented wide-eyed glare, the way he stretches his torso up, up, like a cobra ready to strike. If it weren't so fearsome, it would be comical.

But she does not underestimate this mood. And neither do the children. Their chests draw back from him; they concentrate intently, waiting. He is never more than verbally abusive, but she can't be one hundred percent sure.

A tyranny. She is ashamed to let it go on in her home. But this devil is not her husband; her husband would be appalled at his behavior. If only Lee and Rick could understand, they wouldn't be so resentful.

"No one should be forced to—"

"No one should be forced to," he mimics her in a nasal whine.

Incensed, she wants to slap his face. But it is up to her to keep control of the situation, for the children's sake.

Mike scrapes his chair away from the table, menacingly, still scowling at her. A threat? She must get up, too. She mustn't let him think she is vulnerable. How can she diffuse this?

He points a finger at her. "You undermine me all the time."

Does she? Is that what she did? When one parent is directing a child, the other parent shouldn't interfere. But he was being unreasonable—wasn't he? Confused, she cannot think. She feels responsible for his lack of happiness, every minute of her life. She has done poorly as his partner. If she had done well, he wouldn't need to drink.

"Hey, listen. I'll try it, Mom. I changed my mind."

Mike smirks triumphantly. "He changed his mind, Mom."

"Okay." It's the best strategy after all: humor him. Eat the pudding or whatever. That way it's over sooner.

* * *

Rick lies on his bathroom carpet, staring at the night light. The room is a black tunnel with the light as his goal. From it flows wellness; he can be well if he concentrates on drawing forth its power. He has been nauseated for about an hour, hovering in the uncertain territory between feeling better and tossing his cookies. He should throw up and get it over with. He is stricken with abdominal pain from time to time, which gently eases off.

A cool, reassuring place to be, the floor. Nothing to fall from. He wishes for a pillow though. And a small glass of Coke with cracked ice. Yes.

Perhaps Lee will find him; he has left the adjoining door unlocked on her bedroom side. He estimates that it is four o'clock. She usually gets up once during the night. He could call to her. But he has heard his father prowling through the house for the past twenty minutes or so, clicking on lamps, sliding books in and out of the family room shelves, opening the doors to the pool area. Is it because he sleeps so much before bedtime that he is nocturnal? Rick has inadvertently run into him a few nights, toward morning. His father seems to be at his peak during those hours, reading trade journals and making voluminous notes on legal pads.

Footsteps pause in the hall outside the bathroom door; a soft rapping comes. Rick ceases breathing, struck by another thunder jolt of bilious cramping.

Above his head floats the thin rasp of the doorknob. He prays that it is his mother.

"Champ? That you, buddy?"

"Yeah."

His father moves inside and quietly closes the door, kneels beside him, checking him over. He is never this physically close to his dad; it makes him uncomfortable. He has a definite circle around himself in regard to his father, and it is at least three feet. Why doesn't he back up? The bathroom is as big as his old bedroom used to be.

"What's the matter?"

"I'm sick."

He can hear his father sigh, not a sound of exasperation but one of concern. "Well, geez." He touches Rick's cheek with the back of his hand. Rick closes his eyes. Abruptly the hand is withdrawn.

Rolling onto his side produces a new queasiness.

"Don't you want to get in your bed? I'll help you."

"I can't."

"Do you want a doctor? I could at least call for some advice."

Dead on. This man's as straight as he's ever been. Relief pulses through Rick; the person beside him is a familiar stranger, long time gone. The Good One. When had he last seen him, the daddy he could trust? He had begun as a boy to recognize there were two.

"I don't need a doctor."

"Okay." He folds a towel and slips it under Rick's head, struggles to his feet. "We got Tums and all that."

"I can't right now."

"Sure."

"Just . . ."

His father leans eagerly over him, as though listening through every pore.

"A Coke. Please."

His father leaves the room and returns, jiggling a glass. He bends down and hands it to Rick: a small one, crammed with cracked ice and fizzing Coke. Exactly what he wanted.

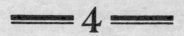

4

As Mike backs his navy blue Mercedes around the side of the house and out into the street, it occurs to him whimsically that he looks like an actor on one of his own storyboards. Main character: nattily dressed ad executive, leaving for work in tranquil A.M. Photo One: our boy taking a last look at his humble abode, a cedar and stone ranch on a scrap of property. Photo Two: he shakes his head. House cost him four times what it's worth. Photo Three: he perks up as he winds through stately avenues lined with chest-high bird-of-paradise plants in full splendor; orange, purple and green. Photo Four: he approaches the freeway entrance, wincing. Photo Five: car climbs up the ramp to merge. Photo Six: close-up of exec cursing. We cannot hear his words because view is from the front, through the windshield. Photo Seven: aerial shot of eight smoggy lanes. Zillions of metal bubbles, all going like hell. Final Photo: bumper sticker on car ahead. ONE PLANET, ONE PEOPLE. PLEASE.

But what would it be an ad for? Staying where you are? Not letting your company promote you to an overpriced overcrowded garden? A reverse chamber of commerce spot, maybe: Yankee Go Home and Take Your Damned Car with You.

He confirms that he is sane every morning when he weathers this lickety-split flume ride. A lesser person couldn't make it. It affirms his strength.

The first day. Lord! Being sling-shot between neighborhoods, mystified. He remembers even now the irrational urge to pull off the road, to let the ambulance driver carry him out, eyes slammed shut against the careening onslaught.

For Chrisake, what a city.

This isn't even a city, for Chrisake.

He is not hurtling but being hurled down a path cut between weird settings; the surreal TV music channel has nothing to top this. Tomblike department stores with glinting mirror eyes. Quarries: gravel mountains next to shallow seeping craters. Two-room frame houses in fenced mud yards; refrigerators on sagging porches; yellow-skinned children dragging each other around with ropes, digging in curbside muck. Lollipop palms—fuzz balls on comically long sticks. Condominiums as wide and seemingly uninhabited as the sheer, abandoned cliff-dweller caves.

And always the drifting white gases. A constant curtain. Not just a curtain but a tent, redolent of old rubber and ash.

Lee deals the Swiss cheese slices like playing cards onto pieces of white bread. Katy follows, heaping mounds of shaved ham on the cheese. They crown the sandwiches with more bread and seal them in foil, popping them into paper bags occupied by apples and small cans of tomato juice. Even Katy takes her lunch these days, munching it in the car between job interviews.

"Gotta run!" Rick gallops by on his way out the kitchen door. Lee neatly folds the top of a bag and sends it sailing to him over the counter. He catches it in one hand.

"Bye." He is gone, with a swish and click of the screen door.

"Whatever was ailing him, he certainly got over it fast," Katy says, sweeping crumbs to the edge of the scarred cutting board and catching them in her fingers. She taps her hands lightly over the sink.

Lee is gulping a banana-orange blender drink the tennis coach has recommended. Her heart-shaped gold earrings twinkle with sunshine filtered through window squares. *Pierced ears, at thirteen.* Katy regards them with an equal mix of disapproval and admiration. Lee's hair is a bisque shade, nearly white in spots. She wears it shoulder length, flipped up on the ends and curved away from her oval face in hot-combed feathery wings.

The most special time of day: these ten minutes or so alone. Lee is her closest friend. She listens to Katy with the unjudgmental expression of a psychiatrist. Confidante par excellence, this little girl with the comforting softness pinned to her sleeve.

"I need to get some work," Katy says. "All these payments are putting the bite on us. The corporate masquerade! Trucking us out here and telling us which suburbs we had to live in—for prestige. Giving us the down payment on a house with a giant mortgage."

"I know."

"The trick is to tread water until the next transfer." Lee nods solemnly, unblinking. Katy wishes she could hug her, but Lee has lately gotten too grown up for that. Too self-conscious.

"I don't want to go to work full time for a theater, but I thought I could tag onto shows that travel in here. That way there'd be no long-term commitment. I feel pretty sure we'll be gone by June."

"I hope so."

"We just need to watch what we spend. L.A. is horrendously expensive, and your dad doesn't seem to know a hundred dollars from a thousand anymore. I feel like the Dutch boy with his finger in the dike." Katy stops, struck by the concern in Lee's expression. "Don't worry."

Lee makes a fist and hits herself lightly on the jawbone in a mock gesture of bravery.

Katy laughs.

He has been pitching for thirty minutes, using flip charts and multimedia, market surveys and glossy scrapbooks of previous campaigns. No teasers for Mike Stockman. In an age when advertising and public relations agencies fear revealing too much in prospective-client proposals lest their concepts be stolen, he's built his reputation on pull-out-all-the-stops presentations. He's only been skunked once—in Chicago. But then again, he's not fooling with local shoe stores or mom-and-pop restaurants. The deals he cuts are national. He's a gladiator, repeatedly squared off against men whose names end in the Roman numeral three and who sport fifty-dollar haircuts.

Now, nearing the end of his pitch, he assesses the prospect's receptiveness. This one is inscrutable. What's his name? Shoot. They're always Trey or Tripp, or sometimes Chip. Well, he can fake it, sneak a look inside the brown suede, gold-embossed folder containing the typewritten proposal. The name will be on the first page.

He ends his speech and comes to sit at the burnished mahogany table. Campaign planning and pitching are what he does best. God save him from being an account executive again, a veritable drone. He is idea-happy, full of himself. In a modest way, of course.

Come on, baby. He's given blood for this one. All of it. He's been embalmed. The company is desperate to snag this designer of pleasure boats, purveyor of yachts.

"Well?" Mike asks.

Trey/Tripp smiles. "Book it."

He has shish-kebabbed himself into serendipity with the powers that be, a long narcissistic lunch in which each of them took a turn tap-dancing at center stage. Beyond that, he has decisively refused wine from a thirty-dollar bottle and ordered instead two drafts of cold tea with lemon.

In the red-carpeted company elevator, their voices boom: three men, finishing each other's sentences, punching buttons with competitive flourish. They need little excuse, but today it is because of him. Boy genius.

He floats from the elevator and down the hall, away from the bumping bodies and thumping doors, straight into his office. Maggie is out, her chair pushed back from her desk, a drawer open, burping its jumble of paper. He half expects to see her shoes sitting on the acrylic mat as though she's been unexpectedly yanked out of them and pulled through the ceiling. She always departed that way; a mistress of organization and yet a leaver of assorted droppings.

He crosses to his domain and goes to sit in the big chair, propping his feet up in a deliberately satisfied pose. A stack of pink phone messages is stuffed into the open bill of his ceramic pelican, the slip on top written in red marker, Maggie's code for emergency status. Even before he lowers his feet to lean forward, he can read it. *"Dan called. Has been waiting for you since noon at the Tiki. Did you forget? Client mad as blankety-blank."*

* * *

"It was a gift anyway," the principal says, standing up to arch his back in a stretch, hands on his hips.

Rick notes absently the large circle of sweat on the back of Dietrich's tapered white dress shirt.

"You were barely under the wire—you got in mainly on your board scores—now you want to flush it down the john." He shifts, and perches on the end of a narrow table laden with tarnished trophies. "The guidance counselor said she talked to you."

"She did."

"And you couldn't tell her why you don't study."

"I study."

"Look, all this is beside the point." Dietrich spreads his arms. "Study or no study, it doesn't make a difference. Grades. You got 'em or you don't. And you don't."

The guy is fairly young, with a decent hairline and no gray; his orange kinky waves have been brushed into submission. He peers at Rick now through black-rimmed glasses. "Don't be surprised if UCLA takes away your early acceptance. They have the right to revoke it, you know."

This man reminds him of his mother's father, the Lutheran pastor. Part of his face is frozen, doesn't move when he talks. The dead part is a horizontal rectangle extending from the eyelids to the upper lip. The nose is especially detached from his emotional message; a graft. It seems to have less pigment than the rest of his skin.

"So, what are you going to do about it?"

Rick shrugs.

"Don't give me that shrugging business. This is serious." There is disdain now, tangible. Men don't like him, have never liked him. He doesn't meet their secret standards. Perhaps they sense from the outset the quiver at his core—not fear but a fine vibration. He is impacted by everything. Girls have it, this perception of things unseen,

31

unsaid; things not even here yet, traveling through time to their targets. Is he a faggot? Is that what he is? Was his Y chromosome weaker than his X chromosome? He has asked this of himself in locker rooms, watching boys flick each other's naked butts with towels.

It's as if Dietrich and other men knew something he doesn't know: he has a sign, a mark, etched into the back of his head. They ride him, each in his own way, as though a constant beating will turn his hide to leather.

"Listen," Dietrich confides. "I can keep a confidence. If there's some reason you're having trouble, how about telling me? Maybe we can work it out."

A reason.

He doesn't know, really. The numbers and the paragraphs just gradually stopped making sense. He noticed it as early as fourth grade. Well . . . he can get sense out of them if he scratches at them long enough. But they aren't interesting. Where he used to see pictures in the words, he sees only printing now, letters and spaces. They mean, but they have no motion or color. He can memorize them, but he cannot travel *in*.

"I can get you any kind of help you need. No one else has to know. Does it feel to you that this is someone's fault, other than your own?"

Whose fault would it be? Nobody studies for him. He's the one who's screwed it up.

"I was looking over your record, all the way back to elementary school. You used to do all right. And you have a rather exceptional IQ." He waits, through an awkwardly lengthy silence. "Don't you have anything to say to me? Isn't there anything I can do for you?"

Rick shakes his head.

"You're going to let it get away, huh?"

"I hope not."

"You can trust me. Can't you tell me what's behind this?"

"I don't know."

"If you can trust me?"

"What's behind it."

Dietrich frowns. "Okay." It has a kiss-off tone to it.

The torches of the Tiki have been extinguished; there are only four cars in the parking lot. Mike pulls up under the overhang and leaves the flashers blinking while he crashes shoulder-first through two sets of doors. Dimness accosts him. He pauses for his eyes to adjust. To the left, the bar with its floor-to-ceiling aquariums is empty. He plods through gloom to check out the dining area. The tables have been stripped of their cloths; he hears a merry racket in the kitchen. Weakness swoops down on him. He leans against the vinyl bamboo wallpaper, feeling the drum of his pulse gather just above his navel.

5

"Maggie?"

"Mike?"

"I'm going to go home. I'm not feeling well." He fingers the cold enamel metal of the pay phone in the Tiki's lobby.

"Where are you?"

"I'll be in tomorrow morning."

"Wait a minute . . ."

"Yuh."

"What about your three o'clock?"

"Who is it?"

"Calhoun and Freeman. You've put them off twice now."

Prelims to pitching. He needs to interview these cats. Two terrific prospects—promo officers for a brewery. He hesitates. "All right."

"You're coming back?"

"I guess so."

"Good."

"Do me a favor. Call Dan Arno and tell him I got hung up with a really critical snafu. Sorry about missing lunch. Reschedule it for me, will you?" He can picture her closing one eye as she listens to this; there is a corresponding pause.

"Okay," she says.

Katy's feet are swollen inside her toeless pumps; her makeup has turned to oil and is gradually sliding down her face. She takes a Kleenex from her shoulder bag and folds it, blotting the slick patches: nose, chin. She rests her head against the back of a red brocade chair as she waits in the dinner theater lobby for her fourth interview of the day. Her surroundings have the look of a first-rate bordello—everything scarlet, from the flocked wall covering to the antique satin draperies with their tassel pulls to the over-sized central ottoman. Ornate, gilt-edged mirrors compound the assault.

The man coming toward her is sixtyish, with a fringe of white hair. When he smiles his cheeks pucker next to the corners of his mouth, a sign of dentures. His body suggests burliness, toned down by age. He has the vigorous step of a dancer.

"Cakewalk."

"Pardon me?" She stands up.

"You say something that goes with cakewalk."

"High-button shoes?"

"You have passed the first test!"

Corny opening. She is put off by it.

He shakes her hand convincingly, but using his fingers only; she notices a pear-shaped topaz pinkie ring. "Résumés are crap. What I need to know is, can you fit it all together? I'm Lyle Taglia, the resident director."

"Katy Stockman."

He leads her in absent-minded corkscrews through the theater, continually backtracking to explain items he has overlooked. She decides it has dignity, this intimate house with its graduated balconies of dining tables and somber oil portraits of American presidents.

Backstage, she feels the blush of intimidation drain from her; she has coordinated productions bigger than any they could handle here. *But not for two decades.* Despite that thought, she is moved by a rising self-assurance. It comes to her concretely when she spies the butt cans—old coffee tins parked just out of sight on each side of the stage apron, their water golden with the juice of tobacco and littered with white tarry stubs: *all theaters are the same.*

Lyle's sentences are becoming less showy, more offhand; he is speaking to her in a new rhythm, the humor-based, confiding tones of a coworker.

"One night a bird got in here and kept circling in the spotlight during a solo, then skimming the crowd. He had come down the fireplace in the bar and was covered with soot." Lyle shoots her a sideways glance with a burlesque lift to his eyebrows. "Can you imagine the cream-puff prima as she caught it in the kisser?"

This is the place. She is sure.

Three girls clustered outside the school snack stand keep peering at him and then turning their backs to whisper and giggle. Annoyed, Rick tears the wrapper from his Clark Bar, swivels a hundred and eighty degrees on the open-air picnic bench and focuses on the scattering pack of students who have been dispatched by the final bell. Half of them are heading for the parking lot, half are emerging in the yellow-and-green T-shirt/shorts combinations of extracurricular sports. He glimpses Joe Dillon striding toward the weight room. Dillon has arm and shoulder muscles like bundles of fat rubber bands; if you look closely you can see each strand, taut and round.

Rick bites into the crumbly peanut-flavored candy. He

has daydreamed but he cannot project himself into fantasies of physical prowess or team camaraderie. Other people are breathing different air; he is strapped into his own atmosphere, a spacesuit.

He checks out the snickering trio who have picked up their books and are sauntering away, still tossing glances at him over their shoulders. They pull together in a hushed hum of conversation. *Get lost, you little twits.* He has always felt like a creature in a cage, an oddity to be stared at. What do they see? When he dissects himself in the mirror, he pronounces his face and body ordinary. Not deformed. In all fairness, the boys seem to like him well enough, but he has nothing in common with them. He plays no games.

He finishes eating and flips the waste paper into a metal drum. The courtyard has thinned out now; the snack bar window is being lowered. He takes a slow pace in the direction of the bike rack. He does not like to be the first one home; his dad is too often there. Don't they miss him at work? How does he get away with it?

He approaches the parking lot, considering with his usual respect the viciously spiked treadle under the entrance gate, over which a sign proclaims: DO NOT BACK UP. SEVERE TIRE DAMAGE.

Do not back up. It is his motto. He is fixed upon a single goal: escape. He applied to California colleges, banking on his family's return to the East. He wants, has always wanted, simply to be free.

Some idiot has left his Porsche illegally parked behind a line of other vehicles; a new blue pickup truck is creeping back and forth in its slot, trying to get out without hitting the car. As he gets closer, Rick recognizes the driver as one of the girls who has been taunting him. Guilt ripples through her expression; she tromps on the brake and waits for him to go past. He sees that there is enough room for her to squeeze out if she turns the wheel sharply. He walks by, then pivots and approaches her.

She shrinks, staring at him. Her brown hair is helmet-style, wrapped with a slender white gauzy scarf, the bow perched on top like perky ears. She has a round, plump face accented with vivid makeup.

"Hey," he says, coming up to the window. "How about if I help you?"

"I'm afraid . . . I'll hit it." He can read her reluctance; she thinks he will deliberately direct her into an accident.

"You back up, and I'll tell you when to cut it."

She considers him for a moment, then some logic registers in her brown eyes, pushing her over the edge. She nods.

He steps behind the truck and gauges the distance. One slip-up and this will be a costly assist. "Come on back. Slow."

She lets it drift toward him.

"Okay, give it a good yank now."

She slides it past the door of the Porsche by inches, but she is not going to miss the fender.

"Hold it!" he shouts.

She jams to a stop.

"You're going to have to pull forward a little."

She leans out the window. "Look, why don't you do this and I'll get back there?"

He could. Easily. He aced Driver's Ed. But he has no license. The humiliation of it rankles him all over again. "No. You'll make it."

She nudges the truck forward, angling the tires, pauses and starts back. He stands over the passing fenders, monitoring the gap; she holds it even and swings it gently into the lane. He can see that she is smiling.

He flashes a quick wave. As he jogs toward his bike, he hears the truck gliding behind him. Now what?

She keeps pace. "Want a ride?"

As they snake into the foothill subdivisions, Rick assesses her outfit: a gray-striped balloony jumpsuit, yellow pumps with pink ankle socks. The socks are the kind you see on babies—edged with white lace. She has a silver pin there, too, on the sock nearest him. A Chinese symbol.

"What's that?" He points.

"Long life."

"Oh." Of course. The high school has been infiltrated by Asians, all speaking their native tongues. She probably got it from one of them.

"I'm Eva," she says happily.

"Rick."

"I know."

He is not startled by her clothes; the whole student body is wealthy-trendy. It's a tongue-in-cheek costume party every day, with participants split into three groups: Preppy, New Wave and Heavy-Metal. Generally—he has figured out after lengthy observation—the kids declare their educational ambitions by these garbs. Preppy for college, New Wave for nondegreed office jobs, Heavy-Metal for trades. She's New Wave.

The mini-alligator on his shirt suddenly draws his attention. When he gets thrown out of UCLA in a few weeks, will he have to take it off? This amuses him. A drumming-out ceremony.

"Whatcha laughing at?" She has tensed, across the shoulders.

She's one to ask *him.*

His silence seems to unsettle her. "Did you think we were making fun of you earlier?"

"Yes."

"Damn. I thought you'd think that. I told them. It's just because Dali wants to meet you."

"Who's Dolly?"

"Dali. Like the painter. Dali Caputo."

"Why?"

"She thinks . . . you look like a nice person."

He is flattered by this. "She's wrong," he says.

She eases the truck over to the curb in front of his house. "Is this it? Forty-two forty-one?"

"Yep." He has taken a fancy to her elegant gaudiness; she is stunningly clean and her trinkets look expensive. He imagines what it would be like to sit on his patio with her, tapping the source of her antics. He has stepped into an entertaining movie and doesn't want to step out.

He squints at the house, hoping for X-ray vision so he can know whether his father is home. Best not to chance it. "Well, thanks," he says, climbing out and lowering the tailgate to retrieve his bike. She stays in the truck, watching him through the rear window. Her hair bow and pink lipstick merge with reflections of bobbing palm fronds.

He isn't sure, but he believes he sees her wink.

He is affected; the phantom wink feels like feminine fingers touching his mouth. Perspiration is spilling under his collar as he opens the kitchen door.

"Hi!" His mother. Her seated profile, against the dining room glass doors, is backed by a blurry amber halo. He moves through the kitchen toward her. She is figuring with a pencil on a square pad of paper, holding a coffee mug in the other hand. She looks skeleton-tired. "Are you feeling better?"

"Yes." He wants to describe Eva. But it would be a poor re-creation. She is a visitor from another planet; he can remember reading such a story in his *Jack and Jill:* a friendly alien, bringing wonder to a young boy gazing out his bedroom window on a dark summer's night. She is real, but if he tells anyone about her she will go away. "How were your interviews?"

She brightens. "I got a job. Part time—coordinating costumes and sets and props for a theater."

"That's great! Congratulations."

"Thanks. I was really pleased. What's on *your* mind? Looks like something is."

"I want my driver's license," he says steadily.

She appears disappointed, then nervous. "Your dad doesn't think you should do that yet."

"It's ridiculous."

"I'll take it up with him again," she sighs. "When the time is right. Don't *you* mention it."

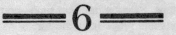

6

Who let *him* in?

Dan Arno reaches Mike's desk in four deliberate strides and bends across it.

Mike forces himself to continue writing his signature. "What's the matter?" he says coolly, glancing up at Dan whose eyes have narrowed into slits.

"I want to talk to you."

"Sure. Sit down." He tucks the Cross pen into a small pewter mug with six others.

"No, thanks."

Arno is a gaunt, rangy man who smells of cigarettes. In his thirties, he has the stooped bearing of an older person. He is generally expressionless. But not now.

To slide his chair away would be to lose the upper hand. Mike folds his arms and meets Arno's gaze. "Well, at least back up."

Dan ignores this, drawing in closer; Mike can feel heavy breath moving his hair. "Where were you at noon?"

Mike studies a staple stuck in the pile of the carpet near his feet. "Something else came up. Suddenly. I should have called you, but I figured you could handle it."

"I did."

"Well, I appreciate it." He outranks this account exec. They aren't going to tangle.

"I want to tell you just how it is," Dan says flatly. "I see through you. And you'd better get some help. Because I'm not going to carry my load and yours, too."

The words slam into Mike, summoning a murderous rage. He struggles to control it.

He can get rid of Dan, get him fired. Maybe.

"I don't like your work," he says to Dan, rising to eyeball him. "I've been sidestepping the issue for a long time." He thinks he detects a slight tremor in the man, but it goes by. What was it? A clue as minute as the dilating of his pupils?

"You think you can edge me out? I doubt it. You might be Golden Boy, but my record is solid. You want to try?"

Panic begins to tingle Mike's skin. *Take a different tack.* He shrugs apologetically. "Hey, I missed lunch. I'm sorry, okay? It's not life or death. Why are we talking like this? Come on, sit down and let's rap about what the client needs."

Dan reaches into the breast pocket of his suit coat and extracts a clip of folded papers, which he tosses onto the blotter. "These are the notes from the meeting. Get some help, Mike. I'll give you four weeks."

Tina sounds far away. It isn't a faintness or slight ringing on the line. It's her voice, so thin it seems the telephone cable has been dissected and reduced to a single wire.

"I called to see how Nathan's doing." Katy is standing at the kitchen phone, her stomach muscles pulled into a shield.

"Better."

She draws air more deeply into her lungs. "I'm glad. What about his eye?"

"He's out of the woods."

"Are you sure?"

"Yes."

"Thank heaven! Is there anything I can do for you?"

"No." It is leaden, final.

"Well, I'll call again to check."

"Good-bye," Tina says. A mechanical humming overtakes the word.

Damn. What did she ever like about Tina? She can't think now. Tina is rude—concerned only with her own feelings. No compassion for the agony of Katy and Mike. Is this a friend? She visualizes Tina's petite, jewelry-bedecked frame, the pert shape of her nose, the slant of her Mary Kay blusher under her freckled cheekbones. Too perfect, too packaged. Her sentences have the dense self-important cadence of a teacher's.

Anyway, they hadn't been that close.

How many was that?

He knocks twice on the lacquered finish of the bar: his signal for the tab. Once for refill, twice for tab. He tips the shot glass up again; a couple of errant drops roll onto his tongue.

People have the wrong idea about saloons, for God's sake. In England, pubs are a whole way of life. Community centers.

Granger slides the bill to him, and he puts a foot on the brass rail to read it. He's always careful not to sit down; he's not in here to lose himself, just gain a little fellowship.

Our gang. They wait for him every day at five, their faces alternating on the bar stools in each twenty-four-hour period like a game of musical chairs. The laughs he extracts from these puffy faces are, he is sure, the only laughs they ever get. It's a pleasureful task to select his stories before he fumbles his way from the concrete glare into the dim, friendly clatter. He likes the round beer-ad clocks that glow overhead, the familiar smell of wet wood.

Six dollars! Four shots. Hell, he hasn't been in here long enough to do that. Granger probably slips a few extra in now and then. These poor jokers wouldn't know the difference.

Oh, well. He peels a ten-spot from a tight roll and shoves the wad back into his slacks. People who really have money don't quibble over a buck or two. Call it vanity, but he's not about to reveal his financial status by squaring this up.

"Not taking off, are you?" Middleton gives him an amiable thump in the ribs. "You were killing us with that bull story."

One of his best. The true tale of Our Boy escorting the Merrill Lynch bull to a stockbrokers' hotel luncheon, twelve stories up. Brilliant promo idea. Except that the freight elevator had stalled, in total blackness. His fear of the bull was quickly surpassed by his recognition of the bull's fear. *It* was a lot more fragrant.

"Yeah. Gotta go."

As he walks behind the hunched bodies, a couple of hands reach out to tug his suit sleeve. "Give us one more, Mike."

He steps between two of the men and leans forward so they can all see him. "One more, huh?"

A chorus of congenial grunts.

He will make this short and punchy, followed by a quick exit. That's top-flight technique.

"I'm working as an announcer at a radio station, right? New job, right?"

Heads wagging, crooked smiles.

"And there's this stuff all over the console—you know, in the booth where the microphone is? There's this junk, dots and splotches like you get when you have dirty windows. It's transparent and I can't figure out what it is. I keep cleaning it off but it comes back, once a week. I track it down to Monday. Every Monday morning, the thing's a mess."

He's the pitcher winding up, the circus diver leaving the board to plunge fifty feet into a miniature pool, unscathed.

"So I finally ask somebody, 'What is this yuck?' And they tell me. 'You know that evangelist we have in here on Sunday giving people hell on the air? He gets so damned fired up he spits all over everything!' "

He has put just the right spin on it; he can see them lift their shoulders, their mouths opening, sucking wind for the great guffaws that are coming. He darts away from the bar and pushes the door, tapping his forehead in a salute. Laughter erupts behind him.

And then he is in the clear, chuckling, patting his pockets for the car keys. Sunset dapples the sidewalk with rusty gold; it sparkles on his shoes.

In the parking lot, he pauses beside his Mercedes, peering through the window at the ignition. Empty. Where the heck did he put his keys? The car is locked. *Doggone.*

He begins an orderly search of his clothing, but turns up nothing. He slumps against the car, thinking, letting his eyes defocus so that he can mentally retrace his steps.

He has never seen night come so quickly. Is it an eclipse? He is lost in a puddle of shadows. The neon signs across the street are on and he has somehow missed the slow, traveling glimmer that precedes their full blaze.

The keys are in his hand.

He has feared Katy's expression, but it is one of relief. No judgment in it. None at all.

"Where were you?"

"Stuck on the freeway."

She comes to him joyfully, putting her arms around his waist and turning her face up to his for a kiss. She has exquisite lips, full and soft; his kiss is eager. If she detects a sourness on his breath, she does not indicate it. They cling, pressing against one another, exchanging strength. She has told him his embrace energizes her. And she is the wellspring of his courage.

The overbright, overwarm kitchen secures him. Gratitude is in his mouth like sugared bread.

"Are the children home?"

"Yes. Studying. Hungry?"

"Almost."

Their martini time is a ritual. She has already gone to the liquor cupboard to begin preparations. He loves her for this: the precise way she sets the glasses in tandem and rinses them with the vermouth. The pinnacle of the work day, this sharing.

"Did Sistaire Yacht buy?"

"Yep."

She glances up at him in delight. "Congratulations!"

"The whole package."

"Marvelous." She finishes pouring the gin. He can hear the tinkle of ice as she twirls the spoon in the metal shaker.

"But I'm having trouble with Arno."

She stops stirring. "Dan Arno? I thought you got along real well."

"Did." Why does he visit this stuff on her? She doesn't have to know all his troubles. But even as he asks the question, he has the answer: she is his comfort, his greatest defender.

"What happened?"

"I missed a lunch date and he's out of whack about it."

"You forgot?"

"We were celebrating the Sistaire account. By the time I remembered, it was too late."

"Well, anybody can forget a lunch date." She hands him a martini and leads him into the family room, where they sit in the corner of the white L-shaped sofa. "He wouldn't accept your apology?"

"No. I think it's going to be a wedge."

"Why?"

"He's taken a dislike to me."

"Can't you talk it over?"

"I tried."

Sadness seeks her husband out. He gives things his best shot, but they come to nothing. How can that be?

Corporate America. Backbiting. Power plays. The clash for the corner office. No wonder his confidence has been undermined.

"It's not your fault," she says.

Rick eases back the glass door in his room and creeps onto the darkened patio. What's taking so long? He's tremendously hungry. The light in the pool is on; he stays away from it, close to the house. His father sits alone on the couch, sipping martini number two. Rick knows it is the second because he can hear his mother bumping around in the kitchen. She drinks the first one with him, then shuts him off after two by serving dinner. Tonight they are late. Nearly eight o'clock.

"Pal?"

Drat.

His father is squinting toward him. "That you?"

"Yeah."

"Hi! How you feeling?"

"Fine." He has no choice. He edges into the family room.

His father smiles. "Come sit down."

Rick circles the coffee table and perches on the far end of the sofa.

48

There is a different aura about his dad tonight; he has a pleased, receptive look to him.

"Tell me about your day, son."

Watch it. "What do you want to know?"

"Well, just about what you're studying and doing."

He searches for a safe subject, but it is no use. Anything can be a bone to pick. "Computers."

"You like that?"

He nods.

"Good for you. I'd never be able to figure it out, myself. Is it hard?"

"Not too hard."

His father finishes the martini in a single gulp. "I admire you, being able to do that. Do you remember Clint Haggarty?"

"In Kansas City?"

"Hell of a neighbor. He and I were twins when it came to mechanical ability. Zero!" He grins now; toothy genuine glee. "Clint got a new lawn mower one day and I could see him over there sitting on his driveway reading the directions. After a while, he rang the doorbell and he said to me—in all seriousness—he said, 'Mike, I can't for the life of me figure this out. It says in here to change the oil every twenty hours. My God, that's once a day!' "

Unbidden laughter seizes Rick: strong, beating about in his brain. He has to release it. His voice, his father's voice, echo together out along the river-rock floor of the patio. Fragmented, scattering. Pebbles of sound.

His father gazes at him with a jubilant intensity. "So, tell me . . . what's happening with you? Your senior year and all. Are you having any problems? I mean, I understand about the grades. And I know you're working on it. It'll get straightened out. Is there anything else you want to talk about?"

"Not really."

49

"That's what I'm here for. To help you. If you'll let me."

No way. Whenever he has attempted such intimacy, it has backfired. If not at the moment, later on. He would never tell his father anything meaningful, any portion of his heart. His father would either totally forget it or taunt him with it in times of conflict. Still, he will have to come up with an item—to satisfy him.

His dad waits, leaning in his direction, forearms resting on his knees. An earnest pose.

Couldn't this be a beginning? Couldn't it happen, after all, that one day—maybe now—they could communicate? *Try.* "I . . . want to ask you . . ."

A tilt of the head, sympathetic.

". . . about the driver's license."

"You think you deserve a license." A statement, not a question.

"I'd like to have one."

"That's not what I said, *like*. Do you *deserve* one?"

Alarm grips Rick; his foot is in the snare. "Never mind." He puts a hand up. "That's okay."

"Are you trying to get smart with me?"

"No." Rick jumps up.

"Because, I'm going to tell you something. If you deserved that license you'd have it by now."

"All right."

"When you earn the first installment of the insurance money, you can get it. That's what I mean by 'deserve.' Participate. Cooperate. You know what it costs for an underage driver? Three hundred extra bucks! For *six months!*" It is a half-shout. Splotchy redness is spreading from his dad's neck up to his eyebrows.

Rick retreats slightly. He hears Lee open the door to her room.

"Don't walk away when I'm talking to you."

He senses Lee coming up behind him.

"You stay out of this, little girl."

"Daddy, I wasn't . . ."

"Get back in your room!"

"Don't yell at her!"

His dad is cat-nimble, springing from the couch to grasp his shoulders. Instinctively, Rick pushes his chest. Mike leaps at Rick, crooking an arm around his neck.

Survival. Rick uses the strength of his upper back to catch his father under an armpit and slam him against the stone fireplace.

"Stop it, stop it!" His mother. Pulling at him. Why is she pulling at *him?* "Michael, don't!"

The pressure on his neck subsides. He moves quickly away from his father, who stands panting and wild-eyed, staring at nothing in particular.

Death glides through Rick: a brutal force, fighting to be born. He could kill his father, kill him with the savage hatred of his mind alone. He would not even have to touch him. "You drink too much! You bastard!" he screams. He isn't saying this, he never says this. He can't.

"You don't love us anymore!" Lee. Shrieking at Mike, her face contorted with terror.

Mike searches like a sleepwalker for the hallway and, without urgency, goes into his room, quietly shutting the door.

Damn it, she's had enough. He can't treat them this way! She'll knock his teeth down his throat. Katy flings the bedroom door wide and slams it with unnatural strength; the explosion causes only a slight twitch in Michael, who is perched on the edge of the bed with his back to her.

"Don't you ever touch the children! Don't you dare! They're *good* kids. I can't leave you for a minute without

51

there being some kind of trouble. You *are* drinking too much and we're all sick of it!''

He turns toward her slowly; she is unprepared for the helpless remorse she sees. She has witnessed the grieving of many people, but none as stark and complete as his. Tears rain down his face from eyes that seem almost concave, so full are they of self-loathing. He holds his arms up to her for mercy, and she knows beyond doubt that she is his single hope. He is being swept away, inexorably. To deny him would be to dispatch him forever.

She is too old for this, to be sitting in the closet. But she needs an enclosed space; walls wrapped snugly around her, unchanging, solid. Absence of light, of any vision. And the layered, sweet fragrance of her own belongings.

Her father is crying; the sound works its way through the porous plaster, muffled. ''How can she say that? How can she think I don't love them? I do, Katy. I do. I love our babies.''

Babies. The word is a hook, tearing the inside of her cheek, her tongue.

Her mother's voice murmurs under his; she cannot decipher it. The vowels all run together in a mournful strand.

Their laments drop in pitch and gradually fade. She jerks herself awake and crawls from the closet, up onto her bed. Her mother will come to her soon.

In the mist of early sleep, Lee feels Katy kneel beside the bed. She does not open her eyes and is careful not to flutter her eyelids; she maintains a steady rhythm in her breathing.

''He's going to quit, honey.'' A whisper, cracked. ''He knows he's been drinking too much lately. He's sorry. We love you.''

* * *

His body is a board. He lies awake, staring through an imagined hole in the roof, hands beneath his head.

The figure of his mother suddenly fills the doorway. He does not move.

Her dress rustles as she walks to him. Can she see his eyes in the blackness?

"He's not going to drink anymore." Her tone is hushed, the message broken into two- and three-word pieces. "He wants you to know he loves you. And all of us."

Tears begin at the corners of his eyes; he applies his anger and they harden into crystal points.

"I know you can hear me. I hope you'll give us some help on this. It's hard to be parents."

She starts away, then turns slightly, inclining her head in his direction. Her profile is bowed like a slender tree in a gale. "You brought up the driver's license thing, didn't you? After I asked you not to."

7

"Would you like to finish up with some fudge cake?"

"I don't think so, Pop."

"This was a good idea of yours, to pick the Huntington for your birthday lunch. A great way to spend a Saturday, too."

"Um." Lee glances uneasily away from him and watches people jostle each other at the restaurant's main French-style doors.

He has tried to engage her all morning. Why won't she talk? She meets his efforts with fragmented answers, not cold—she is never cold to him—just hollow. And she initiates nothing. Has he screwed it up permanently?

Clients like him; surely he can handle his own family.

But this is more difficult. He never dreamed it could be so delicate, the father-daughter thing. How can he please her? What does she want? Clients make requests and he produces. With her, he has no guidelines.

Is she holding a grudge because he yelled at her? That was five days ago. Things happen. Parents get upset—it goes by. Can't she forgive and move on, like they do?

She is uncanny in her perception—almost extrasensory.

Could she somehow know about the couple of sips he's had in the meantime?

You don't love us anymore. An ache grips him. She doesn't really think that, does she?

"I'm proud of you, honey. I hope you know it."

Her reaction is not one of pleasure; the blue eyes are kind but joyless.

"Listen, I . . . I love you. I'm not the best—"

"That's all right," she interrupts softly, lifting her purse from beside the chair. "Let's go see the gardens. I'm tired of sitting."

"Wait."

She pinches her lips into a slender line and stares at him.

"I love you. Believe me. Never think that I don't."

Nothing will satisfy him except the phrase she doesn't want to say. He has badgered her into a corner; she is afraid. Not to give the response he wants can have shattering consequences. He has no midground between calm and fury; there is constant jeopardy. And she fears her mother's disappointment should she fail to pacify him. What if she should be the one to set him drinking again?

"I love you, too," she says.

They wander through the palatial gardens of the Huntington. No blossoms grace the rose arbor. The thousand bushes are bundles of bare thorny sticks; brown, pruned severely. From these a stark thought comes, poking at her sharply, cruel: *she hates her father.* The realization makes her tremble.

"Not much to look at, is it?" He is on a separate, parallel walkway, smiling at her over the bleak, clawlike shrubs. His appearance is transformed by her insight: he seems to be a puppet, a shell inhabited by growing evil. She had always clung desperately to the goodness in him,

55

grappling for the old father who receded from her. Time and again she had reached down to find that essence and pull it forth, peeling back and shucking away the terrifying bad parts.

Now she understands. He couldn't possibly love them and act the way he does.

He acts mean. *Mean.* Baiting them, nasty. He wants to make them miserable; it is a sport. He says differently—and so does her mother—but she sees the truth.

He never apologizes; just hides for a night, then reappears with his suit pressed and his hair combed, speaking to them of weather and the legislature as if nothing had happened, as if she hadn't cried herself to sleep. And behind him, her mother's insistent nods to her and to Rick: *answer him politely, show respect, make him feel wanted, loved.*

They wind their way to the steep, descending path of the desert garden. It is alive with jagged brilliant plants that overflow the cobblestone walls: lush bearded palms, tall candelabras of orange-red aloe flowers, golden cacti as big as barrels and crowned with triangular spikes. The lane curves beside bunches of white pincushions and clustered leaning yuccas. She is not moved. She pictures him in his coffin, a charcoal shadow gliding swiftly across his waxen skin as she slams the lid.

She is swinging gently to and fro in a carefree place; not a happy place, but one devoid of worry. Suspended—as in a hammock between two creaking trees. She rests inside the moment, letting her body sag with the cushioned motion, her head against the seat back, drowsiness networking its way from her head to her limbs.

"I have a birthday surprise for you." The car shifts suddenly under her, rolling to the right.

Beneath the rising curtain of her vision, a street of shops

shimmers. Her father guides the vehicle to the curb and slickly parks it in a tight space.

"I want you to select your own present." His sentence has the tenor of a grand announcement; it fills her with apprehension. Money is always an issue. She does not like gifts because they subtract from the other family members; her gain will mean that someone else will have to forfeit. It will mean grief.

And another price must be paid as well: freedom. Her mother and father bind her this way; the gifts are little tethers. Even the kisses they bestow can increase their power over her, if she returns them.

Her father rapidly comes around the car to hold her door open and escort her a few paces into a jewelry boutique. A man in a dark suit hails them with a wave from behind the back counter; he is on the phone.

Her dad touches the back of her hair. "I want you to choose a necklace, sweetheart."

Stones and metals wink at her from their glass-and-velvet cases. She can tell from the size of the gems and the angles at which they are displayed that this is an expensive store. The pink plush carpet is new; it gives off a synthetic odor that makes her eyes water.

The man hangs up and strides toward them. "How may I help you?"

"This is my daughter's birthday. And we are interested in a gold chain."

"Congratulations." It is offered like a prerecorded message. "We have many. All are at least fourteen-karat, of course. My own favorites are in the flat, polished style. Do you have a preference?" He dons a refined smile, obviously calculated not to be too eager.

She knows her father's pride; to protest in front of this distinguished shopkeeper would humiliate him. They shepherd her to the collection. She glares down at the chains with rising panic. How much do they cost? She must not ask.

She doesn't want them. If her mother has to work, if Rick can't get his driver's license, then why should she be forced to buy one of these?

No reason. Crazy reasons. Nothing makes sense. Her life is strung out before her like the fifteen-inch chain the manager is now dangling from his immaculate fingernails: an endless loop. She has learned not to trust the man beside her who has the same color eyes she does, the same shade and texture of hair, the same narrowness to his cheeks, the same slight jut to the jawbone at the end of his chin. He has no wisdom, exercises no judgment; it is broken in him, loose, flapping. She is wary of his outbursts and even more wary of his silences. The most threatening times are those in which he does not drink. A single word can send him back. Peace is a fragile peace, at best.

"Do you like this one, Lee?" His affection flows to her, real, unabashed. She is being crushed by it.

"Yes, I do."

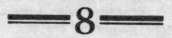

8

Eva touches the remote control in her truck and the wooden garage door slides up.

This is a damned wild hair, coming all the way to Newport Beach with Eva on a Saturday. What if something happened at home? His folks wouldn't know how to find him.

What if something happened *here?*

She guides the truck gingerly into the narrow box and presses the unit again, leaving them in near-total darkness. Daylight glistens behind one small window.

She smiles at him triumphantly; he can see that much. "We made it." Reaching in front of him, she opens the glove compartment and begins to rummage through it. Her perfume smells like wet talcum powder; her right breast brushes his knees. He is stricken with embarrassment and infatuation.

"The overhead's been burned out for a while. Sorry." She finds a flashlight, snaps it on. "Let's go."

Eva climbs from the truck, taking the circle of yellow glow with her. He gets out shakily and follows her through the gloom to a flight of stairs; they emerge into a rectangular living room with a cathedral ceiling. A kitchen curves along one end of it, a bank of picture windows fills the other. He walks to the glass and scans with wonder the bay's tangle of sailboat riggings and the stack of huge modern houses on the opposite shore. The homes perch in two horizontal lines across the hillside: waterfront and crestview. It occurs to him for the first time since his move west that southern California is fabulously, preposterously opulent. Money here is not like money anywhere else. It is enormous; he is staggered by the veritable jumble of vacation homes and yachts and forty-thousand-dollar cars he knows exist in just this one location.

She is watching him now, evidently seeing something amusing. "Ever been to Newport before?"

"No. It must be nice to have two houses."

"Three," she says, lifting her eyebrows to wait for his response.

"Where's the other one?" he asks halfheartedly.

"Arrowhead."

In the mountains. Cripes. What does she want with *him?* He thinks he's figured it out. His unsophistication is the day's entertainment. He resolves not to talk too much.

Eva opens the door of a red-lacquered Chinese armoire, a four-shelved liquor stash. "Want a drink?"

"No." She's pushing all his hot buttons.

"Neither do I." Eva closes the armoire and puts her back against it, studying him.

She's a caricature, he thinks: the hair chopped at those geometric angles, the blousy turquoise dress with its teeny-tiny skirt. White knee socks and strappy toeless flats. One end of her hair scarf is shaped like a foot. "What's this?" He touches the top of her head.

"What?"

"This." He tugs at the cloth. "Looks like a foot on a . . . I don't know . . . stocking?"

"It is. It's the leg out of a pair of pantyhose." She says it defensively.

Why did he let her talk him into this? Her parents aren't even here. His father would take him apart if he knew.

A thrill snakes through him. He has effectively disappeared. For once, his father cannot control what happens next, cannot badger him to death with instructions and opinions, cannot jerk him around.

"I take it you're not exactly getting a kick out of this." She seems hurt.

"It's nice."

"Whoopee-doo."

"Really. It is."

"You know what you need?"

He's heard this line a dozen times before. Everybody thinks they know what the hell he needs. He needs to be more respectful, he needs to study more, he needs to get into varsity baseball, he needs to stay home, he needs to clean up his act, he needs to use his manners, he needs a good fuck (this suggestion courtesy of Joe Dillon). *A nice boy like you. Nice parents who give you the moon. What is your problem, boy? Insufficient gratitude. Don't know how good you have it. Look at me when you talk to me. Stand up straight.* How could anyone else possibly know what the shit he needs? Especially this rich deb who thinks he's today's toy. *He* doesn't even know what he needs.

"Do you?"

"Religion?" He injects it with sarcasm.

"No."

"Plastic surgery?"

"No." She giggles.

"Natural foods?"

"You're making fun of me."

"Natural childbirth!"

"No," she howls, laughing, pinching his arm. "Sunshine."

When he wakes, the first thing he feels is the borrowed bathing suit snug across his behind. The plastic lawn chair has etched ridges into his bare chest; sun is strong on his back. He can hear water smacking a dock far below the redwood balcony. A brass wind chime inside the house tinkles isolated high notes.

Guilt courses through him. *Should have.* Should have done what?

Two glasses of lemonade are sweating on a green enameled-wood table beside him—loaded with ice and topped with Mickey Mouse fun straws. Eva, nestled into an oversized redwood chair with seashell-print cushions, is reading *Glamour* through rhinestone-rimmed sunglasses.

Minutes go by, ripe with delicious emptiness: the silken swish of pages, the skitter-hop of a bird on the porch rail. A giant black ant weaves along one of the deck's floorboards beneath Rick's gaze, pausing to explore a six-inch split in the lumber.

Rick sits up slowly, takes a swig of the lemonade; Eva continues to read. Her bikini is orange and strung in dabs. He glances away quickly, still seeing the plump wide breasts and soft mound of flesh just below her navel. He tugs the back of his chair to a semi-reclining position and relaxes against it.

A peculiar energy is beginning to possess him. Not purely sexual. From all the silence beneath the speckled sky-dome, he is being fed, and from sheer lack of motion. Tranquillity and exhilaration are his in equal measure. When did he ever feel such ease? He is *happy*.

The thought astounds him. In the long ribbon of events, he has had times of comfort, but this pulsing satisfaction is foreign to him. If he dissects it to its components, perhaps he can reassemble it in another location.

Impossible. He owns no space—no corner that is his alone, where others cannot put the spurs to him.

Anyway, he could not maintain it. He spoils his surroundings. Some bewildering mechanism inside him causes others harm and sorrow.

"Hey there, folks!" A man, emerging from the living room.

"Dad!" Eva cracks the magazine shut.

Christ. Rick stands up so rapidly he knocks his chair over.

"I was going to say don't get up, but I wasn't fast enough." Mr. Metsinger smiles and sticks out his hand, walking toward Rick.

"Yes, sir." Rick accepts the handshake and, after a couple of fumbles, straightens the chair.

"Sit down, sit down. Don't let me interrupt. I just brought the kids for a sail."

Eva grins at her dad. "I think I wet myself."

"Doggone, Evie, I didn't mean to do that. I'm sorry. The boys went tearing into the bedroom to get their suits on. I thought you heard us."

She leaves her seat and passes her father, giving him a playful punch on the elbow. "I'd like you to meet my friend Rick Stockman. I'll get you and the doodles some drinks."

"Call me Carl," he says amiably.

He is uneasy being alone with Carl; he crosses to the railing, a healthy distance from him.

"Glad to have you here. Any time." Carl picks up a watering can, half full, and begins to douse the petunias and poppies in a trough under one of the windows. Rick is taken with his unassuming looks: the red and gray expanse of slightly unkempt hair and beard, the crystalline eyes. He is wearing a sweatshirt with the sleeves cut off, wash-rumpled white jeans and moccasins with no socks. "Eva told me that you were at school with her."

Careful. "Yes, sir."

Carl lowers the watering can and drops it to the floor with a bang. "Want to go sailing with us?"

"I need to get home fairly early. It's my sister's birthday."

"I'm not running you off, am I?"

"No."

Eva and her brothers appear at the same time, in a turmoil of chatter and an eager draining of the mugs and soda cans she holds on a tray. Over the noise, Carl offers, "These are my sons, David and Wesley. Dave's eleven and Wes is nine. We'll catch you later. Nice to meet you!"

They churn down the steps, the kids helping their father with coolers and beach towels, dragging fold-up stools and inner tubes.

Exteriors don't fool him. The guy could be a dictator. "Your dad's nice," he says.

"The best."

He can't see her eyes through the outlandish Elton John shades. Is she lying?

She seems to receive the thought from him, whole. "He *is.*"

"Where's your mother?"

"Home. Sailing makes her sick."

"Why don't you drive this time," she says as they prepare to leave. They are scraping bits of salad and sandwiches into the garbage disposal.

Lord. Here we go again. "I might have an accident."

"That's not the reason."

"How do you know?"

"Before you answered me you looked to the right."

"So?"

"People look to the left when they're trying to recall something. They look to the right when they're making it up."

"Come on."

"I read it in *Psychology Today*. Certain parts of the brain have certain functions, and they're connected up to your eyes."

"Very scientific."

"What's the real reason?"

"I don't have a license. I can't afford the insurance."

"Your parents won't pay?"

"Look, I don't ask you personal questions. I don't ask you why you've got all these bucks and you're not going to college."

"Who says I'm not going to college?" They have finished rinsing the dishes and she is beginning to toss them into the dishwasher with swift, impatient movements.

"Are we having an argument?"

She slams the dishwasher closed. "I just don't see what the big secret is. I'm going to Stanford. I've already been accepted. We're paying for it with the trust fund my dad set up when I was three. Your turn."

To tell anybody about anything that goes on in his family is dangerous. It can get back to them. It can slip out in innocent conversation and blow him to kingdom come. If there's one lesson he's learned, backed up by childhood spankings, it is never to reveal a solitary fact about what goes on at home.

"I have to earn the money."

"Why don't you?"

"Three hundred bucks? I'm spending all my time getting my grades back up so I won't lose my early admit at UCLA."

"I'll give it to you."

"Hey, I don't want . . ."

"Then how about a loan? With no interest. Pay me when you can."

On the way downstairs to the garage she, a single step behind him, places a hand on the back of his neck. He stops. The breath of her is at his shoulder. He isn't equal to this. Whatever he does will be foolish.

She slides her arms all the way around his neck and hugs him, pressing her cheek to his. The embrace is exuberant, undemanding. A gift.

His anxiety ebbs. The center of her power is contentment. Her confidence, her unfettered affection calm him to the core.

"This was only a test. Had it been an actual alert, you would have been instructed what to do," she whispers against his ear.

He turns, pulling her closer with one hand across her back, the other under her chin.

She kisses him first.

He can share it. The secret of happiness is being happy— milking the day. Uncomplex, really. Appreciating the symmetrical rainbow-heart of a poppy, listening to the music of a wind chime.

He chooses the front door, letting himself in to the artistic formality of the foyer: silver-edged photographs and prints, an oaken table adorned with spiral aromatic candles. As he passes the living room they never use, he hesitates.

It arrests him. He usually walks right by, but today he stares at it. A setting from a model home. The white carpet and new semi-circular couch and the chrome lamps are only for company.

What company? It is a museum.

"Check out the sunburn," his mother says, smiling. She

is standing in the family room doorway with a load of clean laundry slung on her hip.

He is suddenly aware of his feverish skin.

"Where you been, Rick?"

He crosses the glazed hall tiles to her, startled to glimpse his dad at the dining room table with the newspaper spread out in front of him. His father looks up, the reserve he saves for Rick slowly taking possession of his posture. "I wish you'd at least leave us a note. I thought I was going to have to pay ransom."

"Been to the beach?" His mother gives him a penetrating gaze, as though she can view his day through the bone of his forehead.

He superstitiously blanks out the images of Eva and her Newport house.

"We'd like to know." Her words are kind.

California glory shimmers outside the patio doors: the aqua pool and abundant camellias, the mountain crevices, which today are clear and laced with textured shadows. *Simple. To be happy.* Perhaps no one has taught them how; he's only just learned it himself.

"I was with a friend," he begins. He will tell it piece by piece, abandoning the attempt at the first sign of a problem. "A girl. From school."

A ripple of surprise flows from his mother. He thinks of giving up. Friends have always been intruders; for some puzzling reason, his mother and dad have tried to discourage his attachments.

"It was a quiet, wonderful day."

"Well, that's nice," his mother ventures. "You were at Long Beach?"

"Newport."

"This girl, she has a car?" His mother again.

"Truck. Pickup truck. New."

His father seems mildly impressed, although Rick isn't sure why. "How come Newport?"

"She . . . has a house there. Her parents do. I met her dad. He's a real estate developer."

The warmth leaves his mother. "Is that what you were thinking when you came in?"

"What?"

"It was written all over your face. I couldn't figure it out."

"What do you mean?"

"You were looking at us with disapproval. Now I get it. We're not ritzy enough for you." It is said quietly, but it explodes at him.

No, no! Her view is cockeyed, all out of shape—he doesn't think *that.* What kind of expression did he have, for God's sake?

He knows. He wanted them to be happy—happy when he came in. And they weren't. They aren't. Because they can't.

They *can't.* They put circumstances in their way. People. Cities. Money. The conditions are never right. It is like the game where the ball is tied to a tall pole in the center of the play yard and the children hit it around and around and back and forth and it doesn't go anywhere.

Hopelessness takes him. Terrible. He is owned by it. Why did he ever think he wasn't?

If God Himself were judging his heart on pain of hell, he would swear to this: he does not covet anything but the gladness of others.

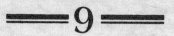

9

Her fourteenth birthday: a serene family portrait, in color. Four smooth faces clustered around a candlelit, linen-swathed table in a restaurant where the waiters sport tuxedos, and flaming desserts dot the dimness.

She wears blue. Pastel blue wool and pink frosted nail polish. Pearl earrings. Ivory foundation, rose blusher. She is clean everywhere, all the hairs shaved from her legs and from the pebbled skin under her arms, her eyebrows plucked—but only beneath the arch, as the beauty books insist.

She pretends they can start from here, from this distinguished pose. A photograph from Olan Mills: spotless clothing and fresh haircuts, intelligent eyes. She would add the hint of a smile along each mouth. Satisfaction. An observable air of devotion. Their bearing would imply family-based strength, an unintentional clannishness.

If she wishes hard enough, they will stay exactly like this when they step out of the evening.

They will Become.

"Would you care for a drink before dinner?" The barmaid, in a short black skirt, blond bangs fringed across her eyelids.

Lee rubs her thumbs slowly against the edges of the open menu she is holding; comfort seeps from the heavy parchment.

"A martini, dry," her father says with elation.

He *promised*.

Her mother nods. "Same."

"Iced tea," Rick growls.

"Tomato juice." *It will be all right*. They are different now, transformed. Why shouldn't they celebrate? Any family would order drinks on a daughter's birthday.

But weakness is stemming through her. She's a damned Pavlovian dog: ring the bell and she salivates. She despises that in herself. If she can understand it, why can't she control it? It has her by the throat; a pressure on her collarbone, deliberate as an assailant's foot. She feels silly.

Frightened.

His wife taps his knee.

Yes, yes. Enough is enough. Two is all he ever has anyway. Did she think he'd order a third? He blots out the sudden vision of the bottle he keeps in a paint can in the garage.

She couldn't know about that; she was in the shower when he sampled it before they left. Bunk, this stuff about sneaking drinks. People sneak drinks because other people are intolerant, not because of compulsion. She's a dear heart, but a stickler.

"Another cocktail?" The ski bunny again. Outdoorsy charm. Yikes.

"No, thank you."

The waiter presents them with shallow wooden bowls of salad: three kinds of lettuce garnished with tomato wedges and home-style croutons. The bleu cheese dressing is awfully runny, like chunks in soup.

It incenses him. Here's the way for a restaurateur to save

a buck: water down the sauces. Well, he won't dignify this effort by putting a fork to it.

He looks around for their waiter. Blast. Which one was it? They are all young, with pink in their handsome cheeks and the same snooty set to their chins. Someone's told them to stretch their necks, to act like British butlers.

A busboy begins to refill their water goblets.

"I'd like to speak with our waiter, please."

"What's the matter?" Katy asks.

She does not like to complain about anything. He touches the back of her hair to reassure her. The movement causes a wavy sensation across the room: ripples of diagonal lines. He focuses on it; it vanishes into the mirrored wall behind a crop of diners. Not a very good grade of glass. Puddles. And streaks.

"Yes, sir."

Mike pulls his gaze back from the mirror to the offending salad. "The dressing is too thin."

"Too thin?"

"That's right."

"I will bring you a new salad. Which dressing do you desire?"

"Bleu cheese."

"Sir, our dressings are specially made by the head chef. This is the only bleu cheese we serve."

Mike perceives a sneer. Camouflaged, of course. It reverberates through him like a sound. He is shaken, literally shaken, by it. He wants to stand up and strike this arrogant snob. "Then get the chef." Several people at adjoining tables twist to stare at him; he stares back stonily.

"I will see if he can come out at this time."

His children say nothing, but their lips are parted in surprise. Why did he bring them here? This isn't a fit place for a birthday dinner. He wishes he could undo it, start

71

over with the Yellow Pages, his finger traveling up and down the list, selecting a number to call for reservations.

Why is he never right? It infuriates him. He plans. He chooses only the best. And is disappointed. Things begin well and run aground. Lack of quality, that's what it comes down to. As if he wouldn't know the difference.

His daughter has encircled her stomach with her arms, her eyes closed. Don't make a scene, that's what she's thinking. She is too tender. She acts as though these things are his fault. When she's older she will understand the value of assertiveness.

The chef walks toward them from an alcove: a squarish man, bound in white and topped with the standard high cap. He has the distracted grimace of a person wrested away from many tasks, all more important than this. "You are not pleased with the bleu cheese dressing?"

"That is correct."

"My apologies. May I suggest, instead, our house dressing, which is a blend of walnuts and oranges in a sweet-sour sauce."

"The point is that I would like to have an edible bleu cheese."

"Edible?" The slight shrug of the man's shoulders as he says the word indicates stifled anger.

Anger moves up in Mike to match it.

"Pardon me. I can understand if it does not suit your palate. But edible it is. I brought the recipe myself from a French culinary academy. It has the finest ingredients."

He feels Katy's hand close over his in warning, but he is fed up. He searches for the most effective sentence, the one that will end the game. "I wouldn't even taste it."

"You have not tried it?" The man's amazement tickles Mike. They are suddenly equals. The chef recognizes that he is not dealing with a customer's naïveté.

72

"Well, if you will not even taste it . . ." His shrug is broad now, tinged with disdain.

The waiter leans between them. "May I suggest an appetizer? Courtesy of the house. Our clams casino are excellent tonight."

"Mike, please," Katy says.

A phantom punch moves rapidly up through the center of his body, from his crotch to his windpipe, unleashing so much adrenaline that he wants to fight, has to fight. His ribs and armpits prickle with instant wetness. He rises, taken down quickly by a blow across the bridge of his nose. He is astonished to realize no one has hit him; they are all in their places, peering at him with varied expressions.

Birthday. The word glides to him over their heads like a magic carpet. What has he been thinking of? To make a scene would destroy Lee's evening.

He gets himself in check. Smiles. "Yes. Clams casino."

She sits on the edge of her bed, shivering with suppressed outrage. Her mother's sorrow and sympathy fill the room, emanating from a body suddenly frail. She is adding to her mother's grief, making her feel terrible. Katy, in the desk chair, bows her head from time to time.

Their sharing has been mostly wordless. She wants to lay her unhappiness against her mother's shoulder, innocently believing—as she used to—in her mother's immense power to heal wounds; her unique fragrance, her mysterious soft curves had salvation in them. She was the source. One had only to ask. Or, beyond asking, believe.

She is her mother's mother now. The helpless posture begs for grace. If she can nurture her mother enough, her mother will be strong again, will reach down to her daughter and take care of her once more.

The two women and the surrounding bedroom change

73

for Lee like images on a pond. She is big, she is small, her mother is big, then small. They are not both big or both small at the same moment. Their tangible gifts to each other undulate around them. The draperies and bedspread and decorative pillows her mother has sewn in summery green and white grow magnified, curved. They cradle Lee with their brilliant folds and patient edges of lace, each stitch a caress. She can count the stitches. They are that visible. The expanse of green shrinks, the walls stretch at the ceiling and corners: a misshapen collage of recorded glory. Framed certificates, red and blue satin ribbons with gold lettering, plaques bearing brassy laurel wreaths, type-written letters crowned by embossed seals. *I give you these.*

"I'll talk to him again, honey."

Her husband, reading *Art Direction* under a subdued light, glances up when she enters the family room. She recognizes that he has passed into a reasoning state. His late-night personality approximates that of the man who courted her: assured, cerebral, magnetic. He gives her a peaceful smile; she goes to stand behind him and put her arms around his neck, captivated by the illusion.

He pulls her gently around to sit with him in the recliner, which is big enough for two if she leans against him side-ways.

"Everything all right?" The question answers itself with its confident tone.

How can he be so unseeing? Is he pretending? She must *tell* him. And now is the time. She has made a science of knowing when to approach him: assessing the tinge of his skin, his carriage, the angle of his head. There are fewer and fewer opportunities.

"You embarrassed Lee."

"When?"

"In the restaurant." She will keep rein on this. It will not get out of hand.

"Because of what I said about the salad?" His words smack of astonishment, the tolerant dismissal of a father bemused by adolescence.

"Yes," she says, careful to keep the hard edge of condemnation out of her speech.

"Oh, it's all my fault." Defensive.

"You didn't have to make an issue of it."

He slams forward in the chair. "I have the right to be satisfied. I'm paying the bill!"

"Shhh."

"Don't shush me!"

How did this escalate? She must finish it, say what she came to say. "You promised us, about the drinking."

"That's not the reason I asked for a new salad! I only had two martinis!"

She mustn't let him get any louder. Lee is upset enough. "Okay!"

"You can never let me be who I am," he whispers. "I don't please you, no matter what I do. You are *so critical*. How do you think that feels, to never quite measure up?"

He's right, in a way. Practically everything he does irritates her. Has he been drinking to combat her dissatisfaction? A cliché, the nagging shrew who sends her husband to the bottle or to other women.

"Can't you be on my side *once?*" he asks, his breath hooked and faltering. "You've done this to me from the start."

Has she? A wrenching possibility: his precious life entrusted to her, she ruining it by consistently making him feel inadequate.

She could have done that, in her ignorance. She knew so little about men and about marriage.

* * *

In bed beside Mike, the circles of delight and exasperation he has created for her close themselves into the same worn question: *What can I do?*

Their long-ago meeting plays like a new piece of film, the colors vivid, the sound undistorted. *A party. Given by an artist couple she barely knows. Her date is an artist, a somber entombment of a man whose canvases record only the ass-end of life: fish skeletons on a wharf, a crumbling chimney, picnic litter among meadow buttercups. The decor of the aging bungalow is electric yellow, all but the hardwood floors. Three white cats spring and tiptoe along high places: the top of an ornate player piano, skinny shelves crammed with a collection of owl figurines. In the crush of guests, she is introduced to Mike and Janine Stockman. Janine paints abstract murals on city buildings, Mike is in radio. She wanders away to peruse the hall gallery, pedal the piano, to cradle one of the cats in a wicker-bottom rocking chair. Mike finds her, again and again. On the fourth time, she notices his effort because it is physical, sensual. He has—at her elbow—inspected the artwork, sat beside her on the piano bench, knelt next to the chair arm while she played with the cat. Now he looks over her shoulder at a book of German lithographs. Stunned by the realization of his attention, she cannot generate conversation. Why would he choose her? The house is full of pretty women with more interesting jobs than hers. Besides, he is married. She hides from him in the kitchen, globbing deli dip on crackers to help the hostess: he stands in the doorway with undisguised infatuation. It is the most flattering thing that has ever happened to her, she with the quiet religious upbringing. Her skirts were always too long and her hair too short, or vice versa. She was not permitted to date until she was sixteen; by then only the most pensive, awkward boys asked her.*

Of all the love stories she had seen or read, hers was the

strangest, the most romantic. She had done nothing to encourage Mike that night except keep very still when he came close to her.

He left his wife the next week. For her. He told her that, straight out.

Katy, I have prayed about this man, her minister father had said, his tone saturated with disapproval. *I think you are making a mistake.* He was not overly harsh or pious, but he believed in the response of God to prayer; it moved his innards infallibly. "I have prayed about it" was his shield. It meant that she had better not argue, he couldn't possibly be wrong, he got it from the Holy Spirit.

Mike . . . no mistake. He loved her. All these years. And she loved him. It was meant to be.

She sees the drinking, she sees that. But what, short of betraying him, can she do?

═══ 10 ═══

The bump in the middle of the otherwise empty bleachers is her uncle Ted. Surprising. Distracting. He has been sitting there for half an hour. What does he want? Her game was uneven anyway—late for almost every shot in the match with Elizabeth. Now the coach's eyes narrow with displeasure as he plucks ball after ball from a wire basket and lobs them to Lee as a cool-down.

Finally, the basket empty, he approaches her around the end of the net. "Whatever you're carrying, how about dumping it before tomorrow?"

Their chemistry is all wrong. Garcia is a thinly veiled chauvinist—which matters to her on good days and bugs the hell out of her on bad ones. She feels she has to prove herself in every encounter.

She has become accomplished at stonewalling him. If he knew how he affected her, he'd really dig in. "Okay, Coach. Stay tuned for another thrilling episode."

He grins, displaying a dazzling lineup of perfect teeth; he has at least twice as many as normal people. She lifts a sun-warmed towel from the bench and presses her face into it. The approval of men. Who cares? She is tired.

She zips the racket into her bag and leaves the court with

the towel around her neck, pulling the chain-link gate shut behind her. Ted has started down through the rows. She waits for him: a lumbering ex-jock with football-flattened arches. An inflated version of her father, wider, bigger. But not fat.

"How're you doing?" He arrives jubilant and kisses her on the temple.

"Fine." This uncle has been a snapshot, a signature all her life. She has seen him at family dinners three times since they got to Los Angeles, and only twice before that. "How's Aunt Monica?"

"Super. I had some calls to make in your neck of the woods, so I thought I'd stop by to watch you practice. Hope you didn't mind."

"Insurance calls?"

"Yeah. More folks dying than buying these days. I got a line on a whole corporation that needs protection for senior execs. It's at the far end of my territory, but still in. Can I ride you home?"

"Thanks, but I usually walk. To unwind."

They have been moving in the direction of the street, along brick paths. He stops curbside and unlocks the passenger door of a black Lincoln Continental. "Lee, please— come with me. I want to talk to you."

Startled, she gets in. He settles beside her, putting the key into the ignition, but does not crank the engine. She notices the rivulets across his forehead and beside his mouth. How much older than her father is he? Four, five years?

He tugs at his blond-gray hair and then brushes it back with spread fingers. "It isn't fair to put you on the spot. But I don't get answers from Mike. Why haven't I seen you more?"

Embarrassing. Her parents have been avoiding Ted, she has sensed that.

He turns his left ear to her; she remembers that the right ear is nearly deaf from college tackles. "Lee?"

"We've seen you."

"A few initial visits. You'll be in L.A. just a year, huh? I know we live an hour apart, but I was expecting some interaction."

"Well, we've been pretty busy." She catches herself beginning to lie. But she can't help it. The product of honesty would be terror: Ted confronting her father. *Mike, we need to talk about this drinking.* Her mother's cold incredulity.

She can't risk it. Besides, what could he do? Her father resents—is jealous of—his brother. Studying him, she cannot figure it out. Quite ordinary the gray-blue eyes, the slow speech, the strain at the shirt button above his belt. Was Ted the favored child, as her father hints?

"I don't get answers," he says again, apologetically. "Mike sidesteps me, your mother doesn't call Monica. I care about you. I want to see you. I would have gone to Rick but I thought you'd be more receptive."

His frankness stuns her; she has to look away from him.

"Will you talk to me?" he whispers. "Am I to blame? Or have you got trouble at home? I did ask Mike—and Katy . . . I *did.*"

His intensity evokes an interior storm of weeping. She wants to cling to him, to tell him—to belong to her uncle and aunt and cousins as other families do. But her mother and dad have drawn a blind between their nucleus of four and all other relatives. They are suspicious somehow, believe their siblings and parents look down on them.

To side with Ted in any way would bring further exile from her mother and father. Intolerable.

"Will you?"

She reads his pain—and his kindness—but cannot answer.

He starts the car sadly and drives her home without speaking.

Ted lets her out two houses from her own. There has been no mention of his coming in; he does not ask. She has the sensation of dragging an air cord behind her, pure oxygen, bubbling, flowing from his concern. It stretches thinner, thinner, breaks. She is in the house, where her mother has been watching from behind the sheers.

Stricken, she stutters, "Mom? He just showed up at tennis. Between insurance calls. I didn't know he was going to. He said . . . he never gets to see us."

"Then why didn't he come in?" An accusation, of conspiracy. Of disloyalty.

The inflection wounds Lee. "He had another appointment."

"What did you tell him?"

"That we've been busy." Is this the right one, is this what she should have said?

Her mother does not comment.

11

For God's sake—it's like he's under anesthetic. Katy bends over the bed and slides an arm under Mike's neck. "You're going to be late for work, damn it. Hey!"

Mike's eyelids open halfway, revealing the lower half of his pupils; the lids close again.

"Mike!" She hits his shoulder with her fist, gently at first and then harder. "Get up!"

"Don't." It is a groan.

"You're making me so mad!" She gives him a final thump and walks away.

Sweating already. Into her silk blouse. She feels disheveled and she's only been dressed half an hour. Her jewelry seems heavy; the fabrics stick to her skin. She accidentally catches a glimpse of herself in the full-length mirror, surprised to find that—except for her frown—she looks fine. Totally put together. Anyone passing her on the street would think her sophisticated and poised. She relaxes her facial muscles. There. She can control things; they will not control her.

Wetting a washcloth with cold water, she carries it to Mike. Who is she kidding? This *is* out of control. Why doesn't he stop? You'd think one of these mornings he'd wake up and say, *I've got to cut back.* And do it. She drops the cloth onto his forehead; he flinches in his sleep.

"Mother . . . good-bye." Lee has come to the bedroom door and is peering cautiously at them.

"Can't get your father up." She shrugs.

"I've got to go. There's a test first period."

Lee's agitation stirs the air between them. Guilt flashes through Katy. She is the mother, she should know how to fix all this. Is it her fault? She crosses to her daughter and kisses her on the nose. In a rare moment of demonstrativeness, Lee embraces Katy, putting her head against her shoulder. Katy, overwhelmed, strokes her daughter's hair. *She needs me. Still.* A sacrament, this holding of her child's flesh; the ancient bond of protectiveness fills her. *In the dark rumple of blankets, she wakes with panic. Where is the baby? She knows she shouldn't bring Lee in bed to breast-feed her, but she has been so sore and exhausted from giving birth. Tiny person—barely seven pounds. Frantic, she searches the covers. Has she slipped down under, toward her feet? Oh, God! Mike, where's the baby? I put her back, Katy. She's in her crib.* How many times had she done that?

Mike scrambles from the bed and rushes heavily into the master bathroom, slamming the door. She can hear the click-click of the toilet lid and seat being raised against the tank. Instantly, Mike begins to retch—nonproductive convulsive gagging that resounds from the porcelain and tile.

Lee tenses, draws away from her. "Bye, Mom."

"Bye."

Katy goes to the bathroom door. She hates this. *Hates it.* Why does almost every day have to start like this? The digital clock winks from 7:38 to 7:39. He can't make it now. She will have to call in for him. And—*Jesus*—

she can't be late to her own job, she can't afford to get fired.

The noises in the bathroom intensify: periodic splashes accompanied by loud belches and the spitting of phlegm. She cannot go to him; a smoldering rage has begun to possess her. She yanks the sheets off the bed with furious energy. They reek. Throwing them into a pile on the floor, she can't think of what else to do. She has begged him, yelled at him; she has tried to handle him tenderly, believing that time and winds would change his direction. She has intervened between Mike and the children, to keep the peace; she has taught them to be considerate of their father. Mike's refusal to cooperate baffles her.

She needs advice. But who can she tell?

No. It's nobody's business. And he would kill her. Word of this could cost him his job—she doesn't want that. They're in over their heads already. She pictures her father's face, Ted's face, should she tell them: disgust, confirmation of their prejudice. Judgment of her as well. Her mother's trusting, ambitionless gaze passes before her: *the husband is the head of the wife, just as Christ is the head of the church. A man will not go wrong if he has the obedient support of his wife.*

She dials the ad agency, Mike's private line, certain that Maggie is at her desk dipping powdered-donut pieces into a Styrofoam cup of coffee.

"Maggie Vanderburg."

"Hi. This is Katy."

"Mike sick?"

A flush of shame. She has done this too many times. "He had a long-distance call. He'll be there shortly."

"Does he want me to cancel his nine thirty?"

Katy feverishly calculates the dressing time, transportation time. "Can you move it to afternoon?"

"I'll try."

Humiliating. In spite of Maggie's pliability. "Thanks. Sorry to rearrange your day."

"Oh, it doesn't matter. We'll see him when we see him."

"Right." Katy cuts the connection.

She doesn't have time to help him dress. She's behind schedule as it is. Mike opens the door and walks past her, his shoulders stiffly raised as though controlled from above by a puppeteer. The rest of his body seems rubbery, weak. He crawls onto the mattress cover and lies on his side, his hair slick with sweat.

"I called your office and said you'd be there soon."

"Umm."

"I can't stay." What if he falls back to sleep? She shouldn't let that happen. But she's meeting Lyle at eight thirty in a warehouse that has no phone. "Get up now."

"In a minute."

"Now."

"Go to hell." He says it lamely but it inflames her.

She kicks the bed. "Go to hell yourself!" Screaming, was she? She doesn't care. "Just go to hell."

The kitchen door slams. Rick, working a few last-minute math problems on the floor of his room, hears a car start up and back out of the garage. He shoves the papers into his book and scouts the hallway. His father's bare feet are hanging over the end of the bed.

Did she leave? The absolute silence of the house assures him that he and his father are alone. He sneaks toward his parents' bedroom, realizing as he sees more of his father's legs that he is facing away from Rick. Stepping closer, he has a full view of his dad's bony back above white underpants. His thinness jolts Rick. Without his clothes he is a skeleton. Why didn't he ever notice this when his father wore a bathing suit? Is it the pose? In lying down, his father's skin sinks between each rib; the vertebrae stand out in knots. He is not fearsome anymore, not even real: a weightless, inanimate thing.

It scares Rick. When his father is ill, he is the Good One. Toddler memories pour down a chute; he is mystically connected to the father who used to cherish him; he can feel the bumping motion of being carried atop his daddy's shoulders.

Mike thrashes onto his back and blinks at Rick.

"You okay?"

"I need to go to work. Will you get me some clothes?"

"Where's Mother?"

"She had an early meeting."

Rick thumbs the light switch in the walk-in closet, uncertain. Wear to work . . . He scans the row of garments. A suit, shirt, tie and belt are hanging together, separate from the rest.

"She usually lays it out," his dad says.

"I found it." He drapes them over a chair.

His father sits up slowly. "Give me a hand." He droops onto the pillow again.

"Maybe you'd better stay home."

"Bring the shirt."

Rick unbuttons it and slides it from the hanger.

Mike stands up in one desperate lunge, swaying to find his balance. He takes the shirt from Rick, pokes an arm into one of the sleeves.

Isn't he going to shower? A stench, radiating from his dad, pervades the room. But to say so—to even suggest it—might set him off.

Mike struggles with the other sleeve and, mastering it, looks helplessly at the cascading line of buttons.

He doesn't act logical, his dad. He never drinks in the morning, but it doesn't matter. He acts nutty. "I've got to get to school."

"I'll drive you. You won't be late."

"Pop . . ." He can't let him go to the office like this. He can't let him be so vulnerable. Pathetic. "Don't you want to shower?"

The forehead creases. "I don't have time."

"I'll help you."

Rick keeps watching the rippled glass of the shower stall; his father leans against it now and then. *This is taking forever.* "Dad?"

"Yo."

"You about done?"

"Almost."

"Listen, I can't miss math. It's second period." He checks his watch. Unless he leaves the house in the next five minutes, he won't make it.

The water stops; his dad reaches over the top of the stall and pulls in a towel from a plastic hook. He steps out, pink from the heat, the towel tied to his waist. Pausing at the sink, he extracts a razor and can of shaving cream from under the vanity.

"I can't wait."

"You said you'd help me."

"I didn't think it would take this long."

"You're going?"

"I have to. You're all right now, aren't you? You look better." Two things he knows about where this is heading: one, nothing he can say will make a difference, and two, his dad's anger is mild in the morning. He will chance it. "See you tonight." He splits, ducking into his room to snatch his stuff.

"Come back here," his father shouts from the bathroom.

Can't. Besides, he will have forgotten about it by dinnertime.

* * *

Katy follows Lyle into the prop bin, a huge area enclosed with chicken wire. Under bare overhead bulbs, furniture and racks of costumes sprawl.

"Home, sweet home," Lyle says appreciatively. "We have to keep it in a warehouse—there's so darned much."

As her eyes adjust to the glare, she begins to pick out gems: a cabinet crank-style victrola, rolled Oriental rugs, feathered hats cased in plastic. The scent charms her: the must of antique wood, the airy nostalgia of taffeta and leather. A subtle order pervades the confusion. She sees that the furniture has been grouped by era, the clothes similarly sorted. She strolls the aisles, squinting at each item, Lyle behind her.

"What say you?"

"Wonderful!"

"The players think I'm an old maid, but I go bananas in here. Historic costume's my specialty. I show up at every estate sale between San Jose and Tijuana." He produces a box of beaded flapper clutch-bags. "Authentic. Can you imagine people don't want these? They came out of an attic. Literally."

He *is* swishy, but she's tracking with him; they are soul mates in this environment: waistcoats and tutus, boas, bustles, spats, ruffled flamenco garb, saris and sailor suits. Petticoat hoops. Monocles. Garish colors, pounds and pounds of sequins.

Lyle winds the victrola; a sour "Carry Me Back to Old Virginny" warbles at them. He beckons to her, grinning. Not swishy, no: just theatrical.

They dance together, sedately but unselfconsciously. The act is comfortable, devoid of sexual current. They're all dilly—theater people. That's what she likes about it. Jolly make-believe.

* * *

In the house alone. A rare opportunity. Mike considers taking a sip of attitude adjustment. Seems to refresh his system, get it moving again. He finishes tying his wingtips and stands up, straightening his suit.

Better not. Reckless he isn't. If there's one rule he never breaks, it's the one about drinking before work. Alkies do that. It's the first sign.

"You're not exactly perfect yourself," Rick hisses.

Eva glances sideways at him from the card catalog. "Just because I said you should study more?"

"I don't give a rat's ass about it."

She scowls, then smiles at a thought. "I am so, perfect."

"You dress like a dork."

Now he's got her. She snaps the drawer shut. "It's fun. What's the matter with you today?"

Rick peruses her prisoner-striped knickers and squarish blouse, the black chain bracelets that circle her ankles. "Fun, fun, fun."

"I don't do this," she whispers indignantly.

"What?"

"Argue."

"I'm discussing."

"This is *your* fun?"

Is it? Sure. His style is alternately sparring and silent. He's a shit.

Her brown eyes wait for his reply: she has glittery pink junk around them. A tiny glazed green star rides one of her cheekbones.

He wants what she has, covets it: the depth of satisfaction, the quirky, delighted view. Is that why he's trying to hurt her?

"It's not fun," he says.

She accepts his attempt at apology by kicking his shoe

once. They sit at the library's center table, she writing a series of index cards for a term paper, he mesmerized by the flourishes and circle dots of her script. He opens his book as a covenant. She fumbles in the zipper compartment of her purse, bringing out a green eyebrow pencil with which she gently draws a petite star on the back of his hand.

Lee stares into her locker: scratched enamel, rusty places. She doesn't want to try anymore. Listening to his vomiting every morning repulses her. He doesn't do it on purpose. He has stomach trouble, her mother said so. Why does everything happen to him? The constant sickness, the scuffles at work. She is ashamed of her feelings: sympathy and disgust.

A lightheadedness causes her to sit down quickly on the concrete of the outdoor corridor. Cecelia Wilkinson, standing five lockers away, slings her books into one and hunkers next to her. "You sick?"

She wants to lie down. Ugly, the world. This battered school, Cecelia's big tits, the globs of grape and pink gum in the water fountains.

"Your period? You should go to the nurse. I'll take you."

In the health room, Cecelia announces, "She has cramps." Mrs. Mellendorf, the white-haired RN, croons at her. "Would you like to go home, dear? I'll call your mother."

"No."

"Then why don't you rest on the cot?" She pulls the shades and gives Lee a wad of wet paper towels to cover her eyes.

She doesn't want to get up again. Ever.

Mike riffles through the mail on his desk, sorting the letters into two piles: winners and losers. The winners pile is a considerable chunk of today's take. One of the notes is a favorable response to a recent airline pitch; it has words like "thoughtful" and "complete" and "well conceived."

"King me," he says aloud. He may be slow starting, but he puts in his share of hours and—except for an occasional boo-boo like the Arno lunch—pretty well meets expectations.

═══ 12 ═══

He couldn't have said that.

Wilson Koppel's face is composed, the mouth undistressed. Neither is it smiling. Motes of dust shimmer in the shaft of waning sun between Mike and his boss.

If he had said that, he would be sitting behind his desk. They are fifteen feet from the desk, ensconced in twin brocade wing-back chairs obliquely angled on an oval rug. The polished facets of the office turn themselves to Mike one by one, ironically serene: the ashless slate fireplace, a brass urn of plumes, the rubbed reddish grain of a Colonial secretary, Chinese silk prints studded with horses and iris.

"Excuse me?"

"I'm considering letting you go."

"Why?"

"Now, Mike, I think you know the answer to that."

"I don't." He *can't* let this happen. How could this happen? Katy . . . she'd be devastated. How would they live? What would he do? "I've been with this company almost twelve years."

"Personally, I like you, Michael. You're a stitch—most of the time. And you've got ideas to burn. I should have such a fertile imagination. They say there's nothing new under the sun, but you sure can rearrange the elements. It would take a committee two weeks to come up with what you can concoct in a single day." He pauses, placing his elbows on the chair arms; monogrammed cuffs peek from his suit sleeves. "But you're irresponsible. I can't trust you. You're not here when I need you. You argue with everybody—doesn't matter who it is. A lot of people refuse to deal with you, did you know that? Not just in this building, but clients—even prospective clients. What good is having you if I have to work around you?"

Mike shakes his head.

"Is this news?"

"No."

"It shouldn't be, because I've told you before. But things slip your mind. You ask me the same questions over and over. I've been chalking it up to genius. People like you operate on a different plane. They're called eccentric. At this point, I don't like it. Not a bit. You've become a liability rather than an asset. I spend too darned much time fielding complaints about you and picking up what you drop."

Pain fringes Mike's vision: dots, darting at him. He believes this man. Wilson Koppel's unwavering dignity is based on a single tenet: uprightness.

"You've been booted sideways in this firm through a number of cities. I don't know how they managed—others took up slack for you, I guess. No one wanted to kill the goose that's laid so many golden eggs. There are only three cities left. What are you going to do when you get to the end of the line?"

This is exaggerated, these grievances. He's not that bad.

"I won't transfer you. Come up to my standards, or I'll ask you to leave."

Can't *anyone* understand? Doesn't Koppel see? It's *hell*

to be the goose. A dozen pressure-cooker years of project after project: creativity on demand. Putting facts through that strange mental distortion that mixes client and market in totally innovative ways. That frenzied, hopeless ritual. *Mike Stockman, Image Builder.* The circus of his mind is tentative, at best. After the endless string of early successes, he had begun to woo his own energy. The connections became fragile, could disappear entirely in the middle of molding a concept. He would bash his head on his desk in furious despair, coaxing back the magic myriad of credible TV spokespeople, graphics, hook-oriented jingles, stationery weave and hue (ivory most effective, according to paper industry surveys), annual report layouts (full-color, 20-lb. glossy), slogans (simple but double-edged), brochures, news releases, campaign kick-offs, banquets, stunts. An errant mosaic, with him slamming the pieces into place, hammering them down. Dazzle the client. Sell the product. Be clever, but oh so subtle. *It's been done before? Are you sure? What doesn't the client like about it? The printer says he's sorry but— Upside down? Fools!*

Banks, pharmaceuticals, cruise lines, die and tool works, sporting equipment manufacturers, stockbrokers, hotels—even the water company, for God's sake. The water company! Why would *they* need to advertise?

He wants to quit, has wanted it for so long. But at his salary level, where could he go? Not back to radio, that's for sure. He's the victim of mortgages and dictated status and imminent college tuition; the hanged man, rope unremittingly tight around his neck, feet flailing air, praying to lose consciousness.

He stands at the end of the bar, thinking: they burn him out, then find excuses to fire him. Young blood would command only half his salary, a big savings to the agency.

Granted, he's testy, but folks seem to take it in stride. Is a protégé waiting in the wings, is that the deal? He won't give Koppel a single opening; he'll be a model player. A team player. He'll even kiss up to Arno.

Arno. Is he the heir apparent?

Granger smacks a shot glass down in front of Mike and pours the first one with pizzazz, raising the bottle rapidly higher, then tilting it back to cut off the stream with the bottle's slender silver tip.

"Got a story for us today, Mike?" Beatty asks.

"No."

"Awww. Have a drink. You'll come up with something."

A rumble of half-laughs.

The implication insults him. He does not need booze to perform. He's had it with other people's low opinions of him, open season on his character. He doesn't rob banks or molest little girls. Or cheat on his wife. He's never even padded his fucking expense account.

He has a story, *right now*. He has a thousand of them— all crackerjack—but this one's the king.

"When I was in radio . . ."

A surprised hush.

He affects his deepest announcer's voice. ". . . we put together a thirty-minute special on the new pope, who had agreed to reconsider the birth control issue. Every week we had to send in our lineup for the newspaper listings all over our area. I was supposed to proofread the pages each week before they went out. But that week I forgot. And a hundred and forty newspapers had received this description: *Friday, 7:30 P.M. Vatican at the Crossroads. The world waits while Pope Paul weighs his birth control device.*"

Shouts of glee. Raucous laughter. People at nearby tables stop talking and give him quizzical, amused glances.

He garners a spontaneous standing ovation and flips a five-spot onto the bar, leaving without touching his whiskey.

After the freeway, the roads lead through well-lit patches of restaurants and bars. As he gets closer to the mountains, the streets widen, sidewalks are clean, devoid of loiterers. Traffic lessens. Storefronts become intentionally quaint or slick, their names more Anglo and newly lettered.

Just beyond the next Gulf station will be an establishment Mike has eyed: a neighborhood place, elegant in its use of brick and glass. He suspects that important people mingle within; top-of-the-line executives stopping six blocks from home to share Happy Hour and exchange corporate secrets. He has been wasting his time with deadenders when he could have been making connections in his own posh suburb. He gives himself three demerits for having missed such an obvious in. It's not what you know, it's who you know.

The circular windows framing Tiffany-shaded lamps are enhanced by a haze of rain beginning in the windless night.

Lucky. He glides into the parking spot closest to the corner. Damn the agency. He will plug into new outlets.

He trips through the drizzle and pulls the brass door handle. Polished to a fare-thee-well; that's a good sign. He was right: an upper-crust watering hole, a plethora of designer suits. Definitely not the Junior Club either. He sees a lot of white hair. Music nudges him along the perimeter of the bar and he makes camp next to three Cardins with breast-pocket handkerchiefs.

Katy marshals her good intentions. He's on time tonight and what happened this morning is over. She can

determine the course of the whole evening by her attitude.

He comes in shyly, as though he expects to find a different decor, a different family, and is relieved that his own
are still here.

She and he have an unspoken pact: they do not refer to
past events, but simply begin again. She wavers for a moment, then reassures herself that she has done her utmost
to prevent a clash. Old-fashioned, maybe, but she has used
her mother's formula: wife bathed and perfumed, dinner
inventive and ready, house orderly, children's homework
complete or nearly complete. *Start with the positive* (one
of her mother's maxims): "I have terrific news."

"Oh?"

She crosses to him, lowering her voice. "We got a note
in the mail about Lee. She's going to be tapped into a
special honor society on Friday and we're invited. But it's
a secret—we're not supposed to tell her."

He smiles. "Fantastic!"

However out of step they may be at times, the wonder
of their children binds them. She is aware that they especially linger at the mirror of Lee's accomplishments: the
medals of their parenting, proof that they are doing something right. "How was your day?"

Hesitation. "Okay."

"Arno again?"

"In a way." He sheds his jacket, tossing it onto a stool,
and shoves his briefcase into a corner. "He's after my
job."

"What makes you think so?"

"Koppel. We had a talk—at his request. He's disen-
chanted with me. Doesn't care for my style, I guess."

"He might . . . move us?"

"Can't count on it. He plays hardball. Thinks he knows
what's best for every branch. And it isn't me."

If only she could look inside the words, actually watch Koppel talk to Mike. Is she getting this through a filter? Her feet are cold, up past her ankles. "But you've done so much for him. For the entire company, all along. He's not going to just throw you away."

Mike shrugs. "It happens." He brushes past her, to the liquor cupboard.

"Don't you care?"

He slams his open palm against the cabinet. "Of course I care! But you can't fight City Hall! If he wants me out, he'll get me out. Our styles don't mesh. He's got the imagination of a first-grader. Totally pedestrian. He doesn't appreciate what I do because he hasn't the skill to understand it. He's not a creative type. Came up in sales."

Such a brilliant man, her husband. Ideas float spontaneously from him like festival balloons being released in droves. Impossible, that he not be appreciated. She puts her arms around his rib cage. "I'm sorry." She hates the Wilson Koppels of the world, the hollow creatures who eventually hollow out their slaves, render them impotent. She believes now the old saying that most people live out their lives in quiet desperation.

Mike begins to mix the martinis; she stands to one side, thinking of the morning's scene. She should have stayed with him. "Was being late today part of the problem?"

"He latched on to that, but he knows I work like a Trojan. I'm at it lots of nights when he goes home."

Still . . . the drinking might be a factor. *Has to be.* How does Mike behave at work? The possibilities horrify her.

What if . . . she went to Wilson Koppel, asked him for the truth. Told the truth. Would he help Mike?

Crazy notion. She has seen Koppel only once, at a dinner-dance. An impeccable man—self-assured, somber. Wealthy. She can't approach him.

What if things aren't that bad? She could ruin Mike's career by interference.

A mistake, to enter his domain. Better to wait it out.

He consents to begin the meal, though only half through with his second martini. Watching the way he seats himself at the table, Lee analyzes his mood, predicts the direction the conversation will take. His spine is an arc, his shoulders droop. From the well of his obvious discontent, he glares stormily at them, chin tipped at a defiant angle. For once, she is hungry. If she eats quickly, she may be able to finish before a major hassle.

The dining room table seems to be the altar of their sacrifices to him. Night after night, the three of them make any concession, agree with him on utter nonsense, simply to get through the meal.

They bow their heads. "God is great. God is good. And we thank Him for this food. Amen." Roast beef, mashed potatoes, gravy, peas and mushrooms, tossed salad; all are passed under his darkening countenance. Lee slices her meat into little rectangles, jabs a valley in the side of the potato mound and studies the gravy as it flows from the crater onto the flowered plate.

"There's no salt in this shaker." Her father's tone is soft but incredulous.

"There isn't?" Her mother rises nervously and takes the offending shaker to the kitchen. Presently, she is back, smiling. "Here you go."

They busy themselves with cutting, munching. Across from her, Rick eats with swift, purposeful strokes of his fork. Maybe she can decoy her father with rosy gossip, keep him off Rick. She flips through the events of the day:

This joke? The results of the language arts test? The Spanish teacher's pregnancy?

"My gravy's cold."

They all look toward Mike.

Rick passes him the gravy boat, which her father tests by touching the sides.

"Not very hot."

A choice. Offer to heat it, or stay silent while her mother gets up again.

"Give it to me, Dad." She carries the gravy to the kitchen and pours it slowly into a pan, turning the dial up to high. When the liquid bubbles, she returns it to the container.

In the dining room, she positions the gravy boat at her father's right hand, careful not to clunk it down or otherwise indicate impatience. She sits, staring at her food, which now does not seem to be food at all but a photo or ceramic of food. She tastes the salad; saliva springs up under her tongue. The avocado dressing is delicious.

"How come the candles aren't lit?"

Her father is staring at the yellow tapers with a foolish perplexity, as though candles came lighted, right out of the box.

"I forgot." Her mother leaves the table and returns with a pack of matches; controlled resentment has begun to possess her posture. Satisfaction ripples through Lee. She wants her mother to be angry with him. He deserves it. The beef seems rubbery now, slippery.

Her father is chewing with the deliberate meditation of a pie judge at a county fair. Ludicrous, this game: everyone jumping up and down, thinking—each time—*this will be the end of it.* If they fill the salt shaker. If they heat the gravy. He cannot be pacified. And no one is to leave the table. Endure.

What mechanism in her continually convinces her she

can win? Absurd, and yet . . . some soul, not her own, has perpetual faith. When the salt shaker is full. When the gravy is hot, he will be satisfied.

"Mrs. Jackson's pregnant," she says. "Isn't that nice? We're going to have a baby shower for her at school. She might have to leave before the end of the year."

"Isn't she the one who had the miscarriages?" Rick.

"Twice. The doctor says she's past the danger point on this one."

"Lovely," her mother nods. "I'll try to find time to sew her a baby quilt."

Her father's instantaneous sullenness implies she has insulted him. Thirty brooding seconds go by. "She's going to get away with that? Breaking her commitment to the school board? Leaving the students at mid-term?" He confronts Lee pugnaciously, as though the teacher's pregnancy were her fault, an event she can rectify. She should have kept quiet. Picking on the meal is standard, relatively safe territory. She has, by her comment, moved his pique into a different realm.

"Asinine. Just *asinine!* Family planning is common knowledge. Is she so stupid she can't figure out how to have a baby in the summertime?"

Rick's face drops closer to his plate. Lee glances at her mother for support. The rule is that Lee and Rick must never reply in a belligerent way. They defer to their mother, who will wrangle with him as she sees fit. "You can't always hit it right on the money," she says good-naturedly.

"She was trying too soon." Those hot eyes have narrowed to vicious slits.

"Christ," Rick mutters.

"Okay, buster," he snaps. A challenge.

"That's enough," Katy warns Mike.

Let him have it, Mom.

"I'm sick of this kid's remarks." Her father shakes a finger at Rick.

"You're the one who's not being nice." Katy says the words evenly, her mouth tightening with each one.

"Get up and help your mother with the dishes." It is said to both of them.

Rick piles his dishes together; the salad bowl on the plate, his glass in the bowl.

"How dare you smack that stuff around!"

Her mother jumps up. "Don't speak to him that way!" They all stare at Mike with hatred: his bluish fists, the bloody eyes, the deranged wag of the head.

He sees their spite and goes blank. The indignation drains from him. Like a whipped dog, he retreats to lie curled on the couch, instantly asleep.

Sometimes she thinks she will take the children and leave him. In her fantasy, she loads the car under streaks of dawn, wipes heavy dew from the windshield with paper towels. *They lumber away from the house, the cold car whining as she shifts gears, her boy beside her, her girl at her shoulder. Earth and sky are beginning to draw apart from one another: the land black, the horizon white, shades of gray resolving to either side.*

Katy pauses, nightgown in hand, in front of the bathroom's full-length mirror, solemnly considering her naked body. Try as she might, she cannot envision where she and the children would go, who would want her. There is no money for starting over. She has invested eighteen years of her life in a man's career. She is hopelessly behind in her own, could not command enough money to support her kids, let alone send them to college. She can't do that to Rick, eight months away from UCLA. Is she to discard everything she's worked for?

Her gaze assesses her firm breasts, the trim line of her

hips. Her fanny's gone a little flat, but the abdomen is still taut. Except for a slight pad of fat along the outside of each thigh and a few broken veins near her knees, she looks twenty years old.

She isn't. Katy unfolds the nightgown and slips it over her head; it settles into place with a faint rustle.

Maybe he sees something she doesn't see. Something unattractive. She could exercise more and start coloring her hair. Admiration and envy consume her when she watches other couples, their mutual affection, their pride, their snowballing affluence.

She suspects herself; a flaw. She is missing a key ingredient in her person and can't figure out what it is.

Mike awakens with his cheek in a tepid puddle. He must have been drooling. The blackness at the windows and the hush of the house tell him it is late. He sits up slowly on the couch, the inner parts of him divided into small weighty squares that shift precariously as he moves; he struggles to balance them. An indefinable dread takes over. He has a sense that things are not perfect, somewhere in this house is a blemish and if he finds it and fixes it he will feel better. He ambles through the family room, searching. The books are aligned on their shelves, no lint mars the carpet. In the kitchen, the sink board is clear, wiped clean. He scouts under the sink for garbage and discovers a fresh paper bag tucked into the plastic basket. Drawn outdoors to the pool, he lingers over it, convinced that a film of dust has gathered on the bottom. Yes. Along the steps at the shallow end, lean columns of silt undulate.

Rick's job, Rick is in charge.

The jouncing bed brings Rick to the surface.
"The pool's dirty."

He recognizes his father's whisper but cannot comprehend it.

"Pal?"

"Yeah?"

"There's junk in the pool."

Calmly. "Okay. I'll get it in the morning."

"It'll gum up the works by then."

"The pump's not running. Can't screw it up."

"Better do it now." The combination of pleading and panic in his father's voice rouses him. Groggy, he slides his glass door open and goes to the pool, his father behind him. Through the water he can see the drain, undistorted. "It's clean."

"Look here." His father takes him by the shoulder and guides him along the rim to the shallow end. "See that?"

He doesn't. A normal amount of particulate matter has collected at the base of each step. Barely visible.

A one-way street. No use protesting. The faster he vacuums the pool, the sooner he'll get off the hook and back to sleep. He unbuttons his pajama top and strips it off, activates the pump, retrieves the pool vacuum from the utility closet. He kneels, pushing the instrument down into the seven-foot depth and slowly submerging the hose. When it fills with water, he plugs the end of it into the skimmer and grasps the pole. His wet arms tingle in the frigid air. He propels the vacuum back and forth, spiritless, unhurried.

The chill breeze attacks Mike's sinuses; they ache. His surroundings glide into sharper focus. In the mist of the pool lamp, his son leans shirtless over the surface, brushing the sides. Or is he vacuuming? Mike has the weird sensation of having been fragmented and then suddenly merged into a solid being, as though his spirit has been chasing his body and has caught up in a single breathtaking instant.

The impact stuns him. *He does not want this to be happening.* He realizes that it is past a January midnight and he has awakened his son to do this task. Unreasonable. The child is cold, and there is nothing sinister in the pool.

A nightmare. Of his own making. He wants to cry out, to weep—to explain it to his son, beg his understanding. *I was running after myself and only just got here, don't you see?* But he is the father. How can he admit he is lost?

He wrests the pole from Rick, pulling it out of the water, shoving it onto the river rock, and hugs him helplessly while Rick stands stiffened, arms dangling.

He's going to shut off the damned drinking. He's going to damned well stop. On a goddamned dime.

===13===

"I don't understand why you're getting so upset," Eva shouts over the pounding of basketballs in the school's gymnasium.

The practicing players, their choreographed galloping and lunging, go soft in front of Rick. "You had no right to do that without asking me."

"You said your parents had never been to Newport."

"I didn't mean for you to *invite* them."

"Your dad was delighted. That's what he said to my dad. I didn't know it was going to cause trouble. What am I supposed to do, call up and say forget it?"

"Yes!" He walks away from her, pushing roughly through a pack of milling students.

"You're not kind," she says, following him outside into the day's stark tranquillity. "I don't even know why I like you."

She won't like him after she meets his father. He might as well give up now. Then, at least, he'll have the satisfaction of doing it himself instead of waiting for her to make excuses. *I have to study, try me next time.* He turns to her. Today it's false eyelashes, furry.

She sees that he is examining them. "You think I'm goofy. You don't want them to meet me."

"No."

"Is it because we're Jewish? My dad's the only one who's Jewish—my mother's Methodist. We're allowed to go to any church we want. Your parents don't like Jews?"

"They like Jews," he sighs. "It doesn't matter." He sits, dejected, on the lawn, stacking his books in front of him. She plunks down, too, slides her feet out of her chartreuse loafers and sorrowfully regards the polish on her toenails. "I made a mistake."

Her vulnerability touches him. Anyone else would call him a son of a bitch and leave him boiling in his own sweat.

"It's just a brunch, Rick—a Sunday brunch. Two hours. Please don't make me go back on it." She squeezes the calf of his leg. "I promise I'll make it go well. Trust me, huh?"

Shit. He can't keep Eva and his family apart forever.

Maybe she can pull it off.

Katy writes the check to "Cash" and pauses before filling in the amount. The bank counter is sterile, impersonal in its straight-edged organization of deposit tickets and fliers; the plastic calendar reads "Friday, January 13." When did she last do this? She doesn't want to make Mike suspicious. She flips through the checkbook ledger and finds such an entry on January 5. A reasonable interval.

Scrawling "One Hundred Fifty Dollars," she steps into line at the window. A hundred for her actual needs, fifty for the secret account. A paint-encrusted workman ahead of her moves aside; the male teller, a red carnation in his lapel, nods at her cheerily.

She feels like a thief every time she does this. It's not illegal. The money belongs to her, to them. She's not really taking it from Mike—it will all go to the family. She's deceiving him, yes, but in his own best interest. If he knows there's money left, he will spend it.

She doubts he'll catch on. It's been three years since she took over the bookkeeping for him after a quagmire of late-payment penalties and overdrafts. To her knowledge, he ignores the mechanics of money now except to make sure he's got a wallet full of cash. He terms his extravagance "generosity," totally unperturbed by it; presents Maggie with a dozen roses for staying late to type an urgent proposal, sends champagne and caviar to new neighbors.

The teller shoves three fifties at Katy. She folds them into her blazer pocket and strides toward the savings and loan across the street.

While he waits for his wife in front of the junior high, he admires the nosegay he is holding: one pink rose in a nest of violets. For his young lady, his star. He's not too shaggy this afternoon for being on the wagon. He's still got the headache and shakes of a walloping hangover, but it'll wear off. In fact, life is pretty damned good. So much for bad press about Friday the thirteenth. He pulled his weight through yesterday and spent the evening in an agency brainstorming session at which he peaked. This morning, he was solidly prepared for the weekly staff meeting and made sure he was endorsing everyone's input. That's for starters. He intends to retrieve his family, too. The edges are mushy, but he remembers being a little bonkers lately. Koppel was right: he's got some clearing up to do.

Well, one task at a time. He's here to honor his daughter and he'll do it in quiet style.

When the curtain parts, his girl is already on stage with about twenty other ninth-graders in a semi-circular row of chairs. Informed only minutes before the ceremony that they were being tapped, the children are flushed, fidget with excitement. Lee seems the most composed, her expression pensive. He realizes as the principal reads the first few names that the students are in alphabetical order; he will have to be patient. Patience is not his long suit right now. His stomach's uneasy. He wishes he were horizontal. Can he last through this, or will he have to leave?

He tries to get Lee's attention with a slight tilt of his head, a prideful smile, but she absently stares at the hardwood center of the stage, listening to Dr. Martin's peppy but repetitious cataloguing of academic accomplishments.

Slowly, her lashes lift; she scans the audience, her gaze coming to rest on him and then on Katy. The sightless eyes move along. Did she really see them?

So, her mother and father are here. She tightens. She must not give him any encouragement; he might become exhilarated by it. She remembers with unwanted clarity the elementary school graduation at which he borrowed the microphone from the phys. ed. teacher to praise and thank the entire faculty. And a fourth grade PTA meeting where he stood up three separate times to loudly bemoan Lee's inadequate lunch period.

Her name is announced. She receives the certificate and returns to her seat, biting at the skin flap on the inside of her cheek, concentrating on the slim greenish veins around her knuckles.

In the aisle, her mother hugs her. The auditorium shimmers with flashbulbs; laughter surrounds them.

"Congratulations, sweetheart," a man says, shyly handing her a purple and pink bouquet. He is wearing her father's face. Strength and dignity flow at her from his posture. Her real father has come to her like this in the castles of sleep: king of the kingdom, she the cherished princess. Now that he is here, she does not want to leave him; the dream will vanish. But visitors are departing, the pupils being whisked to class.

She looks back as she goes, memorizing his straight-on wave to her, his humble receptiveness to the approach of her mathematics teacher. In the hall, she tucks the flowers onto the shelf of her locker, a delicate triumph rising in her consciousness. The feverish hours of untangling algebra equations, political history and Spanish conjugations were worth the effort. He is happy again. And she did it.

Lee tries to hide behind a knot of girls in a corner of the gym. She wouldn't have come to the Honors party except for the coaxing of Lynn and Jessica. Both have left her to dance. Another boy is heading for the group: Jerry Caruthers, a popular kid who has never talked to her; he has barely crossed eyes, which she has heard him make fun of with good humor.

He speaks to Becky Kerner, his words lost in the power of the music and the undercurrent of a hundred conversations. "Lee! Lee," her friends twitter. She glances at Jerry and realizes he has asked for her. Pressure expands the walls of her stomach. She has to do it. She is being pushed in the ribs by several girls.

He steers her into the crowd. It is less threatening there, as though she has walked through invisible glass into a private atmosphere where the occupants are euphoric with pulsing rhythm and their own free motion.

She and Jerry dance separately: he with the deliberately amusing swagger of a punk rocker, she with restraint but with laughter at his antics. The record burps to a stop. Frozen by the silence, she waits for him to walk her back to her spot. He puts a hand on her shoulder as a signal for her to stay.

A song begins, this time slow. He clutches her closely around the waist, snuggling his cheek to hers. She doesn't like it. Her heart thuds with shivering force; she will be too ashamed to look at him when they quit.

Couples glide by, calling to Jerry, their curious stares unsettling her. If he continues to dance with her it will mean he has a special interest. Does she want that? The distance between herself and the girls on the sideline is great now. It will be a humiliating journey if he takes her back. But she wants to go. What should she say? Other girls seem to have passwords; they shuttle between the dance floor and their circle with nonchalance.

Jerry releases her abruptly; a blond boy has cut in. Jason Gates . . . the one who broke his leg last autumn and had to hobble up and down the school stairs with crutches.

"How's your leg?"

"I got over it."

She has to reach up to hold him; his chin brushes her forehead. Almost immediately, the music ends.

He pats her hair. "I like this. You've let it grow." His smile squeezes his aqua eyes nearly closed.

The elation of a sudden crush makes her glance away. Will Jerry be back? She contemplates the swirls of people, glimpsing his silhouette at the ribbon-festooned punch table next to Suzanna Reid.

"Is he your date?"

"No."

"Good." Jason scoops her to him.

The new lyrics wail of blue horses and a river to be forded in the night. His scent and shape are immediately familiar. She believes she knows everything about him simply from his touch, imagines she can see his home: a sparse, dim, one-story house with clean but worn furnishings and yellowed books. His mother is big-boned and kindly, with a wreath of braids and a guttural accent; his father shorter, a scholar, gentle behind roundish eye-glasses. They enjoy home movies and gardening, porch sitting until dark. She pictures herself perched on the front of that wooden porch, feet on the first step, as breezy dusk gradually creeps over her; she can smell the moist clumped earth of the crawl space under the house. In a framed scrap of kitchen light, Jason's mother slices strawberries for shortcake.

Katy lies still for as long as she can, then squirms out from under Mike's weight, nudging him onto his side.

Blearily, he mutters, "Love you."

"Love you." Sleepy but too tired to sleep. Her body aches with the physical strain of waiting for him, thirty minutes or more, alternating positions, trying. For a climax that seems, finally, like something taken from him involuntarily; a small portion, brief. The world exhausts him, uses him up before he arrives at this bed. Most nights, he hasn't the strength to crawl into it. Why should work break a man's health, rend his family? The plight of centuries: men in steel-toed boots, their labor-thickened fingers carrying black lunch pails along morning sidewalks, away from the monotonously tidy places where women wait. And, in the evening, the empty thermos bottles to be washed while the men age quietly in the well of a favorite chair, folding their newspapers back and forth into readable squares, sinewy veins swelling and shriveling on their arms and necks.

He needs her. A man who could have chosen anyone—and still could—has wrapped his life around her. In passing cars sometimes she thinks she sees Janine, always alone, wearing that faded pink headscarf of hers, rigidly watching the road.

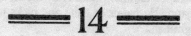

14

Mike stirs the sizzling frittata, savoring its fragrance. Onions, potatoes, green pepper, ham bits. All he needs now are the eggs. He has them ready, beaten to a lemony froth; he pours with precision, covering every inch of the vegetables. Magnificent. And the wooden spoon is exactly right for this experience. Even the slightest flavoring from a utensil can make a difference.

He babies the eggs, careful not to bruise them, and grinds cracked pepper over the top. He used to cook every Saturday morning. The kids went wild for it. When did he quit?

Lee has paused in the doorway and is sizing him up.

He smiles. "Frittata!"

"Great." A mixture of wariness and surprise.

It pricks him. Something slams sideways in his brain, like a drawer sliding open. He feels a queasiness shape itself into a lump at the top of his abdomen. He wipes sweat from his forehead with a paper towel. "I'm the cook, waiter and dishwasher this morning. You three are the guests. I've set the table. All you have to do is come on. Want to get Mom and Rick?" He halves and quarters the omelet, bringing the sections gingerly from skillet to plate with a spatula; decorates each with an orange slice and a sprig of parsley.

Arm service. He's seen this done in restaurants: two plates in the left hand, held sturdily by his thumb, one plate on his forearm. He balances them and picks up the fourth with his right hand.

"Pretty fancy." He grins at his family as he deals his steaming wares across the table.

No reaction. Curiosity, maybe, but not even much of that. Are they asleep where they sit? They're dressed—he didn't wake anybody up. Was he expecting applause? Well, yes. Sort of. He thought they'd be . . . eager. Resentment stirs in him; he holds it in check. He's a new man and this is the third day of a permanent pilgrimage.

The doorbell rings.

Jason Gates.
"Who is it?" her father calls from the dining room.
"It's . . ." Before she can speak, her dad strides into the foyer.
"Who's there?"
". . . Jason."
"Who?" He swings the door wider. "Oh."
"Is this a bad time?" Jason asks.
"Of course not!" her father exclaims. "Come in."
Volume and tone are overdone. Jason looks quizzically at Lee, then steps inside to follow them.
"You're just in time to try my famous frittata. Sit you down. Here." A flourish.
Jason lowers himself into the appointed chair.
"Everybody, this is Jason!"
"I didn't mean to interrupt your breakfast. It was ten o'clock and I thought . . . Lee might like to go for a walk."
"That's quite all right." Her father again. Loudly. "Glad you're here. This is Mrs. Stockman, and Rick."

114

"Hello." Jason's voice is scarcely audible by contrast.

Only God can undo this, erase the past two minutes, start the meal again with no doorbell, no Jason. If she prays hard enough, he will disappear. She can make it happen, she *can*.

No. Nothing's ever been fixed, in spite of all her asking. No phantom floats through the universe, eavesdropping on prayers. That's been proved to her beyond doubt. Like Santa Claus: you know he doesn't exist because it's impossible for one being to get around to all those children in a single night.

But Jason seems intrigued with the frittata and her father's banter; he doesn't notice that her dad isn't eating, has relinquished his portion.

She focuses on her father, dissecting his sentences texture by texture. She has rarely seen him so pleasantly animated, so intent on giving to others. Part of what he says is puffery, designed to convey an image. But beneath that is the traceable outline of soul.

As they finish, he says to Lee directly and sincerely, "You two go on, take your walk or whatever. I'll be the maid."

They end up at Jason's, a freshly painted clapboard two-story in blue and white with a log fence around it. She is timid about going in, but he urges her through the side door. *The dining room.* From it, she can partially see both living room and kitchen. Clutter spills away from her in every direction, between and over the antique furniture: folded laundry, fabric and patterns, newspapers, toys, a gutted radio next to its works, sheet music heaped high on a scarred piano. In a dining room niche, a table-style sewing machine hulks, cloth flowing from its presser foot; an upright vacuum cleaner stands in the middle of the living room carpet, an iron and ironing board by the front door.

They round the corner into the living room where a boy wearing a Walkman reclines across the arms of a bulky chair and a woman is changing a toddler's diaper on the end of the sofa.

"Mom, this is Lee Stockman."

Mrs. Gates smiles broadly at her, lifting the child up by his arms and giving his rubber pants a swat as he scoots away. "I'm happy to know you, Lee."

"Thank you."

"We're going to look at the birds."

"Good idea!" Jason's mother is on the skinny side, her clothes comfortably wilted. As she rises, Lee notices that she has one of those bodies on which things seem to have been slightly misplaced: the nubs of breasts too high and far apart, the waist too long. Her rolled-under hair misbehaves in brittle patches; her blue eyes protrude over an undersized nose and mouth. "I made some cheesies. They're on the counter. Help yourself, kids."

Jason wraps a bundle of the rippled cheese cookies in a paper napkin and carries them upstairs, Lee at his hip. The second floor is a repeat of the first: sweaters hung to dry over the railing, scattered toys and discarded clothes. She can see into several rooms, which are splashed with posters and flags, their beds unmade.

"How many brothers and sisters do you have?"

"Four."

In his room, he has strung a tightly woven fishnet from opposing walls. At its center a deep, narrow wicker basket rests under mosquito mesh and a suspended heat lamp. He uncovers it; baby birds are clinging to the side. "Swifts. Their nest fell down—the mother sticks it to the inside of a chimney with saliva. The neighbors gave them to me when she didn't come back."

They are a throbbing mass of brown-black, but as Lee's eyes adjust she can see the white throat and open beak of each. Five? *Five.*

"Here, look." He picks one from the bunch and cradles it in his hands. "They have these sharp points on the end of their tails so that they can support themselves on the side of the nest."

"What do you feed them?"

"Mealworms." He points to a dish of wriggling dark lines in powdery grain. "And egg yolk. I give it to them with an eye dropper. We all take turns doing it. They need to be fed constantly. And those are my quail eggs." He slides the bird back into the bunch and replaces the mesh. "See? There were too many for the incubator I bought, so I had to make another one with a box and aluminum foil."

On his desk, in a round plastic incubator with a dome lid and in the homemade version, several dozen miniature eggs are lined up in rows. She leans over them, staring. "Where did they come from?"

"I ordered them through the mail. You should have seen us zoom out to the airport when they called and told us the quail eggs had come in. You have to get them right away. They have to stay at a hundred degrees, no more, no less. The big end of the egg has to be up because there's an air pocket in it so the bird can breathe. If you stand him on his head, he'll drown. But I give them all exercise several times a day by turning the eggs over, side to side. That's what you're supposed to do."

He pauses, with a suddenly self-conscious expression. "Does this interest you?"

"Sure." *Another world.* She has been crawling through a long tunnel and come out here, like Alice down the rabbit hole or Dorothy in the tornado. The house's slightly moldy scent of too many belongings, a myriad of projects started and forgotten for new ones, tempts and intrigues her.

They sit cross-legged on the lumpy goose-down pad of the window seat, sharing the cheese snack, talking of school. She watches with growing adoration the crinkles at the outside edges of his eyes as he laughs. The bright panes of glass behind him are speckled in dusty dabs where raindrops have repeatedly fallen and dried.

15

"Well, for God's sake," Mr. Metsinger says, as though he hasn't been expecting them at all. He pumps their hands and claps their shoulders.

Rick stares beyond him to Eva and her brothers, who stand next to Mrs. Metsinger. He notices at once that they are dressed up: Eva and her mother in skirts and stockings, the boys in collared sport shirts. The table is set with gold-flecked plates and cloth napkins, a tulip centerpiece; along the counter between the kitchen and living room are fruit and cheese assortments, baskets of crackers. He gives Eva a grateful smile. The introductions go round and round in a tizzy of ecstatic exchanges.

"I made a batch of Bloody Marys," Mr. Metsinger announces. "Let's sit out on the deck and take the air."

He didn't think there would be drinking at midday, at a breakfast!

Mr. Metsinger opens the freezer door and extracts four fat glasses, lining them up next to the stove; he pulls a pitcher of tomato juice from the refrigerator.

"None for me, thanks," Mike says.

"Nonsense," Carl answers. "I make the best Bloody Mary this side of the Rockies." He fills the glasses and pokes a stalk of celery into each. "Go on out on the deck and I'll have this ready in no time. What do you kids want? Ginger ale? Coke?"

"I'd prefer a Coke," his dad insists.

"Coke," Rick echoes.

"I'll fix it all up. You go ahead and make yourselves comfortable."

Rick leads the way out into the noon heat, stunned to find that the bay view has changed: dingier and more crowded, with a dull one-dimensional effect.

"Here we go." Metsinger, with a tray of clattering glasses, serves the youngest first. When four Bloody Marys remain, he ceremoniously presents them to the adults.

"A toast. To our friendship," Carl says, holding his glass high.

His father hesitates while the others drink.

"Bottoms up," Carl chides.

Katy winces as Mike begins to gulp the Bloody Mary. How can she stop this? Trying to control him is like trying to bend steel—useless and exhausting. Now that he's started again, her only hope is to regulate his intake. Social gatherings are exercises in mortification—for him, for the children, for herself; she shadows and overshadows Mike, sitting close to him, finishing his sentences or jumping into garbled ones with a distracting anecdote, steering him physically away from people he is apt to browbeat. She must appear pushy, her husband henpecked. It is easier to sidestep invitations, which she usually does.

Having paused a sheepish interval in the downing of his drink, Mike continues to drain it to the ice.

"Another one?" Carl offers jovially.

"I'll get it." Katy rises. She is adept at mixing on the lean side, and adding water or juice to existing batches.

"No—wouldn't think of it. Keep your seat."

This situation has as much potential for disaster as Tina's party: her son's pretty girlfriend, the little brothers, people of a different echelon and faith, a house tucked with imported china, rare fabrics, steep staircases. The odds are too great: she is outnumbered by the dangers. Never in this world would they be here if it weren't to please Rick.

His father has consumed two Bloody Marys before the meal and is polishing off a third glass of wine instead of dessert. Only one person in this room knows the torment in Rick; he eyes Lee across the table. She meets his gaze, then spoons sugar into her teacup. So far, his father has been on target with answers, has not slurred or spilled. Has not insulted the host or criticized the meal or started a political harangue. Could it be that the tender affection among the Metsingers has been a good influence? His dad is seldom in the company of other families. Has he made comparisons today?

"Carl and I want to give you the Dollar-Ninety-Eight Tour," Betty Metsinger says.

They scatter from the table, his father weaving after the others, Rick behind him as a guard. The procession is orderly, from bedroom to bedroom, down to the game room and back. When his father goes into the hall bathroom and closes the door, Rick stands by tentatively. The others pass. It must seem peculiar for Rick to be hanging around like this. He returns to the great room and to the deck, searching for Eva. If his dad isn't out in five minutes, he'll investigate.

Mike watches water bubble in the sink. He was okay until he got up from the table. Quick moves usually cause a rush of lightheadedness. And then all that trekking up and down. He'll get over it in a minute. He went back on himself, having those drinks. But what could he do? You can't turn down hospitality without injuring feelings.

Washing his hands, he has the sensation of a ceiling fan rotating over him. He looks up. Nothing. Just a stretch of white.

He uses the embroidered fingertip towel and lays it on the vanity. The towels match the wallpaper, match the curtains. Snazzy.

As he exits, he encounters the daughter coming out of one of the bedrooms. Eve? Eva? She smiles, Mona Lisa–style. Where has he seen that smile before? There's a bit of the trollop in it.

Oh, hell yes—Naughty Nancy from college. She was the only girl at certain fraternity parties. He hopes Rick is being careful. This is the kind of woman who sneaks a pin hole into your prophylactic to trap you into marriage. They always have prominent breasts, slender legs and a gap between their front teeth. Guys used to joke about that gap being Freudian.

She is ahead of him now, walking with fetching sway. He'll have to talk with Rick. Trouble is, boys never believe their fathers. His kid could end up with a baby when he's hardly more than a baby himself—put a damned dead end on his university career.

He'd better jump on this opportunity—later might be too late. "Are you having sex with my son?"

She whirls, obviously frightened. He's pegged this one right. "Sir?"

"Are you having sex with my son?"

Astonishment. "No."

"If I find out you are, I'll be the worst enemy you ever had."

She blanches; her lips part against rapid breathing. He discovers to his dismay that there is no gap between her teeth.

* * *

They pile into the car. Is his father fit to drive? They'll find out soon enough. His mother would never make his dad move to the passenger side while friends were watching. And his father would never admit he shouldn't take the wheel.

They putt-putt away slowly, the diesel engine warming up. Oh, well. Doesn't matter what happens now. They made it through the brunch without incident. All things considered, it's been a pretty decent weekend.

=== 16 ===

"He said *that?*"

Eva nods, intent on her driving.

Absurd. He doesn't believe her. She's such a wacky dresser—it couldn't be much of a leap from there into a mental never-never land.

"You think I'm lying."

The dense jelly inside his bones aches with the truth. *His father did.* The afternoon trees and houses of Windmill Drive are irregular shapes lurching past him, stretched too high or too wide, dizzying. "Stop here."

"Why?"

"Pull over."

"What do you—"

He pushes himself against her and stamps on the brake, jolted by the shape of her foot under his; his shoulder hits the dashboard with painful force, his right eyebrow smashing into the rearview mirror. The truck strikes the curb, bouncing to a halt.

She gapes at him. Silence filters thickly in through the open windows, pierced by the oddly cheerful twitter of a bird. "Why would he say that to me?" she whispers. "What reason would he have?"

"No reason. Look, let's quit seeing each other. This isn't working out."

"I don't care what he says to me, I just want to know why. Was he looped?"

"Probably."

"Does that happen often?"

He can't talk about this. Won't. "See you around, okay?" He opens the door.

"Wait a minute." She scrambles out after him.

He yanks his bike from the back of the truck and slams it onto the pavement.

She grabs the handlebars. "I shouldn't have mentioned it. Forget it. I don't want you to go away from me. I'll never bring it up again."

He tries to move the bike, but can't without ramming her. "Damn it, Eva." He gives the bike a sharp jerk backward and angles it around her.

"Let me take you home," she screams as he rides away.

He wouldn't dare. He needs to pedal this shit-bird as hard as he can to work off his fury. To keep from killing his dad.

In the garage, he smacks his bike against the wall, panting, still livid. His father's car—and his mother's—are already here. He wants to hit his father, has wanted to for so long; a decisive, staggering punch to the side of the face. Would he be able to stop at one?

Fear courses through his chest. Locked in the ice of his father's eyes is an untried zone of mindless violence. Whatever Rick's fury, his father's could be greater.

No matter. He will do it. His own cowardice disgusts him. He is sick to death of treating the man with honor when he deserves none. He is ass-tired of tiptoeing around, of relaying messages to him through his mother, of getting answers back the same way, as though his father didn't live with them at all but miles away.

He bursts into the kitchen, shocked at the worried huddle he sees: his mother, father and Lee, leaden-eyed. They do not greet him but stare at him the way people stare at someone who is the last to know something awful.

Lee crosses to him, over the invisible line. No one speaks. The news belongs to a single person, he senses that; the others are deferring.

"I'm not creative director of Adams-Wenborn anymore," his father says.

He looks from one to the other, trying to understand. "What are you?"

"Nothing. I'm not employed there."

"Are we moving?"

His father shakes his head.

"There was a reorganization," his mother says. "His job was eliminated." *Don't ask.* He can hear these additional words in his ears as clearly as if she had said them.

He doesn't recognize his father: the glibness, the hostility have gone; his clothes hang on a great emptiness. He is a scarecrow, no longer an opponent but infinitely worse. As an opponent, he was still in command, a presence directing Rick's life. Now he is broken. Pitiable, pitied. Sent home to them from the world.

Katy puts a finger to her lips and closes Lee's bedroom door. "I want to talk to you, honey."

Lee comes toward her mother; Katy notices the blue-white tint of her skin, the listless gait. Impacted by the news, no doubt. Well . . .

"I'm really going to need your help now. Dad will only be paid through the end of next month, so I have to increase my hours at the theater. I've been barely more than part time—I'll need to go full time. And I won't be able to do all the things I've been doing at home. I'll have to rely on you to help me.''

"Okay.''

"It's a shame that the opening of the play is tonight, of all nights. I don't like to go out because your daddy is sad and I should be here. But I have to work. Will you take care of him? I'll be worried the whole time. He's really down.''

Lee nods.

God bless. What would she do without her daughter?

Cutting through the bath, Katy discovers Rick at his desk. He blinks at her. She motions for him to close the hall door, which he does with an outstretched palm.

"I need to talk to you, Rick.''

He gives her that defiant glare.

"I'll need your help with this situation. Starting tonight. I have to go to the play opening and I don't want to come home to any trouble. Dad's upset enough. I'm going to trust you not to add to that. I told Lee, and I'm telling you, that I'm going to have to increase my hours at work until Dad gets another job. It will mean some sacrifices.''

Distaste, that's what she sees in the set of his jaw.

"Do you hear what I'm saying to you?''

"Yes.''

"We have to pull together. Do you think you can do that?''

Is this the same baby she brought home seventeen years ago, the chubby boy she used to carry on her hip? They have no contact now, as though she were watching him on television, recognizing him but at an infinite and insurmountable distance. She reaches for him, to touch the kinky fleece of his hair, startled that he is soft and warm and does not draw back from her.

He has always fought her, fought them. She cannot fathom his reasons, she only knows that springing inside her is a rush of tenderness for him and a sorrow for his self-made prison.

"I love you," she says, getting onto her knees, looking up at him. He is affected by this; she can tell by his swallowing, swallowing again. They exist for this minute inside a capsule, as they did when they were one unit and she could feel his tiny feet thumping under her ribs. She rests her cheek against his knee, waiting for a touch that does not come.

"Mom?" The word is cracked with emotion.

She raises her head, seeking his eyes. They are dark with trouble, their usual pose. A stalemate, the perpetual disappointment between mother and son.

"Please . . ." he says. "I need to talk to you, too."

She sits on the end of the bed, listening.

"It's about Dad. He . . . insulted Eva."

A flicker of impatience. This boy is always on his father, will not defer to him even on such a calamitous occasion. *Self first.* "When?"

"On Sunday, at her house."

"Well, I'm sure he didn't mean it."

"It wasn't nice."

"What was it?"

"He asked her if she was having sex with me."

"Sex? Why would he ask her that?"

"I don't know. He owes her—and me—an apology." Sparks now. A witch hunt.

"Do you know what your dad's been through today?"

"Yes."

"*Hell*, that's what he's been through. He's lost his job. And you're . . . focusing on yourself."

"He hurt Eva." Adamant, fierce.

Well, what if he did? She can't fix it—not now. She's

128

not going to throw this into the hopper. Lord! Eva will get over it, it's not a major thing. Puppy love passes by and when she's gone, they'll still be here, bound by blood. They have to stand by each other. Is Rick going to hassle Mike about this while she's out?

"I don't want you bringing it up to your dad tonight. He's worried enough and I have to be at the theater."

"He owes her an apology."

"I'll handle this. I'll find out what was said. Promise me you'll give your dad some support this evening. He's a person, too. He needs just as much encouragement as the rest of us. In fact, more right now."

He does not answer.

"Will you do that? We're in a tough spot, Rick. Say yes."

The eyes focus through her skull, on a point at the other side of the room.

"Say *yes*, son. Can't you do this one thing for me? I don't ask you very much."

He shrugs as consent.

"Katy, I simply won't allow you to go home yet," Lyle says, hugging her on the dance floor of the quiet dinner theater. "It was a fantastic opening and you were a big part of it. You've got to stay for supper."

Katy consults her wristwatch: nearly eleven fifteen. Late. Two waiters, having cleared the full ashtrays and empty glasses from the tables, return and begin to set them again— for the cast.

"Not going to pass up a free meal, are you?" Lyle winks at her. "The management does this for us every opening night. It's a ball."

A few of the actors emerge from backstage in their street clothes. They embrace her with lavish congratulations and on-the-lips kisses. She had forgotten how unabashed theater people are: a kiss standard fare, approximating a handshake.

More actors straggle in, surrounding her, exclaiming about the vibrant costumes and sets she selected for the play. The jubilation excites her: the bumping, touching, joking, laughing. They still smell of greasepaint and cold cream, these people; their movements are large, their anecdotes long and richly embroidered.

She thinks uneasily of the children and Mike. Are they taking care of him? Or are they at each other's throats? Just once, she wants to choose herself—to let go of responsibility for an hour.

She will. She deserves this salad with the Roquefort cheese, the icy beer, the praise and secrets told directly against her ear, the silly cha-cha Benny and June have started in front of the stage. A feast, and she is so hungry.

Lee stands over her snoring father. Should she try to get him into bed? He will nap on the couch all night if she lets him. It can't be good for his health, to sleep in his clothes on a narrow strip of cushions.

But, if she wakens him, he may start a ruckus. He could have Lee and Rick scrubbing out the refrigerator at midnight or staying up to keep him company as he eats rye bread and sardines. He loses track of day and night, believes others should be up when he's up.

Better leave well enough alone.

At last, his mother is home from the theater. Two o'clock by the fluorescent points on his wristwatch. He tracks her through familiar sounds: the hum of the automatic garage door, the feminine rustling in the hallway, the sigh of hinges as she checks on Lee. He hears her try his doorknob, stopping when she realizes it is locked.

She moves on. The rhythmic whishing grows fainter, evaporates.

He gets up and removes the chair from under the hall doorknob, pushes the nightstand away from the bathroom door. He will not feel safe anymore when she is out; his father's new situation could make him wickedly unpredictable.

When he slips the doors open and air wafts into his stagnant room, he feels the dammed-up wave of sleep begin to break over him. He goes to lie with his head at the foot of the bed, his feet on the pillow, swimming through the neutral current.

Katy and Mike dress side by side, she struggling with panty hose and jewelry clasps, he intricately winding and threading his tie. Interesting, that in all these years she has never learned how to master a man's tie knot. She must have watched him do this thousands of times and yet could not do it herself if she had to. She checks him over for lint, hanging threads, split seams and fraying cuffs. None. He's in A-1 condition.

She experiences a swell of hope. He has rebounded so quickly. Fired yesterday, he's willing to sample the job market today. Maybe it isn't bad, this turn of events—a change of scene could give him new enthusiasm.

When he is dressed up, she forgets their squabbles. This morning, he's more handsome than last night's leading man. She smiles at him, amazed to find it returned. They might be going broke, but gaining something more valuable. Awkwardly, they put their arms around one another.

"Almost ready to go?" he asks.

"Uh-hum. Good luck."

"I feel relief," he says.

"So do I."

His mood is receptive—does she dare to mention the incident with Eva? If she doesn't, Rick will take it upon himself. Difficult, to always be the negotiator. But she does it fairly well, has saved a lot of head-cracking.

"Michael, did you say anything unusual to Eva on Sunday?"

"Like what?"

"Something she could have interpreted as a put-down."

"Of course not. Did she say that?"

"I guess so. Rick's a little upset."

"He stays on the ceiling."

She can't argue with him there. "Did you happen to make a comment about . . . sex?" She says the last word gingerly, afraid of his reaction.

Did he? Oh, Lord. He skips back through the hours of the last two days until he finds it: a luncheon in Newport. She is the one in the blue and yellow outfit, the only Metsinger daughter. Nice-looking, with brown eyes. Was he ever alone with her? They were all together, on the porch, at the meal. What could Rick mean? *Sex?* Was she sexy? No, a young teenager—they barely have their bras on straight.

"What would I have said?" he asks his wife.

"A question about whether or not they . . . make love." Katy giggles.

This tickles him, too. He grins. "Not likely." He searches the murky areas of his brain, seeing the rooms of the Metsingers' house, examining each location where he had sat or walked. Did he speak to her specifically, even in the group? *Hello* and *Good-bye,* that was it. And maybe *Pass the butter.*

As Rick leaves for school, his mother trails him into the garage; she comes close to him, beside the bike, and assumes a confidential tone. "I talked to Dad about Eva. What she told you isn't true. I don't know why she'd say that about him, but I don't like it. And you can tell her I said so."

A few blocks away, overwhelmed, he parks his bike and begins to kick a tree trunk furiously and methodically. *Liar. Bastard. Bastard. Liar.* The tree is his father; he imagines the give of flesh, the crunch of bone. His anger comes in an endless bountiful stream, compressed for years and released with the force of a fire hose. *Bastard. Bastard. Liar. Liar!*

"Here, what are you doing?" A white-haired man has come out of the adjacent house with a collie. He waves one arm above his head for Rick to clear out but, in spite of his scowl, does not move closer.

He must look like a frothing maniac—red all over, snarling. Even the dog seems wary of him, tense and skittish, ears tipped back.

He mounts the bike, still seething. His foot is numb.

Rick does not see her at first because of a bulky van. He rides through the school parking lot dejected, suddenly glimpsing her overdone store-mannequin frame propped against the side of her truck—waiting for him as she waits every morning.

He locks his bike into the rack and crosses the lot. Has she dyed her hair? It has the same reddish hue as her cheeks.

She watches him approach, concern and affection mingled in her gaze. "What happened? I was worried about you all night. I shouldn't have said that to you . . . about your dad. People do funny things when they have a lot of wine. He didn't mean it."

He can't tell her what happened. She will hate his father—and his mother, cut off the whole family including him. He can't be honest; he will lose her. He can't even tell her his father is out of work. His parents, humiliated by the situation, would throttle him if they found out he did.

He takes her to him. He can get suspended for doing this on school grounds but he needs her, needs to lay hands on her reassuring strength.

She hooks her thumbs solidly through his back belt loops as they hug.

17

"Doggone right we're interested," Ray Colquitt booms, walking Mike from the elevator into his office. "Let's put our heads together. Have a seat! I didn't think you'd ever leave Adams-Wenborn. What made you do it?"

This is going to be the bear—trying to explain the fact that he's been canned. Koppel will make it out to be Mike's fault, if asked. He's got to head that off. "I'll give it to you straight, Ray. We came to a permanent disagreement. I did not leave under happy circumstances."

"People seldom do. If we were satisfied, we'd still be there, right?"

"Right."

"What are you looking for?" Ray tips his chair back and rocks precariously on two of its legs.

He's my age. The thought startles Mike. *Head of his own agency.* A vignette from *Success!* magazine: Raymond Tyrone Colquitt, clad in a golf shirt and deck shoes with no socks, his almost impudent elfin face framed by oatmeal curls and an Addy Award collection that haphazardly climbs the wall in back of him. "I'm not sure, Ray. I think I'm tired of being a creative type."

135

"Who could blame you? How many years did you have with them, ten?"

"A dozen."

"You're pulling it out of your ear after a while, aren't you? In one long green strand."

Mike laughs. "You've been there!"

"I'm still there. But now I delegate, delegate." Ray smiles. "Seriously, what did you have in mind? You want to be more on the administrative side?"

"I'm weary of the front-line duty. I'd rather direct the battle."

"Well, I'm pleased that you came to us first. I've admired your work and I've got a whole lot of possibilities here. I'm doing some shuffling of my own. Let me have you fill out all the usual forms—I'll take you down to Personnel and they'll give you an application. We can get something going fairly quickly. I've got a lot of projects in motion, more than I can juggle. I'm glutted with résumés, but I don't have time for on-the-job training. I'm glad to have somebody who's really a pro ask me for a slot." He thumps his chair down. "And I'd give my top two accounts to see Koppel's expression when he finds out you just walked across the street to us. Call you in a day or two, whaddaya say?"

One or two days, he said, and it's been nine. Mike holds the family room telephone in his lap. Should he contact Ray?

He's had three turn-downs, following spectacular interviews: two by letter and one at the hands of an inept secretary who was told to call and inform him the ranks were full. He presses the numbers slowly, having memorized them days ago. He has gone through hours-long periods of staring at the phone, willing it to ring, picking it up innumerable times to confirm that it was working.

"Colquitt Advertising."

"May I speak with Ray Colquitt, please?" He is flicked away to silence.

"Mr. Colquitt's office."

"Is he in, please?"

"May I ask who's calling?"

"Mike Stockman."

"Thank you." She switches him to "Hold"; orchestral music pulses from the receiver, the tail end of "Love Letters in the Sand" followed by "Moon River." Why do they always have to know your name before they tell you whether or not the boss is there? Will Ray come to the phone for him?

"Hello, Mike!"

"Ray?" He is grateful, so grateful.

"That must have been mental telepathy. I've been up to my eyeballs in alligators and haven't had a chance to get back to you."

"It's all right. I've been out quite a bit, on interviews." Never hurts to let him know he has competition.

"Good."

"I'm considering other offers and I wanted to see if you were still interested in my coming with you."

"Well, I think we're stuck for now, sorry to say. Over-committed. I have to clear up some of this garbage before I can bring anyone else on board."

He can't let this slip away. He'll have to be aggressive. "Ray, your firm is my first choice. But, obviously, I'd need to nail it down."

"Absolutely. I wouldn't ask you to wait for us. It may be months before we're in a position to hire another administrator."

What happened? It was in the bag. What did he do wrong? "I understand."

"Hate to pass you off to the competition again. Go easy on us, will you?"

"I'd consider waiting if it were in the process."

"I can't ask you to do that." The congeniality is flattening out now. He won't hang on until it goes totally dry.

"Sure. Thanks, Ray. Catch you later."

"Okay, Mike. Let me know where you land."

He keeps cradling the weight of the phone after the voice is gone, wishing he had a tape of the conversation so he could analyze it, all the inflections. Was Colquitt truly sorry? A tremor shoots through him, helplessness. What will happen to his family if he can't get a job? What will happen to *him*? The house is a solitary cage he roams.

He can think of chores he should be doing, but he drags his body behind him, has lost the malleable center from which energy and curiosity once sprang. He envisions himself cleaning out the garage, washing the car, restaining the birdhouse and pouring in the amber seed, raking sycamore leaves out from under the hedges. But he stands numbly at the windowsills while the sun etches its arc and children tumble in the yards.

Once, a few days ago, he knelt in the rain-wet soil along the fence, digging with his fingers to turn up the solid, sour-smelling bulbs of other seasons and, having ripped their pulp from the ground and laid them in a row, could not remember his purpose.

He unscrews the cap on a new fifth of bourbon and, hanging on to the kitchen counter, drinks from the bottle. His body is alien to him, a creature that trembles and sweats and will not be trained. He stands on an island in his own brain, wishing to take charge again, pretending that he can. Perhaps he will fool his flesh.

Intellectually, he sees where he is: a man without a job, *this too shall pass*. But physically, a monster is loose in him: despair that makes the insides of his legs tingle, his skull wobble at the back, his ears ache with a constant far-off whine of swarming bees. If he could kill his body—smash it—and still live, he would. He despises it, despises himself for letting it rule him, is ashamed. He is thrashing about in his skin, trying to get out, to be calm again.

This, only this, helps.

"Can't I do the rest tomorrow? I have a date." Rick looks toward his father, who is ensconced in a director's chair on the driveway. "We didn't have dinner yet. I'm getting hungry." He has noticed that his father's head lolls from time to time, snapping upright when Rick slacks off.

"Keep going."

Rick thrusts the rake back under the hedges and scrapes at the decaying leaves. They are damp-heavy beneath the rake's fan of teeth; he gouges the earth, bringing the wormy brown waste toward him. He has lined up bag after bag of leaves at the curb. And he's already cleaned out the entire garage and washed the car. It's like his father has a list, a secret endless list. "I quit, Pop."

"No."

Fuck you. He scoops the sog into a trash bag and ties it up, dragging it out to the others. He skirts his father warily as he puts away the rake and gloves, checking behind him to make sure he is not about to be attacked. His father sits rigidly glaring at the hedges while Rick closes the garage and goes inside. Rick watches him as he washes his hands at the kitchen sink; his father, his back to the window, does not move in the graying light.

"Are we going to eat now?" Lee says. "I made chicken à la king."

"When will Mom be home?"

"She said she wasn't staying for the third act."

"I have to shower. Eva's picking me up in fifteen minutes."

"You don't want to eat?"

He should stay with Lee, not let her field this craziness alone. But he's got to have relief. He's betraying her, but he can't care. His need is immense; he cannot breathe in here. "Doing that stuff took too much time. I'm in a hurry."

"All right."

He wants to get away from her eyes; they beg him. In spite of his guilt, he will not let her cling to him. He has to be free.

Concealed by dusk, Lee peeks at Rick from the living room window as he hoists himself into the passenger seat. His girlfriend reaches around his neck; they kiss. Gears churn. The headlights dim momentarily as Eva steps on the gas and the truck rambles away.

She turns off the oven. Her father is sitting motionless in the darkened driveway; she goes outside, walking in a semi-circle to approach him from the front. "Come on, Pop. Supper."

He gets up obediently and follows as she carries his chair.

The brightness dispels his glassy gaze. He hunches over the food, which she has placed on the lower counter; his arms hang listlessly across his lap. "We need to help Mom a lot more. I can't find a job and she's working so hard."

"I *am.*" Where does he think this dinner came from? All *he* does is lie around.

"I know, but we've got to do more. She's tired."

A hitch, beneath Lee's breastbone. What if . . . her mother became ill, died? She eyes her father's slouched form. She will do anything to keep that from happening. To be left alone with him is a nightmarish thought. She must guard her mother, take as much worry and responsibility away from her as she can.

"We need to help Mom," he repeats with exactly the same inflection.

Peculiar and infuriating, his habit of saying a sentence over and over. Why doesn't *he* help?

If only she could spill out her concerns—the rude displeasure of her teachers on the days she falters, the contempt of Garcia, who has threatened to cut her from the team. It occurs to her that she has been making an error in excluding her father. By sharing her problems, she may cause him to rise up and take over. He is the leader, she his child.

Where will she find the strength for this? "Daddy . . ." she begins. "I'm having trouble."

Her words seem to engage him.

"At school. I can't keep up with . . . I might be eliminated from the tennis team. But I want to stay. It's because I don't have . . ." How can she explain her distraction, the reflex that tells her—before a match—that she will lose?

Her attempt registers; his brows mesh as he digests her statement. She sees sadness. He focuses directly on her eyes. "I can't find a job."

"You look better now than when you came in." Eva smiles, setting her cue in the well of the bumper pool table.

"Yeah."

"You looked rode hard and put up wet."

"Good night, now," Mrs. Metsinger calls from the upstairs balcony. She leans on the railing, grinning in her friendly way. "Dad and I are going to watch *Invasion of the Body Snatchers.*"

"I enjoyed your violin concert, Mrs. M."

"Wasn't that a riot? You were a great audience. I practice every six months, whether I need to or not. Come back tomorrow and Carl will give you a performance with his ukulele." She waves, then retreats.

"Thanks for the popcorn, too!" He rests his cue stick against the table, glancing around. The Metsingers' main house is even more inviting than the one at the beach: blatant pink and yellow with shots of green; cushions and crannies and keepsakes. Tonight he has learned to play hearts, the boys leaping out of their chairs with excitement when the queen of spades skittered onto a trick. He couldn't get over the unfettered pounding and hollering as the six of them vied. He was the winner, having successfully ducked the queen in several rounds and taken all the hearts in two others.

"Invasion of the body snatchers!" Eva stalks him along the perimeter of the pool table, her hands out in front of her like claws. He likes the pursuit, walks backward at top speed and halts, letting her thud into him. She holds him eagerly around the waist. "I have your loan," she says against his chest.

For the driver's license. Why does she insist? He can't take it.

She fishes three hundred-dollar bills, one by one, from the front pocket of her jeans and tucks them into his; the wriggling warmth of her motion at his groin makes him blush.

"My money," she instructs. "I can do what I want to with it. Get your license."

"No."

"Um-hum." She leads him to the couch. They nestle against each other, Eva beneath the slope of his arm, his fingers touching the side of her breast. Her kiss is shyly receptive, as though he could have chosen anyone but has graced her by his attention. He probes the corners of her mouth with his tongue; they are sweetly responsive.

She acquaints him with his own strength: he discovers

he does not continually have to take, he is ripe with giving. They kiss until he grows sick with desire and she allows him to reach inside her blouse to cup the pointed mound of her nipple. No one in the world is as kind or as funny as Eva Metsinger. The thought of going home fills him with desolation.

Katy is all around Mike, shrieking. She seems to lurch at him in spasms like the figures in an old movie. Wedged into a crevice, he cannot get out. He lies dumbly looking at his wife, hearing her recitation blip on and off. She is elongated, spindly tall. Is this a dream? Her face contorts with anger as she cries out, pulling her fists toward her stomach in gestures of exasperation. A terror begins to spread through him, the certainty of his transgression, the certainty of being abandoned.

What is she saying? The sound hits too many surfaces to be understood. She disappears abruptly, the puzzle unresolved, the pieces floating down over him. He cocks his head, finding a baseboard beside him. For some unknown reason, he is on the floor between the back of the couch and the wall.

Her mother's screams are echoing through Lee as she hurries along the hallway, her nightgown drenched with chill water. She finds her bowed in the bedroom easy chair, her face hidden.

"Mama? I'm . . . I'm . . . upset," Lee gasps, surprised at how thin and inadequate the words sound.

Her mother raises her head; her eyes stream tears. "Me, too."

Katy finishes rubbing her makeup into place and eyes Mike in the vanity mirror. Sound asleep. Today is a beginning. She really let him have it last night. If she hadn't made it clear before exactly what she thinks of his behavior, he knows now. She spelled it all out.

He wouldn't dare loaf around here drinking today, she'd yank the rug out from under him. She could tell she scared him silly when she told him she'd leave and take the kids. She's already emphasized her ultimatum by removing most of the cash from his wallet this morning and pouring bottle after goddamned bottle of liquor down the sink. Should she take the car keys, too? She ponders that one, vaguely recalling a scheduled interview. He'll need wheels.

If only someone would give him a job. The resultant gladness and jolt to his ego would squeeze off the drinking. He'd be anxious to please and—out from under the Adams-Wenborn pressures—find booze unnecessary. Oh, for good people to toss him a chance! She thinks of the busy, hardened executives of this city with bitterness. They just plain don't care. Smug in their offices, they forget what it is to be unemployed, the urgency of it. If you're looking for work, you can wait until doomsday.

The longer this goes on, the worse he gets. She has spent half the night considering counseling, but word of that could get around to the ad agencies and nix his candidacy. L.A. seems like a large town, but its grapevine is well connected.

She's even toyed with the notion of Alcoholics Anonymous. But he'd have a roaring fit if she went to that—she wouldn't dare tell him if she did. And *he* certainly wouldn't consent to go. Is he a real alcoholic? She has seen him stay dry for weeks. And he's been productive all these years with his company. Dismal, the prospect of a group like AA. To entrust her story or—God forbid—entrust *him* to nonprofessionals, drunks and former drunks who might make things worse. She and Mike are refined people with a temporary problem. Definitely not in that league.

* * *

Doesn't he have a meeting this morning? Lee lingers in the hallway, clutching her books. Surely her mother would have awakened him.

It's up to her—she's the only one left in the house. She slips the books onto his dresser and approaches the bed, hesitates. "Daddy." She does not want to touch him. He has grown repulsive to her. Many nights he sleeps with a towel over his pillow to soak up the flowing, foul perspiration. Indentations from the towel pockmark the left side of his face; from his slack mouth whooshes rank breath, noisy against his teeth. "Dad."

The eyes slide open, unseeing. She remembers how she and Rick used to horse around, lifting their dad's lids one at a time when he was sleeping, enthralled and amused by the fact that he would not wake up. He wouldn't even stir.

"Do you have an appointment today? I'm getting ready to go to school."

A sharpening of his hooded gaze. "What time is it?"

"Ten 'til eight."

He pitches forward. "What? What day is this?"

"Friday."

"Ah?" He hugs himself, obviously horrified. "Ohhh. I've made a terrible mistake. I need you to help me. Get . . . the phone book for the airport area."

She pulls it from the nightstand drawer.

"Look up the Days Inn, Inglewood. On Century."

She locates it and puts her thumbnail under the number, slanting the page toward him.

"Ask for the restaurant. There's a man, Harley Hudson. He'll be at a table—you'll have to ask for him to come to the phone."

She thought *he* was going to call! She doesn't want to do it. She is scared of Harley Hudson.

"Please! Please! This is important. Tell him my car

broke down, that I'm out on the freeway and that I called you and asked you to notify him.''

No question—she must do it. She can't let him be disgraced. Hudson is someone who might give him a job. She pokes nervously at the numbers and requests to be connected with the restaurant.

"Sunrise."

"I'd like to speak to a customer. Mr. Harley Hudson." Is Hudson still waiting? She hopes with all her heart that he has gone.

A clanking, as the receiver is dropped. Faintly: "Mr. Harley Hudson. Telephone." The beep-beep of a cash register, papers being shuffled.

"This is Harley Hudson."

"Hello. I'm Lee Stockman, Mike Stockman's daughter."

"Where is he?" The voice turns gruff.

"His car broke down. He's out on the freeway. He called and asked me to get in touch with you."

"You can tell your father I'm tired of his antics."

Shame floods her. *Undependable, her dad.* She knows it is true. Why did she think others couldn't see it? "His car broke down. He's really sorry. Could he meet you a little later or make a new appointment? I'd write it down and give him the message."

"Never. I've been sitting here nearly an hour. You tell your dad he'd better shape up."

"Well, thank you. Good-bye."

"Good-bye."

"What did he say?" Her father's apprehension is a chasm into which she can fall.

"He said okay . . . but . . . he didn't want to make another appointment."

The house is his tomb. Rain has begun again, measured and demanding, tapping incessantly over him. At midmorning he slogs to the mailbox. Among the bills, which melt in his hand under the torrent, is a single reply: a mimeographed regret from the personnel department of Media Magic. He drops it through the sewer grate.

In the kitchen, confusion seizes him. There were bottles here, in this cabinet. Or *was* it this cabinet? He rummages through the others and back to the first. Did he drink it all?

He retrieves his wallet, which feels thinner. Where are his credit cards? Has he been robbed? The face on his driver's license fixes its penetrating inquiry on him. Behind it, the cash pocket yields fifteen dollars. Not enough for what he has to get.

He crashes from room to room, illuminating them, hunting. He finds the toilet stash and the one in a boxed coffee urn they seldom use; both supplies are more than half gone. He drains them over a tranquil hour. The children will be home soon; he must buy what he needs and scatter it into safe places.

The checkbook is not in the desk's top drawer, not in any of its drawers. Is he losing his mind? It's always here. Right here.

He has the sensation that if he can get outside, he will be able to think. The ashen hills and staggered marigold plots beyond the pool reassure him. He strides toward them, punched brutally and hurled onto his back by the glass door.

Dozing, he rouses when his ankles twitch. Emptiness still pervades the bleak afternoon. He is alone. He stumbles up, captivated by an idea.

Around the corner to Lee's jewelry box he glides, drawn along a slick track. The gold chain, draped over a clump of earrings, flashes faintly as he lifts it. Two hundred and fifty dollars. She does not wear it, will not miss it for the brief time he has it pawned. Or, if she misses it, will think it mislaid. And he will bring it back to her; it will appear mysteriously under the cushion of a chair or curled in a vase.

His mission is urgent now. He fumbles in his closet for a raincoat or umbrella. Like the sudden squelching of a radio, the havoc in his ears subsides. *What is he doing? Why is this in his hand?* Astounded, he considers the necklace, then weeping, shoves it into the pocket of an old blue bathrobe.

He should have seen it all along—the problem, the reason he can't get a job: Koppel has been blackballing him. He's detective enough to sniff it out and man enough to put a stop to it.

Drenched, Mike climbs the four flights of cement steps, coming out at the rear hallway of Adams-Wenborn, behind Koppel's office. This is one secretary he won't have to fool with.

He bursts into Koppel's den, certain of his three o'clock Friday schedule. Predictably, Koppel is in conference with his five department heads at the hexagonal teak table. Mike is vaguely aware he has a buzz on from a fortification visit nearby, but it will not alter what he has to say. All the better that Koppel's flunkies are here—his present situation could be their future, and they should know it.

With dignity. "I have just realized that you are undermining my efforts to get a job. You're giving me poor references. It's unfair. It stinks." *Control. Suck it back in.* "I'm here to ask you to quit that. I can do the work, I want to be employed. Your personal clash with me, if you have any conscience, should not stand in the way of a recommendation. You said yourself that I can produce more in a day than others can in two weeks. I'm here to ask you to cut it out."

Has he been flinging his arms around? The table glistens

with water and there is a splatter on Frank Brantley's left eyeglass.

He has entranced them into marble; no one speaks or shifts as he exits.

Courage.

That night—it was reported in the newspaper—whole trees left the ground in a wind. He must have subconsciously heard the commotion, for he surfaced several times strangely pleasured and, tracing the source, remembered the nonplussed Koppel and congratulated himself on his eloquence.

= 18 =

Weekend. Rain batters the window above the headboard. Katy, on her stomach, edges downward in bed until her feet touch the firmly tucked sheet at the bottom. The warm nest of blankets is pulled up to her forehead, with a small gap for air. She makes sure that anyone checking on her from the doorway cannot see her eyes; she does not want to get up.

She will sleep and pretend to be asleep. The two days until Sunday night's dress rehearsal are consecutive ladders she must climb. Today she will hide. She's already told Mike she's ill.

A half-lie. She *is* strung out, done in. Between the rigors of work and Mike's incessant carping, she has acquired a permanent nausea. Let *him* handle the house for a day or two; maybe he'll treat her with more appreciation. As long as he thinks she's sick, he doesn't hassle her. He becomes weaker and sleeps beside her for long periods but is solicitous, even tender.

She does feel rotten. The whipping rain rattles the windows without letup as she nestles further into the well of the pillow.

* * *

"Mother's ill today. I want you kids to stick around."

Lee stops pouring cereal into her bowl. "All day?"

"She'll need some help."

Rick glances from his father's feisty pose down into the pores of his buttered toast. *Shit!* A day like this means being cooped up with boredom, with aggravation—shining his father's shoes under his direction or scrubbing mildew from the shower tile grouting with a toothbrush and Clorox. In silence. Radio music and television programs send his father into such fits of nervousness that he rants at length after he orders them off. His senses are raw; he can stand nothing. It is as though he has no skin, no eyelids, no eardrums. His nerves are naked, sent into spasms by the slightest stimulation.

"I have a date," Lee says tentatively.

"When?" Mike snaps.

"Tonight. Mom said I could."

His father peers at her from a darkening distance.

"I do, too."

The gaze spears him. "No."

"Why?"

"Because I said so. It's Lee's turn."

"We can't both be out at once?"

"Mommy needs help."

Mommy? The guy doesn't know what year it is. Rick has suspected for some time that his father thinks of Lee and Rick as little children, regardless of their age. And Rick is repulsed by his own automatic knee-jerk to his father's edicts. The man had quite plainly scared the life out of him from about six years old on, with his checkered moods—everything great and then the instantaneous horror of a frenzied spanking for which Rick could not discern the cause until he was told. Luckily, he gained his full height early, forcing his dad to back off. He's come this far; if he can crawl through seven more months he'll be out, away at college. But that doesn't solve today. The thought of being here without relief, subject to his father's jumpy whims, is stifling.

A prison without bars. On days like this, he and Lee hole up in their rooms as much as possible, sneaking to the kitchen for food when they know he is napping. At least when his mother is sick, there are no formal meals—the ultimate battleground. They lay low.

"Don't look at me like that," his father says.

Does his son think he's stupid? He might be chopped liver on the job scene right now, but he understands that this conflict with Rick has escalated to sabotage. He sees what the child is trying to do in making up that story about Eva: he wants to drive a wedge between mother and father. Who knows what other untruths Rick has told Katy about him? It bears watching. "You can give us a hand today. And, if you've got time left over, you can figure out a way to make a buck toward your driver's license."

"I have the money."

"You couldn't possibly have three hundred dollars."

"Yes." The tone is infuriatingly calm.

"Where did you get it?"

"I borrowed it."

"From whom?"

"A friend."

"Who?" Gall! He's told a friend that his father can't afford the insurance fee. The humiliation of it causes a cartwheel in Mike's balance; he grips the table.

"You don't have to know."

The gyroscope rights itself. His daughter and son are both looking at him with suspicious curiosity. Did they recognize the sudden, precarious ebb of strength? "No deal!'' He creates a voice that is wide and thick, formidable. ''I said *earn,* not borrow. And that's the end of it.''

She knows this ploy, but she can't stop her husband from going to the grocery store. The list of things to get is on a magnetized pad stuck to the front of the refrigerator for all to see. Today it is abundant; she can't pretend they don't need anything.

From the bed, she watches him go through her purse. He's not a child—she can't blatantly withhold money from him. Her open refusal would cause a hair-raising scene. She wouldn't think of it. Success in controlling his actions depends, to a large extent, on subtle manipulation. Head-on clashes never work.

She can hear a branch thumping the roof in the wind, a steady bashing. The wrong time to go out: midnight at noonday, rain pelted sideways in walloping gusts.

She rises and puts on her robe, zipping it to the chin as he pockets her cash. Useless, a conversation with him. She must *act.*

Rick's door is closed; she knocks. He opens it a crack.

''I want you to go to the store with Dad.''

''Now?''

''Yes.'' He will be her eyes and ears, bring him safely home. A stopgap measure, but she must not think back or ahead, only event by event.

''It's raining.''

''I know. But Dad wants to go now. If you help, the shopping will go quicker.''

''You passed it up, Pop.''

''I like the other store better.''

Sure he does. The other store is next to a bar. His father drives erratically, forever tromping the gas pedal too hard and riding the brake. Damned suck-egg weather. The wipers cannot keep up; Rick squints at the road, determined to ward off catastrophe by being his father's second set of eyes, his brain. When his mother is along, she fulfills this function: *Thirty-five miles an hour here, Mike. There's a jogger up ahead.* Travels with his father give him the mental licks of a roller coaster; he finds himself pressing his own right foot to the floor with all his strength, an imaginary brake. *Jesus-God! Look out for the—* His apprehension is not unfounded. His dad has sideswiped a cement truck and totaled a bus stop bench—on separate occasions. Drivers frequently bellow out their windows at him; his dad is always naïvely, righteously insulted as people blow by flipping the bird.

In the shopping center, Mike inches the car into an absurdly narrow spot against Rick's protest. They can hardly open their doors. His father slides out, Rick squeezing after him. They reach the shelter of the overhang with their shoulders damp and their pant legs soaked from the ricochet of raindrops against concrete.

"Now here's the list, buddy. You start. I have a couple of things to get and I'll be right there."

The experience of a thousand occasions has taught him to say nothing. This will go as it goes. He cannot change it. "Better give me some money."

"I'll be *right in.*"

Rick takes the list and commandeers a dripping cart, ramming it toward the store so rapidly that the automatic doors almost don't have time to part. The air-conditioning seals his clothes to him; he moves through the frigid aisles, yanking boxes from the shelves and smacking them into the basket.

He has to wait in line. At the last, his father does not show and he watches with growing discomfort the squarish red prices that tweet onto a digital readout as the items are hauled across the counter's electronic eye by an acne-studded clerk. He is asked to stand aside and wait with his groceries until the money arrives. He has done this before, too, at various ages. It is ludicrous now. But he knows the taboos. To enter any bar where his father is holding forth is tantamount to treason and met with accordingly.

He is a jackass—*he*, Rick Stockman, waiting here like a pissed-pants kid, still letting his father rule him. He has no respect for himself, can only reason that he *has to*. He wants to come out the other side possessing all his teeth.

His father, blinking at the supermarket glare, saunters in with a brown-bagged bottle under his arm and looks around for Rick. Rick walks slowly to him with the receipt and steps aside while his father pays it.

They amble through the parking lot. In the car next to theirs, the rolled-tight windows are fogged and an incessant, mournful barking rises from the interior.

"Some people!" his dad says.

They bolt across the highway, a bronco out of the rodeo gate. A quick jam at a red light. Off again, with trucks flinging muddy waves over them, *crack, crack*. Lightning dances on a ridge.

They turn off the main road; the rain lessens. Silver glitters along bare tree limbs, the drops showering down like dimes. Three blocks from home, his father sails without warning onto a newly graded corner lot, the car coming to rest in a course of ruts and mounds. They stare for a moment at their unreal surroundings: wooden stakes with flapping red-ribbon streamers, stacks of cement block.

"Road must have been slipperier than I thought." His dad bumps the car into reverse. They lurch backward in a sinking wail of tires.

No. That's not the way!

He pauses, tries again. The wail becomes a whine. Rick feels the rear bumper hit the ground. "Don't, Pop!"

He stomps the brake. Another jolt.

"We might have to dig. Let me look." Rick knows before he pulls the door handle that this will require more than a shovel and a couple of boards.

"Stay where you are. I can rock it out."

"I wouldn't—"

A bang of the gearshift. The car leaps forward, nearly stalling. *Reverse.* A smoking grind like a dentist's drill. *First.* The front bumper slams down into sludge. *Reverse.* The car shudders wildly.

"Stop! The tail pipe could be plugged. Dad!"

First. The car does not move; the engine dies. His father tries to start it over and over with the same steadied approach as if he has no memory, cannot learn from the fact that he's already tried thirteen or fourteen times. Incensed beyond his capacity, Rick consciously detaches himself. Whatever happens can't matter now. He has all day.

Sheeting rain begins again, tossed against them as if from vats. Finally, the repetitious straining gives way to a mental connection: *the car will not start.* He stares at Rick open-mouthed.

"We'll walk," Rick shouts over the tattoo of water on metal.

"No!"

"Why not?"

"We can't leave the car here. Call road service."

"When we get home."

"Somebody will let you use their phone." His father gestures at the neighboring houses.

He is not going to prance sopping through a stranger's

156

house when his own is three blocks away. "Why can't we call from home?"

"We have to guard the car. Somebody might take it."

"If we can't get it out, they can't. Besides, we'll lock it up." He hears himself rationally answering his father's nonsense. The man is drunk. No mistaking the bloodshot eyes, the wobble of the head. No amount of coaxing is going to alter the outcome of this. Even if he did appease his dad by calling road service from here, they would not come in this havoc—they'll be tied up for hours with street accidents. Why should he wait for them here when he can wait at home? *Why should he have to convince himself?* His father is not thinking logically. Rick reaches over and gently removes the keys from the ignition. "C'mon, Pop."

"We can't leave the car!"

"I'm going home."

"Stay here!" His father clutches Rick's shirt sleeve, but he twists away and gets out of the car, assaulted by the torrent, fighting the suction of muck around his shoes. Under the waterfall of the windshield, his father has assumed the pose of a captain going down with the ship; defiant, possessive.

Rick wades across the lot, a field of eddying puddles. As he nears the street, he glances back on instinct. His dad has left the car and is advancing toward him, spite and menace in the tight crimp of his eyes, stealthily hurrying, his shoulders high and poised as hunters do when they stalk. A certainty of evil passes through Rick: *he is in mortal jeopardy.* The recognition of it rivets him.

His father is walking faster now, pinioning him with his gaze, speaking orders. He can tell they are orders because the right hand strikes the air and balls into a fist. The words are carried away by wind.

Maybe he's changed his mind and wants to come along.

Wait. And smile. To show fear always brings wrath; they are in direct proportion.

No, this is different. *Holy God.* Kill or be killed.

Rick begins to run, his mud-weighted feet slipping in slime. On the concrete he moves out, trying to sprint, overtaken by a heaviness in his chest. It is a plodding run. He does it mechanically—right, left, right, left—constantly swinging his torso back to center.

After a block and a half, he dares to look. His father is still tracking him, in the same deliberate stride, closer than Rick dreamed he could be.

Rick continues in the two-legged hopping motion he knows is running. Nothing is automatic. He has lost the ability, has to instruct his body what to do. His saturated clothing is a further drag; flames of rain snatch his breath. As his house drifts into view, he looks back again. His father is not in sight.

His mother, in her bathrobe, recoils as he enters the kitchen. "What in the world?"

His painful breathing fills the room. They stare at each other.

"Where's Dad?"

Are they *all* in danger? He has never been so scared.

"I said, where's Dad?"

"The car got stuck, a couple of blocks away. He's coming."

"You didn't wait for him?" She pushes past Rick, peering into the fog of the yard.

He shakes his head.

Comprehension. Her face hardens. "You . . . *snipe!*"

A flash of lightning illuminates the horizon in streaks, outlining every twig, every leaf; she goes to meet it, descending the embattled driveway, immediately drenched.

After some minutes, she reappears, her arm around his father, their heads pulled together.

No use to run again. He stands aside, listening to their approach.

The screen door squeaks. They straighten, wiping water from their cheeks and eyes. His father, with the pale, benign face of a corpse, focuses on him in injured bewilderment. "Why didn't you wait for me?"

19

She can see through walls. Fourteen years of tense listening have perfected this skill. Something bad is happening. Her brother passes her closed door on the way to his room, the pace double time, the footfall weighted with belligerence. *Bam.*

This would be her father: tentative steps clunking slowly from side to side. He is confused and sleepy, the wide-legged stance—to keep his balance—a giveaway. He bumps the jamb as he navigates the corner into their bedroom. Her mother's movements are flurried; she commands the area as she enters it.

"He wouldn't wait for me, Katy. He won't talk to me when we go out together . . . he won't even *look* at me." This plaintive tone is a slingshot that always propels her mother toward the offender. As her father thuds his way to the bed, the door creaks closed at the hand of her mother, who then bustles along the hallway. She punches Rick's door in a semblance of knocking and twists the knob.

"Unlock this. I want to speak to you." A slapping of wood. "Rick!"

He lets her in.

Bam. Their voices rise immediately, topping each other

but held within a threshold, as though wary of being heard by her father. *Does* he hear? There is no indication. Once a conflict is relinquished to her mother, his silence is total. She believes him to be in a sudden snoring pit, not listening as she is. Whenever he lies down, he seems to be sucked to sleep.

They are moving around in Rick's room; her mother's voice the pursuer, jabbing. Rick's answers shift like a shield, defending against the thrusts. She is glad that with the intervening bathroom to absorb the sound she cannot perceive exact words; the shape of them is enough. She covers her ears, overtaken by involuntary shivering. Her fringe of anger encompasses Rick this time. He never tries to make it easier. He never plays along.

The face behind him in the bathroom mirror is his sister's. What is she doing here? It's a good thing he's wrapped in a towel, this is bizarre. The blue saucer eyes seize him. He stops combing his hair and cannot turn around.

She *walked* in, she didn't simply materialize—he had opened the door to let the steam out. Still, it is eerie, her concentration on him, her solemnness. She floats closer, laying her cheek against his shoulder. The sorrow in her is electric.

Comfort? A declaration of being on his side? It's hard to tell. They see each other at such angles now. When did they last talk?

Old Saturdays, old Sundays—when the Bad One was home—they would crouch together in the hollow of the lilac hedge for hours, playing with objects they found: a brick became a plantation house with webs of dirt-scooped lanes and fences, a lavender bud under a curved fragment of glass became the king's treasure. Did they talk then? The memories are a mute parade. She goes, drifting away

quietly like an apparition. A relief. She spooks him sometimes, his sister.

Maybe she shouldn't go out tonight. Her mother has
been in bed since the afternoon's argument. How sick is
she?

Too late now. Jason will ring the doorbell in twelve
minutes. She nervously unscrews a well of lip gloss and
spreads a dab across her mouth with her index finger. She
doesn't know how to do this—dating, not really. She's only
had two others, both to school dances when they lived in
St. Louis. She isn't slick enough for California boys with
their muscled independence and hoarsely murmured jokes;
Jason is from Nebraska.

This sweater? Acceptable. She scrutinizes the earring assortment in the tray of her jewelry box. It's an evening at
his house—she doesn't want to look overdone, like she
expects big entertainment or has an outsized opinion of
herself. But she has studied the latest scenes in *Glamour*
and *Mademoiselle* and the models are wearing ceramic chip
earrings. Mysterious, these vignettes: the kicky stride and
swingy haircuts of the girls, the shyly clowning poses of
the boys. The girls seem to be the initiators of fun in the
pictures, the photographer freezing their antics just after an
act or phrase of cleverness. But *what?* These are portraits
of reactions only, the boys so thoroughly tickled at the girls
that they laugh aloud and dip back from them a little, the
girls amused at their own impishness. There seems to be a
correlation between what the people are wearing and the
ability to be carefree, to evoke admiration. She can imitate
that.

She selects small red crescents, setting them aside on the
bureau top. A ring? Necklace? *Not too much flash with
jeans and a sweater.* Maybe a ring.

An absence in the jewelry case causes her to stare down

into its tangle of Indian beads and pearls, seashells and tarnished medallions. Nothing specific, the merest difference. It flutters by. She guides a gold post through the channel of her earlobe, vaguely nettled. As she clips the second earring into place, she eyes the case again.

The gold chain. Gingerly, she rearranges the contents, searching. Befuddled after a moment's scratching in various compartments, she hesitates. It has to be here.

But it isn't.

Strand by strand, she extricates the pieces, laying them in rows on the dresser. When the container is empty to its green velvet lining, she looks under it, then kneels to search the carpet.

Could it have dropped into her lingerie drawer? She methodically removes the slips and panties, shaking and refolding each. It can't be lost—she never wears it.

In a burst of awe, she thinks of Rick and his three hundred dollars.

"Where are you heading?" her father asks Jason.

"Over to my house."

"When will you be back?"

"Around eleven?"

"All right. Have a good time, honey."

They emerge from the stuffy foyer into a bluish evening. The sun has barely gone; remaining rain clouds piled along the horizon glow violet.

"Does your father nip?" The question rolls between them, friendly and light.

Dumbstruck, she fashions her answer, a camouflage. "What do you mean?"

"Nip. Take a drink."

"No."

"He looks like he's been into the sauce."

How could he see that? They only exchanged a few

163

words. She thought her father did well—better than usual. "No," she says again.

His smile is one of pleasant conspiracy. "I'll bet you're wrong."

The quail are loose in Jason's room.

"Wait—don't step. I'll round them up." He clicks on the overhead and shuffles across the hardwood, the baby birds hopping rapidly after him. How fast they run! He lifts each and places it in a makeshift pen of boards. She counts seven peeping fluffballs.

"C'mon in."

"When did they hatch?"

"Three days ago. I tried to call, but you weren't home. It happened in the space of half an hour. So I decided to save it for a surprise."

"Only seven? Out of all those eggs?"

"Yeah. The rest didn't make it."

"Where are the swifts?"

"In my brother's room."

She sits with him on the floor by the pen, watching the quail dash and huddle. They are no bigger than fat rose-buds, a glossy light brown.

"Hold out your hand over them—down low."

She reaches into the pen and all seven rush under her palm, pulling their legs and wings in until they are one throbbing mass.

Jason laughs. "They think you're their mother. Instinct tells them to get under something, can you believe that? They don't distinguish. At night I put this feather duster on them and they love it. Sleep 'til morning."

Their throbbing, trusting softness stirs warmth.

Guilt accosts her. No one at home is happy, she is not entitled to joy while others suffer. She sweeps mentally through her house: the unwarranted job predicament of her

father, the courageous striving of her mother, Rick's alien-
ation. She cannot be free until she helps to make the situation right, until it comes right. And it will.

"Talk about your dad," Jason says.

"What about him?"

"Does he do the drinking every day?"

She draws her hand away from the chicks. They cry—
almost a mewing—as they disperse.

"He was really wound up the weekend he wanted me to
eat breakfast with you, and tonight he gave me the evil eye
and he smelled."

She can't stay here, she has to get away from him. His
honesty embarrasses her. But, more than that, she feels
sorry for her father. A rush of love. No one can see him
as they do. If he has veils of ugliness, he doesn't mean it,
doesn't even know it. That's what's horrible. She doesn't
see it either, half the time. People must despise him. *Her
father*.

"We had a neighbor like him. On the back of their house
was a sun porch with lots of flowerpots. He used to go out
there and throw them around. Does your dad break stuff?"

Looking at Jason's inquisitive eyes, his cross-legged ca-
sualness, she detects no malice. He is discussing this as
one would discuss a road map, dispassionately and with
the same intent: to get from here to there. To understand
her.

She has wanted to be discovered in this way, she realizes
it now: direct, forceful guessing. A naming of the problem.
Her senses are heightened, the quail and Jason magnifi-
cently real, not filtered to her through deadening glass. She
is aware of every thread in his collar, every pore of his
face. The golden hairs of his eyebrows stand out one from
the other.

"I'll share a secret," he says. "And you can tell it if I
ever tell on you. My older sister had a baby. She didn't

get married, she gave it away. Nobody knows but us. Even my grandparents don't know.''

"How old is she?"

"Nineteen. That was three years ago."

"Oh."

"Is that what's going on, he drinks?"

Should she commit to this? The risk in admitting it is huge. The consequences. But who does she have? Not her father, that's for certain. And her mother, who loves her best, doesn't probe her heart. She thinks of Rick taking her chain—which he deserves, which she wants him to have because he was entitled to that money in the first place. She is mixed up, shut away from everyone. She *needs* Jason. She likes him, his gentleness and patience with the birds. She wants to live in his care. "Yes," she says.

He nods seriously and clasps her wrist, rubbing it with his thumb.

Unlatching the door with her key, she turns to wave at Jason and Mrs. Gates, who wait in the darkness of the car. Inside, the brilliance of the living room shocks her; every lamp is lit and, in the midst of the blaze, her family sits, her parents grinning, Rick appearing calm.

"Hey, where's your beau?" her father hails her.

"He couldn't stay. His mother dropped me off."

"Well, why didn't they both come in?" He gestures generously, arm extended toward the ceiling.

"They're gone now." It has the air of a party, this gathering: paper plates and napkins, sandwich spreads and toasted rye, potato chips, tall iced drinks. Her mother is in her bathrobe but beaming, her color restored. Rick's length is awkwardly draped along the end of the sofa as though he doesn't quite buy into the premise but is complying nonetheless.

"Have some, sweetheart." Her mother motions to her.

"I'll get you a Pepsi. We're celebrating!" She nods at Mike. "You tell her."

"We're moving back to Chicago!"

"We are? You decided?"

"Daddy got a job."

"Where?"

Her father stretches back proudly, hands behind his head. "Remember Jonathan Yarger?"

"He worked with you in Chicago."

"Right! He has his own agency now. Called me tonight. Heard I was on the loose."

"What will you be doing?"

"We'll have to process that."

"Dad's flying to Chicago Tuesday to meet with him." Her mother and father exchange smiles.

"When are we moving?"

"We'll have to process that, too," her father says.

Rick has begun to tear his sandwich into bites and arrange the chunks on his plate. Suspicion creeps over her. "Did he say, *for sure?*" She addresses this to her mother, whom she can usually read. Her father is the prince of leaping to euphoric conclusions.

"They just have to negotiate a salary."

"Will you like that, living in Chicago again?" Her father's excitement dictates her answer.

"I like Chicago." *He hasn't been offered a job, he's been offered an interview.* "I'll get my own Pepsi."

Her mother follows her to the kitchen, whispering, "I'm surprised at your behavior. You should congratulate Dad."

"Are we really going?"

"We're going. How about giving him a hug?"

=== 20 ===

Who the heck would come to the front door so early on a Monday morning? His family has barely left. Maybe it's one of the kids who forgot a schoolbook and didn't take a key. Through the sheers, Mike glimpses the outline of an unfamiliar vehicle in the driveway. Better check it out before he answers. Homes get ripped off in broad daylight.

As he approaches the window, it registers: *black Lincoln Continental*. His brother. Reflexively, he steps to the side, away from the line of sight. *Damn*. Well, he can just get back into his pimp-mobile and snoop on somebody else.

The bell sounds again—and a third time, its metallic strokes bludgeoning sweat out of him. Trickles run behind his ears. He flinches at the motion of Ted passing and perusing the glass. But he can't see in—that's the thing about sheers. He might see an outline if Mike happened to move, but he won't; he'll stay glued to the corner until Ted goes.

Ted keeps his face toward the house as he circles the car and rests his chin on the roof of it.

Go on. Nobody's home. He's glad he can't discern

Ted's expression through the scrim. His brother always looks like somebody's pinching his balls: the furrow down the middle of his forehead, the pained lift to the cheeks.

Ted ducks into the car. *Get going, you.* Still staring! For God's sake! What does he see?

And now, the twirling growl of the ignition. The car glides away.

The sputter of the approaching postal truck magnetizes Mike; he lowers his half-read newspaper and leaves it on the kitchen counter, ambling past the garage doors around to the front of the house. Today the ritual is delicious: no more longing and pouncing and disappointment. If anyone wants him, it's too late. He's the property of Jonathan G. Yarger. First come, first served.

He grins at the mailman, whose truck hisses to a stop curbside.

"Got a bunch of goodies for you. How ya doing?"

"A-l! You'll be getting a change-of-address on us soon. We're moving to Chicago."

"Oh, sorry to hear it."

"I'm not."

"You from there?"

"Yeah. Sort of." He is handed an assortment of envelopes.

"Well, good luck."

Should he have mentioned it yet? All he's got is an interview. Hell, think positive! Jonathan's not going to pay his air fare all the way to Chicago tomorrow and renege on him. He'll have a considerable investment in Mike Stockman by then.

Left in a cloud of exhaust fumes, he flips through the mail. Lots of third class. Blah.

"Hi." *Ted.* His brother is arm's length from him, against the background of a feathery green day and the dark blot of his distantly parked car. "Why didn't you answer the door a couple hours ago when I rang the bell?"

Don't tell him you were out. He's probably been sitting here the whole morning. "You did?"

"Yes."

"Must've been in the shower." He tenses. Cat and mouse. The parry instead of a cordial greeting proves what they both know: Mike was hiding. His pulse begins a steady tick.

"I called your office, asking for you. They told me you hadn't been employed there in two weeks."

"I have a new job."

"I heard you tell the mailman. When were you going to tell me?"

"I was going to phone you tonight."

"Mm." A skeptical mini-grunt, his standard—the kind you give to a pitch for underwater Florida real estate. It pisses Mike off, every time.

"Say, how are Monica and the kids?" He tries to summon their names but comes up empty.

"Fine. Let's cut this. I've been worried about you."

"Why should you be?" He almost believes it. His brother's jowly face is hang-dog, beseeching. They haven't been alone together this many minutes in a row in years.

"Can I come in . . . and talk?"

"I have an appointment. Gotta take off." Interference. Ted will block his access and his thirst is a deep-down itch.

"You smell like Dad," Ted says flatly.

The impact jars the roots of Mike's teeth. He cannot speak.

"Is that what's the matter here? You're into the bottle?"

Clutching the mail to his stomach, he walks away from

170

Ted toward the backyard, wrestling the urge to sprint. It has worked so many times, this deliberately paced retreat. People are baffled by it. They hesitate; when they recover, he is safely gone.

Ted looms beside him. "Didn't you learn *anything?*" he says.

Through the screen door, Mike can see the amber fleur-de-lis of the kitchen floor tile. In seconds he will be barricaded inside. Ted is a peaceable man—he will not touch Mike.

"Wait!"

Now they are scuffling. Who started it? An uneven match. Ted, the bigger, is instantly overhead with a firm knee to Mike's throat. "You listen to me," he whispers, trembling, slipping his fingers up Mike's half-sleeve and pressing the muscles of his armpit. "How can you forget what he was?"

The knee is weightless. The unbearable fire is beneath his brother's hand: a bite mark, inflicted by his father when Mike was ten. Under the slowly growing mat of hair, it had ceased to exist.

It is funny. Comical. A bite under the arm! Mike laughs, his Adam's apple burning with each gasp. An asshole thing to do. Bite your kid in the armpit.

Frowning, Ted gradually releases him and gets to his feet with noticeable difficulty.

"Losing your oomph, old man? My brother, the football hero. What did he earn for it? Bad legs."

"Don't be like him, Michael."

"I'm *not* like him. You pompous bastard. Let me ask you something—Where's *your* scar?" He's picked the right string, the one that causes the deepest reverberation. The concrete driveway feels good under him. There is no reason to stand up. He has the advantage, lying here relishing

Ted's contrite grimace. "Do you think I stayed on the bad side of him all by myself? I had help. Mr. Perfect was always there as an example."

"I know." A hushed apology. It snags him but breezes by.

"And then you moved out. Can you guess what happened after that?"

"Yes," Ted says.

"Bullshit."

"I have scars, too."

"Bullshit."

Ted considers him solemnly, seeming to collect himself by glancing back and forth from Mike's eyes to various spots on the lawn. "Could we—"

"Bullshit!"

He pauses. The stiffly parted lips close. He shrugs, and slouches away.

"Bullshit!" Mike calls.

Lyle brushes by her as she nibbles a sandwich at the pay phone in the theater lobby. "Why don't you use the one in the office?" he says. "It's free."

Lyle's measure of the world: free or not free. It is worth a quarter to have privacy. She glances toward the box-office window where Alice McNamara, the reservations manager, is stuffing tickets into cubbyholes. Why do excess makeup and perfume always seem to go with a loose tongue?

The hiccupping buzz in Katy's ear continues. *Where is he?* He said he'd be home all day. She has to keep him in shape for tomorrow's flight. *Dang it.* She can't be two places at once. How can she work *and* monitor him? The daily lunchtime prodding helps. If he knows she's going to check up, he stays fairly straight.

"Yuh."

"Hello! Were you out in the yard?"

"Uh . . . who . . . ss . . . this?"

Sacked out. On the sofa, no doubt. Drunk? "Mike—"

"Who?"

"It's Katy."

"Can you call back?" The question squeezes out of him, husky and warped.

"No, I can't." She grips the receiver the way she would grip his arm if she could. "Have you packed yet?"

"What?"

"For Chicago?"

"Oh. No."

She sensed he wouldn't do it. It was busywork anyway—to distract him. He doesn't know how to pack, she's always done it. "How was your morning?"

"Katy?"

"Yes."

"Ted was here."

He must be mistaken. "Your brother?"

"He bugs me."

So that's what did it: the visit. He can't abide Ted. Why did it have to be today? "Well . . ." *Don't stick with this subject. It'll set him off.* "Were you taking a nap just now?"

"Yuh."

"It would probably be a good idea to organize your thoughts for the meeting with Jonathan."

"That tomorrow?"

"Yes, honey." Is this what she should do? Maybe she shouldn't have awakened him. If he gets up, he might start to drink again.

"I don't feel so hot."

"Go ahead and rest. I'll help you pack."

"Okay."

"Bye-bye."

173

"Bye."

It is too scary. How is she going to pull this off? Should she fly to Chicago with him? She *can't*, by God. She's behind on nineteen projects. She can't do everything! She'll just have to give him a pep talk tonight.

Damn Ted Stockman.

=== 21 ===

He likes airplanes. The tidiness of jet travel appeals to him, the cabin a miniature Twilight Zone in which you—suspended in time and space—exist in a state of perfection: well groomed, devoid of belongings and bills and relationships, tended by courteous servants. Whatever mess you make is lifted from you and placed in a bag on wheels, whisked out of sight. All future wishes come in clean wrappers.

"Finished, sir?"

He nods. She reaches down to remove his plate, napkins and bottles. He checks his watch, locking his tray up into the chair in front of him. Two hours to go. He's planned it exactly right. Half and half. He's dry from here to Chicago.

A sudden coaxing of Mother Nature. He unbuckles his seat belt and starts back the aisle. A cavernous plane—three movie screens. A bank of rest rooms lines the rear passage; he chooses one and slams the door.

Itty-bitty. How do you sit on the john without bashing your knees? It's a good thing he's left his suitcoat in the overhead. He lowers his trousers. Incredible, the rumors of a Mile High Club. It would take acrobats to make love in here.

He jounces to a sitting position, immediately lulled by the gentle rocking of the jet's tail section and the seashell-roar of pressurized air. The commode seat is cool, the whole compartment several degrees more comfortable than the cabin was. His lunch is talking back to him. Could it hit that fast?

Why not. Food service hoagies are notorious. He rests his cheek against the side of the steel sink. That's better.

Has he been dozing? Of all places to sleep! The muffled whir and shudder of the plane are unchanged; he's been free-floating, somewhere over Kansas.

He closes one eye and consults his wristwatch. Nearly time to land. What a riot! He'll start his own version of the Mile High Club with this caper.

Is he sober? The thought crashes in on him. He gauges the clarity of his vision, the evenness of the pendulum in his chest. Not to worry—the three vodkas are history. What he's got now is simply a cranky stomach and a case of the jitters.

Jonathan bear-hugs him. Refreshing, the absence of a macho arm punch or stuffy handshake. The man is real.

"Welcome home, Mike!"

"Thanks! How are you?"

"Terrific."

That's evident. He's aged about one year in the last nine. As they barrel toward the baggage claim, Mike does a double take at Jonathan. He was always a baldy but sinew-lean and vigorous; funny, unflappable.

Mike finds himself loping to keep up. The crowds slamming by begin to make him dizzy. Jonathan's brown eyes and pearly whites flash at Mike from a surrounding of taut swarthy skin. "God, it's good to see you. Let me zip out

176

and get the car while you're lining up your bags, okay?'' They have slowed to a trot, with the conveyors in sight.

"Okay." Is he going to puke? *Hold on until Jonathan goes.* He loosens his tie and undoes the first button of his shirt.

"Be right back."

They part, Jonathan framed against parking lot snow as he crosses four busy lanes, Mike setting his attaché down and peeling off his coat to fish for his ticket. He'll need the baggage stub.

He's going to have to give up and locate the men's room. *Now.* The floor is moving. He closes his eyes. *Steady. The revolving parade of suitcases creates that illusion. Don't panic.*

He focuses again, hunting for the appropriate sign. It is cold in this corridor, damp cold. His undershirt's sticking to his chest.

There. A rectangle with a simplified man on it. A picture of himself, faceless, weak.

Glinting tile and metal blind him. The atmosphere is tinged with the odor of urine. He gags, realizing that in spite of the pains that streak across his abdomen he will not be able to vomit.

He searches for a towel dispenser, finding only hot-air dryers. What kind of men's room doesn't have a single damned paper towel? He digs for his handkerchief and wets the square, wringing it, placing it to his eyes.

More pain. He might as well have swallowed razor blades. A little brandy would soothe it. Medicinal. Maybe Jonathan could . . .

The crucial mission of this trip sweeps back to him. He *has* to succeed.

"I figured you must be in here." Jonathan's body grows larger in the mirror. "Are you sick? You must have bolted. You left your briefcase and coat by the luggage belt."

"Yes."

"Darn! What do you think it is?"

"Food poisoning, I guess." The only thing it could be—he was well when he left L.A.

"I had a run-in with some clams last year in Detroit. It's the closest I ever felt to dying. Look, I've got the car outside, but I can't leave it there. Do you think you can make it? You could lie down in the back seat."

"Yes."

"I'll take you to the hotel. Bet you'll revive with a shower and a rest. Should I give you the fireman's carry?"

For a moment, he considers it.

He's got to get up out of this tub. How long has he been soaking? He flicks the drain release with his toe and carefully slides to a sitting position. Is Jonathan still waiting? Crawling from the water by hanging onto fixtures and the wall, he selects a towel from the neat stack and rubs it over his body. A sense of well-being possesses him: this is the same pristine environment as the airplane. His wet towel will be gone by bedtime, spirited away by a maid who will also turn his covers down and leave a chocolate mint on his pillow.

He plucks his folded robe from the counter and dons it.

"Any better?" Jonathan asks as Mike emerges. He is slumped, chin in hand, at the table.

"Lots. I thought maybe you'd split."

"I can use quiet interludes for thinking."

"Get rushed off your feet?"

"Who doesn't? And tomorrow I've got to fly to Pittsburgh. That's another reason I wanted to hang around. We need to talk."

"Do you mind if I lie down?"

"No! Have at it. It's a shame that flight was the Ptomaine Special. I had arranged for us to have dinner with some of my cronies."

"I'm sorry." He lowers himself onto the mattress, the back of his head weighted with marble.

"Are you well enough to go over the job description? I can get Phil Jacobs to show you through the agency in the morning."

"Sure."

Jonathan perches on the other bed. "If it's too much for you, stop me."

"I will."

"The main problem we've been—" Two hard raps shake the door. Jonathan laughs. "Well, I said 'stop me'!" He saunters around to it. "I ordered you some tea." In a slick five seconds, the tray is on the table; Jonathan latches the door. "Dinner in bed," he jokes as he prepares a mug and slides it onto the nightstand.

"Thank you."

"Before we start—one last interruption. Don't go away." He fades from the corner of Mike's eye; there is a solid click of metal.

In the bathroom. Mike raises to an elbow, staring at the cup.

Move! A man spends practically no minutes taking a leak. Quickly, he locates his attaché and the airline bottle within, breaks the seal and pours, watching the three-quarter level of tea in the mug rise to meet the rim. There is whiskey left; he chugs it. *Cap.* Tightening it, he shoves the bottle between the mattress and box springs. Back to a prone position, arms at his sides. The toilet flushes. A brief tumble of water echoes in the sink. Jonathan fills the view again, smiling.

"What we're looking for is a troubleshooter, Mike. We've got a couple of stickler clients and a couple of fogies. Rascals, but worth a bundle every year. I won't kid

179

you—it takes the right temperament and a freight-car load of ideas to keep them happy." He plunks onto the opposite bed. "It's three different outfits. Two are in Pittsburgh—that's where I'm going tomorrow—and one is in Cleveland, so it would mean some travel. You wouldn't mind that, would you?"

"No." He inches toward the headboard and, half reclining, sips the warm liquid.

"The first one is a chain of restaurants, headquartered in Monroeville—that's a suburb of Pittsburgh. A family business. Grandpa's dead and Papa's the patriarch type. Got four sons working for him and they all have to bootlick. One of them, Dale, is exclusively in charge of advertising and public relations. He doesn't know the first thing about it. His college degree's in geology or some equally useful subject. He insulates Papa from us . . . to make himself look good."

The tea is cool enough to gulp. He intakes it smoothly, noiselessly, and replaces the cup.

"When we come up with a scheme Daddy hates, Junior—who has previously agreed to it—backtracks and badmouths the project. When we come up with something Daddy loves, Junior makes sure he takes the credit for the concept. Am I scaring you?"

"No." A mood is settling in, working its way up from his feet. Lethargic, tranquil.

"Because I've got to lay it on the line. I can't invite you in and then unveil the skeletons and expect you to like it. The restaurants are making money, there's no way they can't, they're in elite locations in twelve cities. But lately they've been nudged by establishments with more of a flair. When Grandpa started them, good food and attentive service were enough. What I see as their major drawbacks are these: the interiors are dark and lackluster. And the food is standard. Good, but standard. Why should anybody go out to get chicken pot pie or a mustard-ham slice? You can make that at home. And they haven't changed their menu in a number of years and this is a problem, too, because the regulars have seen it all, over and over. But Papa thinks that's why they . . .''

The words are notes of music written on a scale behind his eyelids. Down, down, up, up, up. Down, up. Up, up, up. Down. Down.

He awakens in the dark and, fumbling for the lamp's knob, illuminates a note on the nightstand.

I do that to my kids, too. Am a wonderful sedative. Think nothing of it. Feel better soon. I'll drop you a letter, outlining my thoughts.

J.

22

Dear Mike:

Sorry you had to wait a week for this letter. I was hanging by my thumbs in Pittsburgh.

Mike, I've given sincere consideration to your personality and talents, which I greatly admire. We go as far back as Army buddies, although we are veterans of other wars. I know what fantastic things you can do. But I am concerned that the role I had in mind for you might not be the right one. The folks I'd want you to be dealing with are—to put it mildly—cantankerous. This was reinforced to me by the rounds I made last week. It is not fair to inflict this on you or anyone else.

What I'm trying to say, and perhaps not very well, is that I'd like to wait a while and pursue the matter with you in the future. Our agency would benefit immensely from your experience, but I am skittish about present circumstances. R. L. (my partner) and I have decided to handle these three backbreakers ourselves in the hopes of ironing out what, at best, has been a tangle of miscommunication.

*It was a treat to see you, my friend. I regret it had
to be while you were green in the gills. Hope none of
that episode stuck with you and that you and the
family are all fine. Believe me, I will contact you if
opportunity parts the waters. Meanwhile, I wish you
every success. Give my love to Katy.*

Sincerely,
Jonathan

First of all, it's crap, this letter still warm from the interior of the mailbox. He has written enough advertising
copy to spot the hidden message: *Drop dead.* Was he not
the King of Gloss of an entire decade? He knows nuance,
all the pretty words.

He looks up and down the street; the slants and arches
of the houses, the red roofs and magenta blooms are glamour from a postcard. He wants to rip them apart, wants to
rip Jonathan Yarger apart, his fancy clothes and false
friendship. If he were still in Chicago, he would grab Jonathan by the neck, press the hollow of his collarbone with
his thumbs until he confessed: *I didn't want you, Mike, I
don't want you.*

Why? What has he done?

What will he do now?

He enters by the kitchen, and sits at the dining room
table, rereading the page. In time it grows three-dimen-
sional, becomes a transparent cube, the print floating submerged midway in it: *a clue.* He has been relying too much
on surfaces, the appearance of things. What separates him
from success equal to Wilson Koppel's or Raymond Colquitt's or Jonathan Yarger's is not lack of talent. He has
that—has it in spades. No, it's a spiritual meshing with the
unseen, a courtship of his own psyche. The stars. Fate, if
you will.

183

He must tap in. There are forces that can help him.

He goes to the canvas magazine rack and roots through newspaper sections until he finds the morning's horoscope column. Then, propping it in front of him at the kitchen sink, he nurses a couple of shots while he peruses the cryptic instruction.

GEMINI (May 21–June 21): Answer to key question can be found today. Be considerate of partner. Conditions right for new enterprise.

The middle one is easy. *Partner*—that's Katy. Has specific significance, though. Each word in the message is important. Their anniversary? August 17. And this is only . . . February . . . the tenth. Friday. February . . . Valentine's Day . . . is Tuesday. All right.

New enterprise. Who else could he ask for a job? He's followed every lead. *New.* Totally different. *Enterprise.* Business, initiated by self.

His own agency! Why hadn't he thought of it before?

He lifts a pair of shears from a peg and cuts carefully around the Gemini paragraph, disposing of the rest in the basket under the sink. Distilled, the wisdom of this square scrap has weight, like a precious metal in his palm. He carries it to the family room and stands thinking.

Answer to key question. Confusing. He has to figure out the question before he can receive the answer.

He lies on the couch, held up by clouds, and tucks the wisp of paper inside his shirt next to his skin. The snow-capped crest of an enormous mountain piercing the cloud bed is his only companion in a smoothly revolving sphere. He realizes he is dreaming and tries not to steer, merely observe. His eyeballs are traveling by themselves, winding through the house; the clearest view is peripheral, the path ahead slightly blurred. He lets them take their lead, tugging him along as a dog on a leash tugs its master. They pause at the scrupulous neatness of Lee's room. A scent greets them: the elusive mixture of baby-soft hair and old dolls. Her jewelry case opens without opening, as though he can see through it. Her birthday necklace, serpentine across rhinestones and coins, collides with a man's hand. He strains to sharpen the image, but the dream fails. One must not press too hard. He can glide back in.

No. He has ruined it. He lies listening to the barely perceptible singing of the refrigerator, disappointed by the quickening of his senses. If the sequence had gone on long enough, it might have meant something.

Lee scrutinizes the side of the house, cannot find the profile of her dad in any of the windows. She and Jason take a few steps into billowing shade and rest against the low slate wall at the bend of the driveway.

"Lee!" Mike pokes his head out the kitchen door.

"Just a minute," she whispers to Jason. As she approaches her father, she recognizes from the staring roundness of his eyes that he has an agenda for her.

"I'm glad you're home from school. The dishes need to be done," he says urgently.

"I was telling Jason good-bye. He's going away for the weekend."

Her father does not speak, but the way his eyes reshape themselves into almonds frightens her. He moves inside, out of sight.

Quickly, she returns to Jason. "I have to go."

He responds to her alarm with a suspicious glance toward the house. "Why?"

"I have work to do. The dishes."

"I'll help you."

"No. Thanks."

"I will," he hisses, walking with her. "Mr. Stockman!"

"Don't!"

"Mr. Stockman?" Jason follows her into the kitchen and slings his books onto a chair.

"Yes?" Her father materializes, sizing up Jason with the trace of a smile.

Jason mistakes it for genuine and smiles back. "How are you?"

"Fine."

This is a trap. She must get Jason out of here. He thinks he can control the situation, jolly her father along.

"I'd like to help Lee, okay?"

Her father gives a single nod.

The only way out of this is through it. She begins to rinse the things that belong in the dishwasher; Jason loads them into the machine.

She is aware of her father pacing behind them. "How's your family?" he asks.

"Real good. But my little brother's making my mother go cuckoo. He's eighteen months old. He pulls junk out of drawers and closets the whole day."

"Sticking his nose in where he doesn't belong?" her dad offers amiably.

Jason laughs. "Yes."

"Like you?"

"Me?"

"Aren't you always sticking your nose in where you don't belong?"

A nervous laugh. "I hope not."

"You're poking your nose in here."

She should stop this, but no sentence comes to her. Her arms are hot from the rushing water; she is hot all over.

"I guess you're right, Mr. Stockman."

"Is that what you are?"

"I do that. It's a fault." There is no sarcasm to it.

Her father ceases pacing. The only sounds in the abyss are those of the journeying dishes, one after the other.

"I thought so," her father says at last.

Outside, Jason puts an arm around her shoulders. "I'll call you Sunday night, huh?"

Will he? "I'm sorry."

"About?"

"Him. I feel bad."

"Don't."

Why doesn't his daughter hurry back in? He's got few enough hours to fulfill the instructions. Tomorrow's paper will bring a new batch. He has to be ready.

He prepares the family room desk with freshly sharpened pencils, a blank note pad and the telephone book. He will announce the formation of his agency this afternoon by calling his acquaintances at all the others. By five o'clock, it will be a fait accompli and he will announce it at the supper table.

A tap-squeak-tap of footsteps across linoleum. Lee comes by.

"Honey . . ." He brings out his wallet and slides three twenties from it. "I'd like you to get your mother a Valentine's present from me."

"Now?"

He quells his impatience at her sass. The way she says "Now?" when he asks her to do a job always implies he is slightly daft.

"Valentine's Day isn't until next week. Can't I buy it Saturday?"

"No." The word is rock-solid. He can see it hit her.

She takes the twenties. "What should I get?"

"You decide."

"Are you going to drive me?"

"I can't. I have phone calls to make."

"I'll have to ride the bus."

"Okay. And wrap it, won't you?"

Her lips stretch into a very straight line.

She wanders through the department store aisles, searching. The impersonal jostling of shoppers and faceless legions of blouses and dresses on silver hangers compound her isolation, her weariness.

He does this every time. *Get Mom a birthday present, get Mom a Christmas present.* Usually the day before. But if she didn't do it, her mother would have no gift from him. Her father would not remember to buy it. She has seen that happen twice. Twice was enough.

She surveys the jungle of cosmetics, belts, scarves, hosiery, handbags. Of the ten thousand possibilities, are there any that would please him? Probably not. And the money . . . Sixty dollars. Her mother would rather have a box of candy so she wouldn't have to worry about it.

He can't let anyone go to bed before he finds it: *answer to key question.* It's beginning to upset him. He has obeyed the horoscope implicitly. The Valentine gift is wrapped and hidden in an old suitcase. His agency has been born, properly heralded through an hour and a half of phone calling and feted with champagne.

If people go to sleep, the day is over. He loses his chance.

Katy and Lee and Rick are in their rooms. Will they be turning off the lights soon? He stations himself at the desk, reviewing the list of agencies notified. He even called Jonathan Yarger's.

Key question. The pressure under his cheekbones is intense; he puts his knuckles to them, pushing. It has to be simple. Like the Hitchcock TV episode where Barbara Bel Geddes clobbers her husband with a frozen leg of lamb and then feeds it to the detectives who arrive to investigate his murder. A great moment, that: the officers wondering aloud why they haven't found the weapon, all the while stuffing their faces with it.

Think. A weird dream this afternoon, the eyes rolling through air. The clouds and mountain. The necklace. A man's fingers.

Answer to key question. He is stuck. Stuck.

He goes to Lee's room; she is reading in the rocker, the book large across her narrow nightgowned knees.

He wants to see the jewelry case, has to see it.

"Dad?"

"May I . . ." He gazes at the padded box. A vision runs him through, keen as a memory: the necklace rising away from the glitter-mash. A theft. Excitement grips him. "Do you ever wear your chain?"

"Yes."

"I don't see you wear it."

"I do."

"Would you show it to me?"

"Why?" She closes the book slowly. The rocker dips forward. "I . . . lent it."

"To whom?"

She tucks the book beside her and considers him.

"To Rick? Is that how he got three hundred dollars?"

Her complexion fades to the color of her hair. "No."

"Let's ask him." He is onto it now, *answer to key question.* He strides through the bath, wrenching the doorknob to Rick's room. The boy is facedown on the bed. "Come here a minute, Rick," he commands, departing abruptly to wait beside the jewelry case.

Rick, in an undershirt and jeans, sheet-wrinkles etched into his cheeks, limps in, focusing on him blearily.

"I'd like you and Lee to tell me where her chain is."

"What chain?"

"The one I bought her for her birthday."

"How would I know?"

"It's missing, isn't that right, Lee?"

"What's the matter?" Katy has walked up beside him.

"Rick has something to tell us."

"No, I don't."

"Lee's chain is missing. Correct?" He flicks the lid of the box upward. "Lee?"

"I *lent* it."

"To Rick?"

The children look at each other.

"For the driver's license money?"

"She didn't lend it to *me!*"

"Who was it, then, Lee?"

She edges against the wall, watching Rick's mouth.

"You think I took it, don't you?" Rick says to her. "I don't believe this. *You* probably took it!" His son is pointing at him. "And you're trying to blame me!"

"That's ridiculous," Katy says. "Nobody in this house would take anything. Not you. Not your father. Besides, he *gave* it to her. That doesn't make sense."

"It makes sense to me."

Another wedge. His son will try to pit Katy against him if he can. Ludicrous, Rick's attempt to toss the guilt back in his lap.

Stealing is a quantum leap. How should he deal with it? *Do nothing. Let it cool.* The morning paper will bring directions.

A figure circles his bed; Rick, his head half under the pillow, calculates the person's location in the dark by listening intently. The body halts in the corner formed by the sliding glass and his highboy.

Now who's in here? For shit's sake! This is madness. Why do they think they can stick it to him day and night?

Because he lets them. They're all crazy. He's going to start defending himself.

He sits up swiftly. "Who is it?"

"Me." His sister's voice.

"Will you get the hell out of here?"

"I want—"

She wants to talk about the necklace. *Eat grass, girl.* He knows where it went. Can't she see? It turns his stomach that she would suspect him. It hurts. "Get the hell out."

Her pale hair and gown, faint as smoke, cross the carpet and disappear into the gilded shaft between the frame and the door.

23

A black sun rising at the center of his being tells Mike it is morning. Anxiety flutters all around him, waiting for him to open his eyes. He cannot make friends with it. He has tried.

He forces himself to surface, the black sun contracting into a powerful stomach knot. He experiments briefly with ways to sit up, but the tensing of any muscle causes excruciating pain. Even flipping onto his belly is beyond his ability.

He can't stay here, either; the cramp is growing, making him nauseated. Acid shoots from his stomach into the back of his throat, scorching it and the inside of his nose. He twists violently out of the bed, falling to his hands and knees on the floor and crawling toward the bathroom. Reaching the toilet, he presses his cheek against the side of the cold porcelain bowl, heaving. He vomits convulsively in a single torrent, amazed to find the commode water a bright scarlet.

It is not his, this blood. He pushes the chrome handle and flushes until he can see his reflection in a clear motionless pool. Another wave seizes him, pouring out of his nose and mouth. Red. He chokes on his screams.

* * *

Lee finishes loading clothes into the washer and walks away from its vibrating slosh and burble. As she leaves the garage and passes through the kitchen, she thinks she hears him shouting. For her mother. Doesn't he remember she's at a farm auction, buying props?

She tracks the fragments of sound to his bathroom and lingers in the hallway, stricken by a wafting putrid odor. *Sick again.* She doesn't want to see it. Why isn't her mother here? There is no way to get in touch with her—or Rick, already out on Eva's boat.

"Katy!"

Her mother pampers him in these situations, cleaning the bathroom, bringing him ginger ale in bed. She *can't.*

"Katy!"

She runs into her own bathroom and wets a washcloth, holding it to her lips and chin, trying to block out his voice. Tears squeeze from under her lashes; she waits.

He calls once more and is quiet. She will tell him she was doing the laundry and didn't hear.

In the blessed silence, she rests for a few minutes, elbows on the sink. He will be back under the covers by now, dozing. She peeks as she goes by.

The rumpled sheets are vacant, cased in sunlight. His bathroom is revealed in portions as she tiptoes toward it: the medicine cabinet and expansive mirror, the vanity, a ruffle-curtained window. He is sitting next to the toilet, slumped against the wall, watching her.

"Dad, you doing all right?"

He does not respond, although his expression changes to one of mild surprise. Has he had a nosebleed? She imagines she sees caked blood in his nostrils and a sprinkling of it across the hairs of his chest. His pajama bottoms bear a small maroon stain, at his left hip.

The brilliance in the toilet bowl flashes into her consciousness. She stares at it, uncomprehending.

"I think I need a doctor," he says.

"Hello."

"Uncle Ted, this is Lee."

"Hiya! How's the tennis?"

"My dad is real sick. We're alone. I don't know the name of a doctor to call."

"I'll be right over."

"He's been throwing up blood."

"Tell you what we'll do." His tone has lowered into an artificial calmness that alarms her. "It would take too long for me to drive up there and take him to a doctor. The best thing is to get an ambulance. I'll call it for you. Go ahead and ride with him when it comes. I'll meet you at the hospital."

In the ambulance, she numbly holds his wrist while the female medic continually takes his pulse and blood pressure on the other arm. His head is papier-mâché above the blue blanket and sturdy straps of the stretcher; he appears to be unconscious. She sways on her knees, keeping her balance during a long succession of turns taken at moderate speed. There is no siren.

"Is this your father?" the medic inquires sympathetically. She has the plump, weathered appearance of a woman with many children. Her hair is dye-orange, parted in the middle and pulled back in a casual way that matches her lack of makeup.

"Yes."

"He'll be okay."

She doesn't believe it. She has seen the same web of bruise-colored veins and sunken dry skin on the forehead of a man who died within hours: her Grandpa Stockman.

In the funeral parlor, she was fascinated that the veins had flattened, whitened. He no longer looked distressed. He looked better, actually.

The woman gazes at her with the receptivity of a priest. They are breathing the faint stale breath of her father; their cloistered intimacy overwhelms her. She wants to confess to this woman, to let her wordlessly, competently attend the solutions. She can feel her chin quivering. *I wouldn't go to him when he was ill. I waited too long. I am responsible. I despised him. Wanted to be rid of him and he knew it. Is he sick because he knew it? Did I do this? He drinks. Did I do that? No one likes him. Did I kill him by not coming when he called? Would a few minutes have made a difference? If you hate a person, does it make them drink? If they love you, don't they stop drinking? Does he love me? I still love him. Did I do this?*

The woman merely sighs in answer and pumps the ball of the blood pressure gauge again until it sighs, too. The ambulance is backing up slowly; through the rectangular panes in the doors, she glimpses her Uncle Ted among a flock of white coats.

They stand at the emergency room desk, a cluttered, well-lit island in a sea of echoes. The physician in charge habitually adjusts his bow tie as he interviews her. *How old? When last ate?* Behind her, the curtained cubicle containing her father keeps accumulating people. At first, there were three nurses and a doctor but, one by one, they discreetly departed and returned bringing others.

"Mr. Stockman, can you talk to us?" a woman's voice urges. "Can you answer a few questions?"

A masculine pitch: "Mr. Stockman? We need to ask you some questions. Mr. Stockman?" The lines are offered without conviction, as though to a person in a coma.

Two nurses break from the throng and run down a side

corridor. Seconds later, they emerge flanking a short swarthy man in a rolled-sleeve smock. An East Indian? What kind of doctor?

"You can go to the admitting desk now," the mouth above the bow tie says. "Please wait out there."

Her uncle takes her hand.

The admitting department is a contrast of human agony and glass-encased computers. She and Ted sit for thirty minutes watching mothers with feverish children, auto accident victims, people with home-gashed limbs trussed in dish towels, elderly men with congestive coughs await their turns in resigned silence. Their suffering does not penetrate the glass barrier; pain is translated dispassionately by perfect fingernails plucking computer keys. *Fell from ladder. Smashed thumb in car door. Vomiting blood.* The stony click-click-click hypnotizes Lee. Beside the computer, a machine stamps her father's name and code numbers onto a plastic rectangle as smooth and factual as a grave marker.

She and her uncle travel to the cashier's window, have the rectangle pressed onto a rainbow of layered papers. They work the waiting room soft-drink machine, which hails them in a robot monotone: *Make—your—selection—now. Don't—forget—your—change.* Side by side in an isolated niche, they examine wrinkled magazines without speaking. Between them rests the imagined presence of her mother, through which he cannot hear her despair.

Soon the bow tie seeks them out, bearing the tale of her father's dehydration, a shriveling of veins, you see, one could scarcely be found for the entry of fluids, don't you see, but was, and he is out of danger, for the moment, and here is a shopping bag containing his clothing.

They have cloaked his bed with a hospital-green drapery hung from a horseshoe metal track. He lies alone, resentfully eyeing the steady drip of glucose from his IV bag into a cylindrical reservoir and down a plastic tube. The parade of white shoes and silver wheels beyond the hem of the curtain, the hushed conferences and joking banter, the aroma of coffee, are relics of a former world. He wants to die.

He is hated. By his wife. By his children. By his peers. He can never make up the miles of lost ground.

And he is afraid. Has been afraid all his life—*of* his life—weeping to God in the early years and then accepting the vast dark space he was born to inhabit. Always he sees that hairy arm, his father's, fishing under the bed for him, groping viciously as he huddles in dust.

He digs at the adhesive tape of his left hand with the thumbnail of his right, patiently peeling the strips, unwinding them to discover the raw, puffed hole in his flesh where the needle resides.

Someone has got hold of him, tenderly, around the neck. His wife. He is on his side in another hospital bed, tied by a throbbing ache to another vial of glucose. She lays her cheek against his, leaning over him, clasping him in the old loving way. She kisses his temple and draws back to gaze at his face. Hers is distraught, but she smiles.

"Hi," he says.

"Hi," she answers tearfully. "They told me you pulled out your IV."

"I don't want to get well."

"I need you," she whispers.

"No."

"I do."

His breastbone is cracking; he cannot keep the halves of him together. He begins to sob.

She strokes his hair, weeping quietly. "Come home."

"I'm ashamed."

"We'll start again."

"Help me."

"I will."

"I'll do better."

"I know." She touches her mouth to his mouth, and then to his ear. "Please come home."

Leaving Mike's room, she encounters her brother-in-law.

"How is he?"

"Pretty weak."

He stares at her, processing this information. She has noticed this about Ted, that he pauses after each exchange as though her sentences must travel an incredibly long distance through the synapses of his brain, be received in some central core, an appropriate reply formulated and sent back along the same meandering trail. "Can I see him?"

"Not now."

"I'll come back tomorrow."

If only she could keep Ted away. The advantage of this hospitalization is that she can insulate Mike from the factors that harm him. He will not have access to liquor, and it is possible to control the visitor list. If she can erase stress during his stay, it may truly be a time of renewal for him. She knows the origin of this near-fatal binge: the string of anguished days waiting for Jonathan Yarger's reply. Why couldn't Jonathan have been honest with him in the first place? "Please don't."

"Why not?"

She's going to take the bull by the horns. "He doesn't feel comfortable with you, Ted. Don't you know that?"

"Yes. But I want to change it."

"I really thank you for coming, and I'd like it if you'd go on home."

His head droops, craning his neck forward; his fleshy

face seems too big for his body to balance. "What are you going to do about his drinking problem?"

How would he know *that*? Has Lee been talking to him? Ted Stockman, the jury. She wants him out of her sight. "What makes you think you can pry into our family affairs?"

"I *am* your family."

"No. You gave Mike up."

"I had to get out, Katy. It was a matter of survival."

"You left him in that house. He was the tormented one, not you."

"But that tormented *me!*" He shrugs in exasperation. "I can't explain how it was. We were both affected. He doesn't drink because of me. Or anyone else. It's already in motion. We're just excuses."

Why can't he understand? Her husband has got to get a stretch of peacefulness. She will not allow Ted near him if she can prevent it. "I appreciate what you've done for us and I'll be in touch." She walks stiffly away, turning to check on his whereabouts as she reaches the end of the passageway. If he's gone into Mike's room, by God, she'll drag him out. He is in a swirl of people, gradually moving into the elevator. She pivots to find her daughter waiting.

Her mother comes to her with arms outstretched; Lee lets herself be held. This is the mother of her babyhood, love itself. They cling to one another, her mother's scent musky sweet like forest flowers. It is good to hug tightly, neither of them letting go from chagrin or busyness. The physical contact produces a keen nostalgia. She believes she can remember all the way back: being brought home for the first time, the shining delight of her brother and father and mother flowing in through her eyes, warming her, making her drift to sleep without care.

Slowly, they part.

"Why would Uncle Ted ask me about Dad's drinking?" her mother says in a tone of suspicion and disappointment.

Amazed, she bows her head.

"Have you discussed that with him?"

"No."

"Why did you call *him?*"

"I didn't know who else to ask."

Her mother nods sadly. "I'm sorry I wasn't there. You did right. But . . . he's not to be told what goes on at our house."

"Okay."

"He upsets Dad. Very much."

"What did he do?"

"Let's just say he never took his part. He wasn't a friend. That was the beginning."

Did Ted cause him to start drinking, is that what her mother means? She was fooled by her uncle's mask of sincerity.

"Dad's going to get well, but we have to give him an awful lot of support. It's up to us. His ego's been scraped enough. That's very important to a man, ego. Too many people have been unkind to him lately. We have to build him up, not tear him down. Make him happy. Take care of him. It's nobody else's business what he does or what we do."

"You the family of Michael Stockman?"

She and her mother, waiting in a vinyl-chaired hospital alcove, rise. The man seeking them is a doctor with grayish glasses, gray eyes and a fringe of sparse gray hair circling a fuzzy bald spot. His lenses are so thick that his heavy-lidded eyes seem those of a benevolent monster.

"Yes."

"I'm Dr. Connally. I'll be serving as your husband's physician. I've been in to see him, and he's a mighty sick fellow. We'll need to keep him with us a few days. I'd like to have a little powwow about him.'' He has a Southern accent, crusty and rich. They gather around the brown plastic coffee table, which bears on its edges the melted troughs of forgotten cigarettes.

"You brought your daddy in, is that right?"

Her mother is positioned between her and the doctor; she has to lean forward to see him. "Yes."

"What was he doing before the vomiting incident?"

"Sleeping." She can sense her mother's discomfort. Lee slides back until the doctor is no longer in her sight.

"Your daughter said he's had an ulcer."

"Yes."

"What kind?"

"Duodenal."

"And he's been treating it?"

"Well, it was quite a while ago."

"Did it heal?"

"I suppose so. He was on a special diet for almost a year. I haven't heard him complain about his stomach since then."

"Could we get the records?"

"They're in Chicago."

"If you'll sign a release form, we can send for them."

"All right."

"You worried about your daddy?" As the doctor says this, he comes around to sit next to Lee, peering at her with a gentle curiosity.

"Yes."

"We're going to fix him up. But I need you folks to be real honest with me."

Hope surges through her. Her mother squirms slightly.

"Has he been under stress?"

"He has," her mother says. "He's been job hunting.

But decided to start his own ad agency. I think that's all straightened around now.''

"Could you trust that he hasn't ingested any harmful substance?''

"Like a poison? Oh, surely not.''

The doctor addresses Lee. "What do you think?''

"No.'' She stares at her lap, determined to defer to her mother.

"Mrs. Stockman—does he smoke?''

"He used to. But not for about fifteen years.''

"Is his alcohol intake more than moderate?''

"No.''

He pauses. "What else? Parents' health?''

"His father died of heart trouble.''

"Mother still living?''

"Yes.''

"Any diseases?''

"Arthritis.''

"And you, young lady. Got clues for me?''

She does not dare to look up. She shakes her head.

"He's being poisoned.'' *Her uncle. Standing in the doorway.*

"Who is this?'' The doctor peers at him.

Her mother rises. "My husband's brother.''

Ted does not change expression. "With alcohol. He's poisoning himself.''

"Is this true?'' Connally asks.

"He's got . . .'' Her mother sits down without answering, red deepening into gray across her cheeks. "He'll think *I* told you,'' she whispers.

The doctor regards them all sympathetically, one by one. "He doesn't have to know anyone told me.''

=== 24 ===

Katy slides from her bed and gets onto her knees in the darkness, hands folded against the blanket. She has been away from prayer for so long she does not know where to start. She must be cautious about memorized prayers or selfish prayers that take the form of a letter. They do not garner His favor.

She has never felt adequate for this task. Even when she was in practice, her sentences came out stilted, as though they were to be graded by the Almighty.

Lord God of the Universe . . .

Pretentious wording. Not credible.

Frustrated, she covers her face with her fingers. Whatever form she chooses, it will be the wrong one. Can't He just bless her as she is, know her unspoken plea?

She has been reduced to nothing, a person who tries and tries and can't get results. She is weary clear through her soul. All she really wants is for people to be satisfied, healthy—for things to go well. But she is powerless. Intentions turn into events that are totally opposite.

Holy Father, Creator of Heaven and Earth . . .

Her husband is not inside his body anymore. If he were

dead, she could accept it. But to touch and see him and yet miss him so much . . . is bizarre. Terrifying.

Oh, he was wonderful! His native funniness . . . the grateful embraces. They were two misfits who fit perfectly together: the whipped, belligerent man who hid behind the personality of a radio announcer, the inherently guilty preacher's daughter who cloaked herself in the trappings of theater. They entertained and comforted each other. At first.

You who can perform miracles . . .

She loves her family. Mike and Rick and Lee. Truly.

Lord, I care. Examine my heart.

How can she do so well at work and so inadequately at home? In her office, rows of clean slots bear her achievements: set construction plans, costume sketches. She's already earned a small raise.

The house seems manageable without him here: a stage, meticulously designed and accessorized. Ideal. All he has to do is live in it! Why does everything go awry?

Father, if I am to blame, make me a better person. Help me to try harder. Bring him back as he used to be. Heal us.

He cannot ride this out. The night is endless, the sheet under him stubbled ice or sopping tepid rags. He's got to unhitch himself from this metal pole.

How far would he have to go to get a drink? Could he push the IV stand along with him? Is the hospital coffee shop still open? *They don't sell liquor in hospitals.* What hospital is this? There's bound to be a bar nearby.

They've taped him up royally this time. Like a tight glove glued to a board. Maybe he could lift the glucose bottle off its hook and carry it.

Staff's sparse in the wee hours. He could sneak out, down the steps. Can't go into a bar like . . . Have to get dressed. Where are . . . clothes?

His ribs seem too snug, maybe he can remove them. But once he pulls them over his head, how is he going to slide them off his arms while he's connected to this tube? He'll need help. Better ring now—nurses take forever to answer a light. He searches patiently in the blackness for the button. The ripples along the sheets are snowy hills to climb. Midway up a white glinting slope, he scans the horizon. The distant peaks are shaped like frozen ocean waves cresting. Must be India.

This glorious Sunday morning—February the twelfth—has the promise of Easter. A resurrection. All things are possible. The family room twinkles with reflections from the sliding glass and pool. Katy admires the lace runner she has placed on the low table in front of the couch, the cinnamon-sprinkled peach kuchen, a spray of marigolds from the yard. She will serve her children with silver and china, with linen napkins, with new devotion. A beginning.

They stumble out sleepily to sit beside her where she spreads her arms to take one under each wing. They eat in peaceful meditation. Then she lifts the snapshot album with the scuffed, split binding onto her lap and opens it to wedding and baby pictures. Neither child seems pleased; they begin to stack the dishes and forks.

"The night I went into labor with you," she says to Rick, "I had a suitcase packed and in the front closet. Dad was so excited that he grabbed the canister vacuum cleaner by mistake. He put it in the car trunk and didn't even realize it when we got to the hospital. The nurses cracked up when they saw him coming with one hand on my arm and the other hand holding the vacuum cleaner!"

"I've heard that before," Rick says testily.

"Here you are the day we brought you home."

"You can't see me in that picture."

"I had the blanket wrapped around you because the wind was strong."

"Looks like you're carrying a bundle of laundry." He turns away.

"What about this one?" *Rick at eight pounds, decked out in a baseball slugger suit, his sweet wise face alert under a thatch of dark hair.*

"Yeah," he says, rising.

"Please stay with me."

He sits down again.

"There *you* are," she says to Lee. A baby doll, six months old, clad in a pink gown and nestled in Mike's arms, their close resemblance already apparent. "Remember this?" *Rick at three, proudly clasping a bunch of flattened dandelions.* She laughs. "You told me not to worry, you had made sure there were no bees in them by stepping on each one before you picked it!"

He does not comment.

She flips a page, finding a photo of Mike assembling Rick's first bicycle. Those were the golden times. Rick and Mike roasting marshmallows at the living room fireplace in Kansas City. Lee, five years old, wearing a floor-length velvet Christmas dress. Cutting and sewing that fabric had been tricky and tedious because of the thick one-way nap. But she did look beautiful! "And here's a birthday party. Yours, Rick. I think you were nine." Katy smiles to see the motley lineup of children in cockeyed foil hats and clutching balloons. The day comes back to her with its fresh hot air, the out-of-doors refreshments and games. It was a Disney party. She had gotten a neighbor to dress up like Donald Duck and dance with all the gaping children. "Halloween, the same year. Dad painted that big box to look just like a package of chewing gum. Remember, Rick? What a great costume. All we could see of you were your shoes." Pleasures seem to tumble from the book, rapidly, one upon the other. This minute, too, is a keepsake, this gentle sharing.

Why doesn't her mother stop? They are misleading, these framed split-seconds. She can step back into every photo—reliving the weather and voices, clothing and actions, exactly as they were—and none of them are pleasant. The bicycle was impounded for a week two hours after it was built, for some infraction by her brother. The marshmallow roasting was fraught with instructions as to how to properly center the marshmallow on the stick and evenly brown it—and ended with the children being sent to their rooms. The outdoor party was marred by her father's merciless flare of temper at a guest who flew his model airplane into the cake.

"The Fort Lauderdale vacation!" her mother says. "The first time either of you had seen the ocean."

Her father, refusing to rush to the beach when they arrived, insisting instead on naps for all of them. Her mother, sneaking the children out when he was asleep, down to the shell-starred shoreline, where water playfully tagged and tugged them as they ran in and out of the surf, shrieking. The only thing they had for lunch was ice cream, as much as they could eat. At twilight in their hotel room, after they had been fed and bathed and lay content with exhaustion on unfamiliar cots, their father awoke, cross, ready to go to the beach. After a vehemently whispered discussion with him on the screened balcony, their mother had dressed them in their bathing suits, which were only half dry and stuck chillingly to their legs as they pulled them on. The waves that night were ferocious, popping around them like boiling water. Her father lost his balance and was thrown against a jetty, scraping his thigh. They were summarily marched to bed, where they eavesdropped, disillusioned, on their father's spiteful opinion of Fort Lauderdale. They went home early.

She does not like to speak of the past, and pictures sear her. She has learned to discard each hour as it goes by.

Doesn't her mother remember the truth? It is as though she wasn't there at all but only read these adventures and tells them innocently as her own.

"I have to get a shower," Lee says.

Her mother puts a hand on her arm. "Wait."

"What's the point of this?" Rick stands up.

"The point is . . ." Her mother closes the album. ". . . sometimes I think all you remember are the bad things. I don't understand that. We've always loved you both, and enjoyed you. We're a family. We need to come back together."

We were never together.

"We'll be going in to see Dad today. Let's put the past behind us. We have to forgive each other. If we have to make the first move toward Dad, let's do it."

"Why doesn't *he?*" Rick jams his hands onto his hips.

"He can't."

"Why not?"

"We have to make allowances for him. He had a terrible growing-up time. His father could be brutal. Really . . . it ruined his life. Once, he took Dad—"

Lee jumps up. "I don't want to hear it!"

"You can't hide your head in the sand and pretend it isn't there. If we love him, we have to help him. Dr. Connally is involved now, and things are going to get straightened out—about the drinking. But we have to let Dad know we care. Make the first move," she says to Rick. "If you can't do it for him, do it for me."

Lee locks the doors of her room and goes to the closet. Kneeling down, she crawls in among the hanging wools and cottons that shelter her like boughs. She sits gingerly, and scoots slowly all the way back to a dim silent corner. Resting her head against the wall, she waits for the rocking motion to subside. The vision of her father as a baby taunts her. *Ruined his life.* He was just a little boy, trusting. And his own father hurt him. She must make this, too, go away. Erase it, like the others. *Concentrate.*

He has never seen his father look so bad. For the hour they have stayed with him, he has alternately slept and trembled; the whites of his eyes are yellowish, pebbled, bloodshot. He seems to be in pain yet cannot name it. They have covered him with two blankets, at his request. Still, his heels and knees work up and down restlessly under the covers.

"We'd better go and let you be quiet," his mother says, kissing his father's forehead. Lee, solemn and formal in a cream-colored dress and white stockings, steps to the bed and strokes his hair.

His mother and sister walk past to exit, his mother nodding almost imperceptibly. He can feel her watching him as he leaves the wooden chair by the window where he has been sustained by a sliver of air blowing in between the sill and the slightly raised sash. He reaches the side of the bed; his father stares up at him with the hopeless repentance of a man facing his executioner.

"Bye, Dad." He offers a handshake.

His father clasps his hand tentatively, but when Rick tries to let go, his father holds on.

Rick hesitates, stunned by the beseeching grip.

"Thanks for coming in," his father whispers.

His throat is too tight to say anything. Finally he manages, "Get well."

His father releases him.

25

"I don't think you have the dedication to continue with tennis."

"My dad's in the hospital."

"I heard you the first time. But it doesn't really compute. We all have personal problems."

Garcia's eyes seem even darker, his teeth whiter in the bare-bulbed understairs storage room that is his office. She stands in front of his dusty desk, watching him slant back, back in his chair until he seems to be looking down at her from a high place.

"I'd like to continue."

"Not this year."

"I can't?"

"I need people with guts, Lee Ann. I get the notion life's a little too easy for you. Skip a practice here, blow a game there. You've got talent but no tenacity. Tenacity means you hang on, doing what you know you should do, against circumstance and against the odds. It means being kicked and getting right up again. Perseverance. I don't see that in you, dear. I'm sorry."

* * *

He must have been delirious. The three days since they brought him in are spotty. What the hell is wrong with him? Some kind of a fever, like malaria? Is his ulcer flaring up again? Maybe a combination. He feels downright inhuman.

Well . . . they'll figure it out. They've taken enough of his blood. Vampires.

God, he could go for a martini. He's been all but hallucinating about it. He'd flat damn get his clothes on and quit this place if they'd ever unplug this what's-it.

Who could he schmooze to bring him a cup of relief? Housekeeping can always use a few extra bucks. Where there's a will, there's a way. Men in prisons, staring at concrete long enough, become incredibly inventive—build weapons out of soap and cardboard, hatch ingenious escape plans.

He turns his pillow over to the other side; it is cool against his sweating scalp. He has to go to the bathroom, but he can't even make it to the john by himself. He has to summon a cherub-faced nurse. Why are they all so young?

He consults the clock. Five to five. If he were at work, he'd be packing it in for the day.

Adams-Wenborn. He's a reject, a public one. How is he going to drum up clients for his own agency?

He should have died. What is he going to do?

"Dad, hi. Are you feeling better?" Lee approaches his bed, her sweetness and beauty an instant balm.

"Fair. Where are the rest of the troops?"

"They stopped down in the cafeteria to get dinner. I brought the Valentine gift so you can give it to Mom tonight. It's in that bag."

"Thank you." Is Lee getting thinner, or just taller? Her figure is straight as a straw. "How come you're not eating with them?"

211

"I'm not hungry."

"They'll be along with my tray soon. I'll give you part of it. I don't have much appetite either."

She shrugs, and settles into an adjacent chair. "Do you want to watch TV?"

"No, let's talk."

This seems to make her uncomfortable. She crosses her arms.

"How was practice today?"

"I'm off the team."

"Since when?"

"This morning."

"Why?"

"I'm not good enough."

"Yes, you are!" He presses the knob that electronically raises the headrest so he can see her better. She does not look at him. "What happened?"

"I can't keep up."

Nonsense. There's got to be more than she's telling. "Your coach . . . he's sort of a hotshot, isn't he?"

"Sometimes."

"He make you unhappy?" As soon as he can get out of this bed, he's going to confront that Latin lover. "He do something to you?"

"No, Pop."

"Anybody who isn't nice to you is going to hear from *me.*"

"He's nice."

Can't dig it out of her. She's so darned shy. "I want you to feel free to talk to me. You can come to me anytime, with any problem, no matter how bad. Okay?"

"Okay."

"I really mean it now. We'll work it out."

She nods, teary.

"I want us to talk. That's what dads are for."

212

She plucks a tissue from the box and wipes her nose.

"Okay?"

"Okay."

Lee accepts the heart-shaped box of candy Jason has shoved toward her.

"I waited until I thought you were home from the hospital. Is this too late to come around?"

"No. We just got here. It's fine." She flicks on the track lighting in the living room.

"Happy Valentine's Day." He gazes at her with expectant pleasure, a shoe box tied with a red satin ribbon still tucked under one arm.

In movies and novels, this is what they do, boys—bring candy. Or flowers. But not to her! She couldn't be that lucky.

"Whitman's Sampler," he says.

"It's great. I love chocolate."

He grins at her sheepishly. "I thought you were going to say . . ."

"What?"

"You loved something else."

She laughs, embarrassed. "I didn't get you a present."

"Doesn't matter. How's your dad?"

"He's able to eat now. Soft diet."

"That's good."

"Here . . ." She gestures toward the couch, but he chooses the floor, squatting, and setting the shoe box in front of him.

"I felt rotten about Garcia when you told me on the phone." He takes her wrist, pulling her down beside him. "You've had dumb stuff lately."

She knows what is in the box; she can see the air holes now, hear the delicate whistling. She unties the bow and

213

lifts the lid, startling a quail, which cowers at the overhead motion.

"He'll keep you company. He understands about your dad . . . and . . ." Jason reaches into his shirt pocket. "I copied down something for you. It goes with the bird."

She unfolds a small piece of blue-lined paper and reads: *Hope is the thing with feathers that perches in the soul and sings the tune without the words and never stops at all.*

"Visiting hours are over, it is nine P.M., visiting hours are over." The nasal whine dies away; the corridor lights go dim. He opens the nightstand and inventories its shelves: two sizes of plastic basin, body lotion, assorted coins, magazines and newspapers, a dop kit. He fishes it out and peers into it. A razor, shaving cream, comb, mouthwash, Band-Aids.

Mouthwash. He reads the label. *Alcohol content 18%.*

Wait a minute. Crazy he's not. Basket cases drink shoe polish and vanilla extract, mouthwash—not him. That's insane. He's been lying here too long.

He flings the case back onto the shelf, smacks the door closed. He's not desperate, for Pete's sake. He's not going to drink crap.

He dozes. He can tell when it's past midnight because the faces that check on him have changed. Each time a flashlight looms toward him and a figure stirs the air around his bed, he forces a sleepy squint to see if it's someone with a bottle.

There is an angel above him; at least, it has the winged stoop and praying head of an angel. Its outline is white-white in the gray refracted dawn.

"I see I got here before breakfast," it says.

He focuses on it. It is wearing glasses.

214

"We'll take out your IV this morning and see if you can keep food down without help. I've done a lot of snooping and I'm not sure what ails you. The root cause. We're going to let that stomach rest for a while before we try to do a GI series. I think I'll send you home in a day or two and have you come back for that on an out-patient basis. Meanwhile . . ."

He raises himself to one elbow and blinks, recognizing Connally, the doctor.

"I'd like you to be straight with me, and I'll do the best I can. Is there any reason you know of why you'd get dog-sick like this?"

Connally's words and smile are mellow. The net of drowsiness is beginning to dissipate. He hears the scraping of a chair as the doctor draws one up next to him. "No."

"People put all kinds of things into their stomachs. You been eating hot peppers?"

They grin at each other.

"Could be your duodenum back for more. But that type of ulcer'll usually heal good as new. You see this gastritis in folks who've been on a toot. You been on a toot?" The smile again.

"I do my share, I guess."

"It'll chew you up. I'd be willing to guess you do more than your share. The tests I've done seem to point to that. Your body's giving out on you."

He's not tied to this doctor. Doctors can be dismissed. He'll get a new one.

"We gotta be careful with that stuff. You see, an alcoholic is never us. It's always somebody else. That's called *denial*. We just plain can't see the truth. Truth is, alcoholism's a terminal illness unless we can stay away from drinking, period. Now. I suspect you've got a problem here, and I'm giving you the same counseling I give my cancer patients. Treatment's the only answer. You play around with that and you're playing with your life."

"I don't have a problem."

"Yes, you do."

"Did my wife tell you that?"

"No." The doctor is looking at him as though he is already dead.

His gut flutters with imaginary maggots. If no one told him, how can Connally be so sure? Shit, maybe he *is* on his way out. Has he got holes in his stomach? What's happening to him?

"You could go right from here to a twenty-eight-day treatment facility. They're not asylums, you know. They're hospitals. Your insurance would probably cover it."

Would it? He's lost his Adams-Wenborn insurance. Katy's couldn't be a whole lot. And they'd still have to pay fifteen percent. They're in enough financial trouble.

"This is a disease. Follow? The root cause hasn't been figured out yet, but it could be related to metabolism. You find alcoholism running in some families with diabetes and low blood sugar and such. It's nothing to be embarrassed about."

He's constantly got the urge. He can't deny that to himself. But he can stop. Anytime. In fact, he *is* stopped. He doesn't need another four weeks in the hospital. My God.

Katy tamps the cards of the deck together and slips them into the box, swings the rolling table away from Mike's bed and winks at him. It hasn't been all bad, this hospitalization. In fact, it's been almost a honeymoon—other than the first two or three days. In this room, they have regained rapport; played double solitaire, read aloud to each other, held hands while enjoying television shows. No distractions, worry temporarily suspended. Best of all: sobriety, like a sudden thaw. The times she brings the children with her, he seems uneasy, but she's kept their visiting to a minimum. She still senses a caged energy emanating from him; his movements are often swift and impatient, though tempered by reason.

"Anything else you want before I go?"

"No."

"I'll be in Sunday morning, to take you home." She scans the sparse assortment of floral arrangements, hunting for a dead bloom to toss away. If only he'd gotten a few more dish gardens and notes. It's a lean collection, this—mostly from relatives. The lack of attention is bound to depress him. Not a single greeting from friends except Lyle and the Metsingers. Maybe she should have called around, let more people know.

She stoops and kisses him on the lips.

"Kate . . ." He hugs her around the neck suddenly, sadly. "I can't face them."

"Who?"

"The kids."

"Hey . . ."

"I've used up all my chances."

They never speak of this. She doesn't want to. "No, you haven't."

He lets her go, but she sits on the bed, burying her nose and mouth in his neck. He smells clean, like *that* Mike, the one she's missed so much. He rocks her soulfully back and forth.

"I don't want to lose them. Or you. I'm afraid of that. I'm going to keep a lid on the drinking. I see where I am."

The doctor must have talked with him. How was Connally able to effect this on a single try after all her years of maneuvering? The jolt of relief is coupled with familiar caution.

"I'm all right. I promise you."

He is. She discovers it in his eyes: a frankness she had

217

only barely remembered. He was not absent from his body, as she had feared; he was a prisoner in it, now set free.

He hates these conferences with his mother: hates, hates, *hates*. A new list of instructions, that's what it'll amount to. Won't do any good. He won't win. He has outgrown this house, wants to shed it as a snake sheds its skin. He lives for the day he will not have to sit in front of her, answering up.

"Dad's coming home tomorrow. I want to settle an issue before he gets here," she says, staring at Lee.

"What?"

"Where did the necklace go?"

They study her determined expression across the dining room table. Lee glances at him.

Resentment floods his belly. "I didn't steal it!"

"She didn't say you did, Rick."

"That's what she *thinks.*"

"No." She swallows. "I lost it."

"You did? Oh, Lee . . . why didn't you say so, honey?"

"I thought I could find it."

"You've caused a lot of damned trouble," he says to her.

"I'm sorry."

"Don't speak to your sister that way. Let's put it behind us now. We got it solved."

He is frying, down to his shoes. He avoids Lee's gaze.

"I'm counting on you both to make Dad's homecoming go well. He's not going to drink anymore. If we don't stir things up, there won't be a problem."

Bull. He goes to his room and lies on his bed, pretending it is in his own apartment. The house without his father in it has been deliciously open. Other boys' number-one fantasies are of naked women. His are of a space to call his own, a space to which only he has access. Naked women are definitely number two.

On Eva's sloop last Saturday, he found himself coveting the compact cabin with its pull-down table, postage-stamp stove and skinny beds. Cramped, but he'd take it.

He met a teenager once who lived in the back of an old mail truck. He had fixed it up like a one-room efficiency, wallpaper and all.

Anything. He'd gladly live in a car.

"I'm going to sign the discharge papers, but I have a lot of doubt," Connally says to her in the privacy of the stairwell. "Your husband thinks he can handle this himself. Do you?"

"Yes."

"I haven't broken your confidence, but I wish you'd go in there with me and talk him into treatment."

It's all been settled. Why does he persist?

"Will you do that, Mrs. Stockman? My opinion doesn't count like yours."

The thought of putting all the agony into motion again is impossible. "Let's give him a chance."

"I think you're making a mistake."

She can hear her father in these words. This doctor suffers from self-righteousness. Let him sign the papers and get out of their lives.

He follows his father into the house, carrying his suitcase.

"Well, now," his dad says, staring at the rearranged living room.

His mother and sister place the hospital flowers on shelves and tables while his father gapes at the office they have created for him: the desk and phone they moved in from the family room, the rack of professional books, the brag wall of awards and business photographs.

"We had stationery and calling cards printed for you," his mother ventures. "The typewriter will be delivered tomorrow."

"Who did this?"

"We all did." Her smile is apprehensive.

A complete hassle, the hours they spent tearing this room apart and putting it back together, spackling nail holes, stocking the desk. The books are alphabetized by author, but he won't notice that until later. They used a whole can of furniture polish.

His father fingers the silver letter opener decorously positioned on the blotter; his chin sinks to his chest. He spreads his arms toward them, his face too oblique to be read. The stance cannot be denied. His mother steps into the circle, pressing her cheek against his father's.

The hands remain in midair. His sister leaves her corner and locks an arm around his mother's waist.

He relinquishes the suitcase; its metal studs click against the stone tile of the foyer. No one is looking at him, their eyes are obscured in the awkward huddle. But his father's right hand remains outstretched. Toward him. Woodenly, he walks over and stands under it, feels it grip the nape of his neck, thrust him gently toward his sister and mother. Only by the shuddering of his father's shoulders does he realize he is crying.

26

He lies on the bed with his hands to his eyes. It is better when they are all out of the house; he does not have to pretend, finds himself moaning softly and biting his fingers in a rhythm for distraction. It is not the craving for a drink—he believes that quite honestly. It is a relentless depression in which he is exiled from the joy of life. Foods have no flavor, flowers no fragrance. He has no desires, for sex or money, for activity or ideas. His existence is flat, dry, all the enticements now curios. The clatter of the family when they are home frustrates him, their ambitious little tasks sapping his remaining energy. He becomes restless, retires to his room, the painless pain in him indescribable. When she notices, his wife slides her hand along his brow, but it is an intrusion. Touching makes it worse. He lies stricken much of the time they are away and uses all his strength to stay quiet while they are present. He had thought of severe depression in terms of gray, black and rain; it is not so. He sees the colors of the bedspread clearly, the splinters in the furniture; the room is yellow-bright and a breeze shifts the drapery to and fro against the sill. Things are as they were. He is different.

* * *

Mike comes to the dinner table with a glass of rosé, limits himself to one. She confronts him in the kitchen after the dishes are done and the children gone to their rooms. "I was surprised to see you with that wine."

"You can drop the bossy tone."

"I'm worried about your stomach."

"That soothed it a little bit."

"Mike!" It is unintentionally chiding.

He snaps his head away from her. "You're always on me. Like I'm a kid! I can have a glass of wine! There's no harm in that."

A glass of wine with a meal. Innocuous. Why does she constantly attack him? She must change if she wants him to change.

"Katy, I need for you to leave me alone. There's no trust. It drives me absolutely mad. Give me some credit, will you?"

"I—"

"Stop harping at me! If you'd cut it out, maybe I could get my breath. Maybe I could feel better." He glares out the window.

He's right. A grown man, after all. She's kept everyone away from him—even the children—so that he could rest and recover. Now she's messing it up. She won't make that mistake again.

Lee shifts her textbooks to her hip and examines the new electric typewriter. He must have had a great first week, organizing and planning. It gives her pleasure to behold her father's office; it is sophisticated, dramatic. The creamy amber wall they painted behind his desk makes the metal picture frames and buffed furniture stand out like gems.

She winds through the hall and family room. As she approaches the kitchen, the silence is broken by the unmistakable crunch-shush of a bottle cap being unscrewed.

222

Sloshing.

With disbelief, she brings him into sight: he finishes gulping and lowers the bottle, thumbing the cap into place, rotating it. *Whiskey.* He positions it label-out in the liquor cupboard.

"I'm home," she says.

The swivel of his head seems to be in slow motion; she is afraid of the eyes, but when they find her, they are kind. "You're early! No tennis practice?"

He doesn't remember. "I'm . . . off the team."

"What?"

"I'm off the team."

"Why?"

Fascinated, she inches toward him. "I can't keep up. I'm not good enough."

"Yes, you are!" He glances to the side as if listening to an unseen person. "Your coach, he's sort of a hotshot, isn't he?"

"No."

"He do something to you?"

"No."

"Anyone who isn't nice to you is going to hear from *me.*"

She sets her books lightly on the breakfast bar and sits at it, leaning forward, burying her face in her arms.

"Pumpkin," he whispers close to her ear, "tell me what's wrong."

She looks up into his innocent perplexity.

"It can't be so bad that you can't tell me. I care for you so much. You're my . . . baby." He rounds her chair to sit in the other one, knee to knee with her. "Right now, while there's no one else here, let's talk."

She watches his tongue and lips, which are sluggish and contend with each other in forming the words.

"I promise not to get upset."

Is this her real father? Through the dense scent of liquor and the fog of his concentration, she seems to recognize him. "Daddy . . ."

He nods at her.

"I am—sad."

He nods again.

"Because . . . you drink. I don't want you to drink any-more."

He doubles in the middle as though she has punched him. "It's *me?* That's why you're sad?"

"It is, Daddy. Please stop," she whispers. "I miss you."

His mouth droops in dismay.

Fear washes over her. "I don't mean to hurt your feel-ings."

"No. I'm glad you told me. You're honest."

"Lee Ann!"

She drops the fluttering quail into its pen and faces her mother.

"Did you talk to Dad this afternoon about his drink-ing?"

Instantly paralyzed, she cannot answer.

"Don't you ever, *ever* do that." Her mother's voice wavers with anger.

"He didn't mind."

"He *did* mind. He was furious with me. Wanted to know what kind of line I'd been feeding you about him."

"He said I could . . . talk to him. He asked me to."

"Don't you know better?"

=== 27 ===

Try as he might, Mike cannot visualize the homes of his childhood with people and furniture in them; every remembrance is of a moving day, the last hour, the house cavernously empty, echoing, the windows naked and leaking dusk. There would be one shrine of forgotten promise: a stained-glass window forming a trumpet-shaped lily, a fireplace ringed with blue-on-blue Holland tiles, a burnished window seat curving along the bay front of the living room. He would stand before that item, recalling the moving-in day excitement, the appropriating of the piece as his symbol of a new life, a talisman. In the abandonment of a home, the final desolate sweeping of bare floors with a worn broom, he would meditate before the shrine, remembering his eager anticipation. And his eventual disappointment.

How many houses had he lived in growing up? Ten? Fifteen? Odd that his perspective does not include the daily hubbub of life, just scattered cameos of his mother's dry-eyed sulking, his father's mayhem, his brother's militant pride. His mother would be injured to know that in spite of her constant baking, all he recollects in detail are minutes of forlorn leave-taking in a dozen neutral houses.

Today he has traveled among them, seeing them splinter by splinter in disturbing succession. He has dreamed fitfully, roaming the narrow backstairs, pushing, having fragments revealed to him: the oval lock-knob of a clothes chute, swans painted on a bathroom wall.

A harsh ringing begins. Perhaps an alarm clock left in one of the rooms? But which? Far above him is a white telephone, its cord extending toward him in perfect loops. This house has furniture and pictures, some of himself. The phone is too high to reach.

An urgency grips him. He rolls to a sitting position and scrambles to his hands and knees, crawling around the desk, where—hanging onto the chair seat—he pulls himself up to sit.

"Hello."

"May I speak with Michael Stockman, please?"

"This is . . . he."

"I'm Alex Villanueva, vice president in charge of marketing for the Reynolds Bank Group. You planned an ad campaign for a colleague of mine, Emerson Roper of Finance-Net."

"Yes."

"I contacted Adams-Wenborn and they told me you had started your own agency."

"That's right." He pinches his cheeks to shake the drowsiness, studies the red numerals on his calendar: MARCH 5.

"I'd like you to do a proposal for us. We're expanding into Canada, a venture of forty-five million dollars, and we need to launch with appropriate fanfare. Whoever we select as our agency, we'll contract with for two years. Would you like to build us a package?"

"Be glad to."

"Good, Mike. I got your address from Wenborn. I'll send you the particulars. You look them over, then we'll meet. We're working against time—who isn't? I'd say we'd need your material within three weeks."

"No problem."

"Thanks. Bye now."

"Good-bye." *Hot damn!* Where was the guy calling from, Canada? Sounded like he was in a barrel. Tinny, with a background of intermittent clicks.

Through the front sheers he sees Lee and her boyfriend stroll onto the lawn. She comes in timidly. "Hi."

"Hi." Should he tell her a forty-five-million-dollar deal just landed in his lap? "How was school?"

"Fine. I want to get the quail—to show Jason."

He decides to play his cards close to the chest. "Okay." As she heads back down the hallway, he walks outside.

Jason, waiting on the semi-circle of grass between the driveway and sidewalk, nods. "How are you, Mr. Stockman?"

Nature's glory races through him in a surge of ecstasy, the sky a Dutch-tile blue, cloudless, the mosaic of palms and blooms illuminated by sun filtering slowly through their honeycombed cells. He must confide his joy. "I want you to keep this a secret," he says to Jason, "but I'm about to ice a deal with a forty-five-million-dollar chain of banks. It'll bring a lot of revenue to my company over the next few years. I'm going to get rich, and I'm going to make a lot of people rich. What does your dad do?"

"He's a dentist."

"Then I guess he wouldn't be interested in working for me. But I'll be offering stock, and I'll let my closest friends buy in first. You ask your dad how he'd like an early retirement. This thing's going to take the roof right off."

Lee steps onto the porch carrying a box.

"Let's keep this between us until I get the contract hammered out," he whispers, squeezing Jason's shoulder.

He passes his daughter and pauses in the foyer. It's a

wonder Adams-Wenborn gave Villa . . . nova? . . . his number and address, considering the hard feelings. They could have gobbled this one up for themselves. No, the client was after *him,* specifically.

Doesn't mean Koppel couldn't jump in and undercut him if he got the notion. Stockman and Associates is bound to be stiff competition for A-W. Koppel will probably try to hold him down the way he nixed his job search. Best to be tight-lipped . . . perhaps get a mail slot put in the front door so no one can filch his letters and contracts.

Tinny. Could Koppel have a tap on his phone?

Of course! His son-in-law works for the phone company! The sneaky SOB.

Talking won't do any good in a situation like this. He may have to wave a gun under his nose.

Jason smirks at her, raising his eyebrows.

"What did he say?"

"We're all going to be filthy rich. He's in demand. Getting ready to close on a big one. Millions of dollars."

"Well . . ." He does nothing but sleep. As far as she knows, he goes out only to the liquor store.

"A bunch of bunk, isn't it?"

Maybe. She wishes it were true. There was a time she believed him, the captivating tales of imminent wealth and honor. The demise of such a prophecy was unheralded and unmarked except by a listless chain of days in which her parents no longer spoke of it. She would know then that it had failed—due to the negligence or hostility of an exterior figure or force—and that the facts would be told to her in hushed terms later.

Jason laughs heartily. "The way he says it! Like it's a CIA operation. 'Keep this secret.' " He imitates her father's earnest swagger. "He's so full of gas."

Stung, she gazes at the quail, which is thudding its

chickenlike wings against one end of the slanted box; she tips the container until it is level again.

"Hey, the fellow's getting fat. Do you have trouble keeping him in the pen now?"

"Yes, but I'm building the sides up."

This is the result of daring to share the truth: humorous stabs at her father in the belief that she disapproves of him. There is no way to describe the loving and the hating. She is forever alone.

"Buddy."

He looks up from the garage workbench where he is fixing his tape recorder. "Yeah?"

His father has an air of self-satisfaction; he strikes a pose with his forearm on the bench. "I want to tell you something privately."

"Um?"

"I had a call today from a banking group that I'll be taking on as a client. They contacted Adams-Wenborn to get my number—didn't even want to mess with the folks over there. Within three weeks, I'll sign on the dotted line and we'll be in clover! I'm going to try to get a penthouse office, one large enough to have a boardroom. We're talking a million-dollar client here—*many* millions of dollars. What do you think of that?"

He knows the prescribed answer but cannot work up the requisite enthusiasm. "Good."

"Good? I'd say it's great."

Whew. Nobody light a match. "That's what I meant."

"You'll have your pick of schools. Maybe you should apply to some others. Ivy League."

"I'm happy with UCLA."

"Listen . . ." He crooks his finger. "I wouldn't want your mother to get wind of this, but I'm such a thorn to

229

A-W at this point that I think they've got our phone tapped.''

"Oh?" He replaces the screwdriver in the tool kit.

"I need you to help me put a mail slot in the front door. Security reasons, comprendez?" He shoots him a confidential glance. "Mother doesn't have to know why. I don't want you to tell her anything about this. I know how to get Koppel off my back and he isn't going to like it."

He recognizes the prelude to pugnacious anger.

"If he's gonna horse with me, he's gonna get what he deserves. I'm not saying what I'll do, but I'll teach him to meddle with *me*. Huh?" He smiles wickedly.

His father is fond of this fantasy of power; Rick has grown up hearing brutish threats and plans, the retaliation for imagined slights. None came to pass. He has seen his father bolt for the telephone at the hint of a prowler in the yard.

"If he fools with me, I'll have to take drastic action."

Eva nets the triangles that are bobbing in the boiling oil of the wok and drains them on a paper towel.

"What's that?"

"Shrimp toast. An adventure in eating. Don't you own a wok?"

"No."

"We're having beef vegetable stir-fry. Your taste buds will cave in on themselves." She pads to the refrigerator and removes a series of plastic-wrapped bowls. "Chopped snow peas and mushrooms. The meat's in a marinade."

He loves the sight of her. The yellow jogging pants and mock college T-shirt that reads "Neurotic State," the punky short hair sticking straight up in the middle like a rooster's comb. She comes to him suddenly and puts her arms around his waist, kissing him under the chin.

"Ma!" Wesley shouts from his vantage point in the family room. "Eva's hugging Rick again!"

Mrs. Metsinger's voice, above the rattle of a newspaper, answers, "That's okay. You just mind your business. Take that laundry upstairs for me, please."

"Where are you?" Eva whispers. "Still at home?"

How could he recount his father's monologue? Besides, to bring his problems into this environment would be to lose it, to be shunned. Experience has made him wise. Friendships exposed to more than fleeting encounters with his family evaporate overnight. Thank God that when he's here, his dad isn't. He can leave it all behind.

Tired. Every part of her skull aches: the cheekbones, the eye sockets, the crown. Her scalp is so sensitive she can barely stand to touch it. She sits in the under-stage women's dressing room, waiting for the finale, staring at the ghost of herself in one of the bulb-wreathed mirrors. This is how she would age an actor: powder the hair to remove its sheen, glaze the skin with white panstick. Wrinkles are not as necessary as a general lack of vitality, an ectomy of the spirit.

Above her, the boards begin to rattle with the rhythmic jumping of the cast in the last dance number. Without the vigorous hoofing, she still would know blindfolded where she was. The oily scent of cold cream, the clay-flat pungence of greasepaint, the marriage of musty wood and concrete. Even the candy-striped sheet cloaking the doorway has a smell, of months-old perspiration tempered with dust.

Stampeding for curtain calls, the feet rearrange themselves over her head. And again.

"You decent?" Lyle.

"Yah."

He enters briskly and adds hangers to a rack. "Staying for the party?"

"Not this time."

"Bring Mike to midnight supper, why don't you? I'd like to meet him."

"He works hard. This would be a little late."

"Well, tell him he's invited. Say, when the girls take off the costumes, will you group them by acts? Goes faster that way."

"Sure."

The jeweled, regal women file in and peel false eyelashes and wigs, smear their faces with goop and tissue it off, pull bobby pins out of their piled-up hair, jamming it into a low bun or ragged ponytail, dismantling the facade piecemeal until their utter plainness enables them to exit unnoticed into the middle of the dispersing crowd. She lines up the costumes, goes on stage to reset the props for Tuesday's first act, drives automatically the twelve miles home in a misting rain. On her own street, she suddenly becomes conscious of the road and the steering wheel. *Did she stop for red lights?* Her living room window gleams against the night. She takes her time gathering purse and papers from the car's front seat, anxious.

He is at his desk, filling a page with decisive rows of pencil writing. The startled jolt of his chin in her direction tells her he has been drinking. All day?

"Our troubles are over," he says. "I got the account we've been waiting for! Reynolds Bank Group. They'll be sending a contract. I'm doing a proposal."

Pie in the sky. "Proposals come first, don't they? Then contracts?"

He glowers at her. "I'm the only damned agency they want! I thought you'd be surprised! I thought you'd be pleased!"

"I am."

"Well, give me some support!"

"I'm . . . glad. But . . ."

"For Chrisake, this is what we've been hoping for!"

Tonight she is exhausted enough to get mad at him. Tonight she could wring his neck. "March is the last mortgage payment we'll be able to meet. We'll have to move."

"You're not hearing me."

"I hear you."

"But you don't believe me."

This time might be it. He could be right. To undermine his confidence would be to ruin the chance. "I believe you."

"I'll ask for an advance on the contract. We'll have it by next month. We can send the April payment in late along with the penalty."

"Okay." If she doesn't lie down, she's going to be sick. She takes off her shoes and carries them to the bedroom closet, tosses them in. He follows her and paces with a quickened stride while she removes her earrings and wristwatch. "Give me a few ideas," he says. "I'll give you the profile and you brainstorm with me."

"I can't." Her chest is crumbling; she will hardly be able to change her clothes.

He examines her face, slow enlightenment flooding over his own. "You're tired," he says.

He knows when his wife wants to make love. He darkens the living room and visits the kitchen for a drop of blend. Returning, he discovers her in bed, a streak of gold from the bathroom lamp nudging the shadows. He fumbles until he finds her and, lying on his side, tries to scoop her into his arms. It is clumsy, him on top of the blanket, her under it. He seeks her mouth. She squirms out of reach. The idea of pursuit appeals to him; he tangles his fingers in her hair, gripping it, spurred in his desire by this primitive physical possessing.

"Stop," she says.

He digs at the covers. She begins to battle him, finally eluding his embrace by climbing out of bed.

"Don't!"

The command is spiteful. He could overpower her, but he is struck by this cry of a stranger. He has a sense of two people backing away from him in the filmy night but can detect the outline of only one. He stumbles from the bed, steadying himself against the brass valet. "Kate?"

She does not answer.

The mystery meshes like the slick bite of a sawtoothed trap. "You're having an affair," he says. "Isn't that it?"

The silence enrages him. "Is his name Lyle Taglia?"

She is leaving the room; he follows the sighing of her gown and springs at her, his fury uncorked, pouring from his brain. She leads him quickly away from the children; he can hear her unlock the glass door in the family room. He taps a switch and glare stings him.

She turns, her hand still on the latch. "You're crazy," she says. "Lyle Taglia is sixty years old and wears dentures. He goes home to his canary at night."

Juice is being pumped through him so fast he has to fight for breath. She is lying. He'll drag the bitch to the sink and wash her tongue with soap. He charges, shoving his arms under hers, lifting. She struggles. In the dining alcove, she kicks her feet, toppling two chairs; she grips the door frame so he can't pull her through it.

"Rick! *Rick!*"

"Shut *up!*"

She goes limp.

His son has got him under the chin, from behind. He releases Katy and, ducking, tries to tug the boy over his head. The child clings to his back like a monkey; he twirls around and around, hitting the walls of the kitchen, trying to bash him off.

"Daddy, ahhhhhhh!" Lee hunkers in a corner, making

herself into a tiny ball of pink flannel; from it rises the
most inhuman keening he has ever heard. He halts, nearly
toppling. Rick leaps from his back and grapples with him,
straight on. He is trying to extricate himself and go to his
daughter, but Rick does not seem to understand the retreat;
his son pushes his ribs with four sharp blows, propelling
him backward against the junction of the counters.

"That's enough!" Katy says.

Rick, cursing at him through clenched teeth, quits.

He kneels beside his daughter, stroking her hair. She
raises her wet face to him. "I *hate* you! What were you
doing to my mother?"

"You bastard!" Rick yells.

He looks at his wife and, seeing her unforgiving bitterness, runs from the room, falling onto the sofa, the world
detonating around him. His son has caught up.

"You shit!" he screams, standing over him.

"You treat me like hell!" Katy hollers, punching the
back of the couch.

"You act dumb!" Lee shouts. "You act like a dumb
damned *ass!*"

Her father begins to weep, in great jagged cracked sobs.
The pit of his loneliness rends her heart. She does not want
to live.

Her mother sleeps with her all night; they lock both doors
and huddle together in the bed, waking over and over in
search of morning.

The first instant of consciousness is always painful. Self-blame starts her heart, which had been languidly squeezing warmth through her; its tempo increases in milliseconds to a fine drumming. Before she can see or move, she is planning penance: *whatever she has done, she will make it right*. This does not calm her but at least gives her something to grip as she passes back into life.

A remarkable circumstance, her unchanged room; she expects it to be different because of the night's argument—perhaps not there at all, her bed open to the sky—but the ordered pieces of it emerge into her vision.

She sits up, dispelling a portion of the panic, knowing from the volume of bird song and angle of the sun that she is late for school. *Nine thirty.* Her mother was here, in bed with her, wasn't she? The house has the feel of Grandpa Stockman's funeral day: time suspended; hours like weeks, sorrow inching its way along an endless noiseless track.

Where is her mother? And Rick? Is she alone with her father? Uneasily, she creeps from room to room; the beds have been made, the clothing hung away. She finds her parents drinking coffee at his desk, pens and paper spread out before them in a clutter; her father is unshaven, but they are both dressed. Glimpsing her, they smile, adoring contented smiles, a bit on the side of preoccupation.

"I left a sweet roll and bacon in the oven for you," her mother says. "We decided to let you sleep as long as you needed to. I called the school and told them you'd miss part of the morning. The materials from the bank group arrived, Federal Express. I'll be helping Dad with his work until I go to the theater."

"Come here, sweetheart," her father says softly. She does, and he kisses her on the cheek. "Proud of you."

Beaming, her mother nods.

"Do you know what I resent?" Her history teacher starts down the aisle between two rows of desks, shaping his guide booklet into a long cylinder and tapping it repeatedly against the palm of his hand. "I *resent* reading everything I possibly can for this course . . . *And* writing it into a series of lectures, *which* I happen to think are pretty interesting . . . *And* standing here for forty-five minutes, talking, doing everything I can—short of swinging from the chandelier—to make it entertaining . . . Bringing in Civil War artifacts that I have found or purchased in six states . . . *And* that I happen to think are pretty interesting . . ." He pauses at her side. ". . . And having . . . a *student* daydream incessantly, as though I didn't exist at all . . . Or as though I am the biggest bore known to mankind. Tell me, Lee, wouldn't you resent that kind of treatment? Wouldn't you feel that it was *rude?*"

Without exception, the class is staring at her; many are openly amused.

"Wouldn't you?"

"Yes. I would."

Forgiveness is holy. People who aren't willing to start over are doomed to resentment and despair. If she didn't believe in this quality, her marriage would have been finished long ago. It is not her right to rub his nose in past deeds.

She leaves the desk and stretches. "I have to get ready for work. It's almost time to take off."

He regards her appreciatively. "Thanks."

Now that Mike is working at home, she may be able to guide him back into success. This proposal, as they have mapped it out, is irresistible. She knows how to create a dazzling package—and so does he. None of his competitors will be able to propose so much at such low cost; he has an impressive breadth of experience and no burden of overhead from office rental and salaries. His business could soon be so great that he will need her permanent help.

Still, she has observed his growing restlessness as the day progressed. Will he, in spite of last night's scene, drink while she's gone? Will he go back on the morning's promise: *I don't need treatment, I can cut back myself, hospitals are expensive, we don't want that, trust me, this is it.*

The sound of her car fades. He strides to the liquor cupboard, afraid that she has emptied it, gratified that it is as he left it. He cannot get through the rest of the afternoon without a boost. He locates a shot glass and sets it in front of him. He will measure his intake. She would like for him to have none at all, but it staves off the shakiness, the nausea. He isn't well yet, and a short snort gives him backbone. He'll keep a careful record. He slides open a box of matches; he will lay one out for each shot.

No, no, no. *Count?* One's his limit. He decisively closes the box.

"I'll get us a couple of Pepsis."
"Let me come in with you."
"Wait, okay?"

"I'm not afraid of him, Lee Ann. I'm used to him."
Jason, letting go of her hand, presses the front door latch.

Her father is sleeping spread-eagled on the living room
carpet, clad only in his underwear. She takes it in at once:
the bare bony legs, underpants gaping away from a thigh
to reveal part of a testicle, undershirt sweat-stained in a V,
whisker stubble, tousled hair.

A perceptible attitude change ripples over Jason. He
makes no move toward the kitchen or back outside, merely
stares in disgust. Mortified, she snatches an afghan from
the back of the rocking chair and, unfolding it, covers her
father.

"I'm not speaking to him. I've had it." Her mother
smacks the whole wheat slices into even rows, picks up
the knife and begins to slather peanut butter on them. "Get
out the grape jam, will you?"

"Right there."

"Don't you dare let on you know. He'll be at my throat
again. Just treat him normally." She unscrews the lid and
dollops jelly onto the peanut butter with swift little scoops
of the spoon and an angry flinging motion; she slaps the
tops onto the sandwiches and rips squares of foil from the
box.

"I'll pack the lunches. Let *me.*"

Her mother stops working, sucking in her breath and
holding it. "I just don't know what else to do. I've tried
so hard . . . Lee . . . what can I do?"

"Mommy isn't talking to me."

Has he been lying on his bed since this morning? His
clothes are heavily wrinkled.

"She's mad because I don't have any clients, I guess.
But this is going to take time. You can't build a business
overnight."

He smells of fresh whiskey and, beneath it, the other pervasive odor he carries with him whether he's bathed or not: garbage-can fruit in hot weather.

"She's not talking to me. I don't know what she wants. Come and sit with me, honey. Nobody's been with me all day."

She hesitates.

"Please."

She bends over him; he looks worse than anyone she's ever seen: bruise-yellow, shriveled.

Tears flow down his temples, into his hair. "I feel so bad inside, so weak. Hold my hand. Please. *Please.*"

Her quarter comes back twice. She opens the door of the stuffy phone booth; candy wrappers and grit from the road blow in. The whir of rush-hour traffic, the clanking grind of trucks, reflected heat from the metal and glass of a thousand cars assault her. Closing herself in once more, she puts the coin in the slot and dials the number she has jotted on a piece of notebook paper. Cotton blocks her nose and throat; she cracks the door and sticks her foot between it and the frame.

"Doctors Madigan, Connally and Perron."

"May I please speak to Doctor Connally?"

"Doctor Connally is with a patient. May I have him call you back?"

"How long would that take?"

"I really don't know."

"Thirty minutes?"

"I can't say."

"I'm calling from a phone booth. But I'll wait. Could you make sure he knows it's important?"

"Your number, please."

"Four-eight-two, oh-seven-three-two."

"And your name?"

240

"Lee Stockman."

She replaces the receiver and leans against the outside of the booth, watching the traffic signal's lazy winking. She counts twenty-seven cycles. On the twenty-eighth green, the phone rings.

"This is Connally."

"Do you remember me?"

"Yes, indeed."

"I want you to know that . . ." *Go ahead.* ". . . my father's drinking again. Can you help him?"

"I haven't seen your dad since I released him from the hospital. How is his health?"

"Not very good."

"I'm sorry. There were some additional tests I wanted to do. But I was under the impression your parents had selected another physician."

"They did?" She is suddenly becoming faint. She props the door again, letting in a slash of wind. "Don't tell them I called you."

"No, ma'am." The voice is kind. "But I can't do a thing for him unless he comes to see me."

"I'd be glad to chat with your husband."

"Reverend Gillogly, he won't. He gets mad when I suggest counseling. I can't force him." She covers the phone's mouthpiece and turns to Lyle, who is at the other end of the theater lobby, beckoning to her. "I'll be there in a minute." Never any privacy—damn it—at home or at work.

"How did you say you got my name?"

"A friend of mine goes to your church." *Former friend. Tina would be amazed if she knew.*

"Perhaps your friend could talk him into it."

"No." She checks on Lyle; he has gone.

"There's always Al-Anon. For you."

241

Airing the dirty linen in public. "I know how they operate, and it wouldn't fit with what I believe."

"Well, I'd be pleased to try, but I'm not a psychologist. I can refer you to one."

"But what good would it do for me to go, when he won't? *He's* the one with the problem, not me."

"In situations like these, the family is often contributing—unwittingly, of course."

Rick. "I see."

"It's quite complex."

"Let me ask you this, suppose I went to a psychologist and spent all that money and—"

"Be sure to take the children."

"Oh, I couldn't! He would be furious if he found out. It would be terrible." This man couldn't possibly understand or he wouldn't suggest such a thing. "What I want to know is . . . suppose he wouldn't be helped, after all that. If he refused. What would I do?"

"There's a process called 'intervention' in which a counselor helps to gather a team of relatives and friends to confront him and tell him exactly how his drinking has affected them. It's an excellent way to get an alcoholic into treatment."

"He'd kill me!"

"Well . . . the way I see it, you have three choices: you live with it the way it is—which I don't recommend because it's harmful to the whole family, you get a professional on your side and take some kind of action, or you leave. This isn't a do-it-yourself project. You're bashing your head against the wall."

"All right."

"Are you sure you wouldn't like to give me your name and have me contact you now and then?"

"No. Thank you."

"I'll pray for you."

* * *

"We're going to leave him. That's why I wanted you to come shopping with me—so he wouldn't hear us. If he has any warning, there'll be hell to pay."

Stricken, she does not respond. She and her mother are approaching the cosmetics counter; a blond model in an off-the-shoulder gown and swept-to-one-side hairdo saunters toward them, carrying a wicker basket. "Would you care to try Enigma?" She aims a perfume atomizer at them. Her mother consents.

The floating sweetness spreads a tart taste across Lee's tongue. "We'll just . . . run away?"

"He'd make a lot of trouble for us, honey. Don't you see?"

Her father: arriving home or waking up to eerie emptiness. "Where would we go?"

"Out of town, I guess. We'll have to hide from him." Her mother looks at her with injured resignation.

"Does Rick know?"

"He doesn't care what's happening at home since he got a girlfriend. We'll tell him when it's time. Keep it to yourself."

Her father will not eat. He will die. "Who will take care of him?"

Her mother glances sharply at her. "He can figure that out."

"Why doesn't he go back to Doctor Connally?"

"He won't. He refuses to do anything." She hooks an arm around Lee's neck and hugs her in consolation. "We'll get through this."

Mr. Gates, in the midst of fifteen boisterous cardplayers, waves at Lee; she waves back.

"Let's raid the refrigerator. Saturday bridge club is always good for shrimp dip and assorted nuts." Jason does a double take at his own statement and laughs. "Especially assorted nuts."

She smiles at him.

"You get to know which groups are good for what kind of eats. Poker night is Dagwood sandwiches. Bible study is great for cake. But the best . . ." He brings down two plates and shakes potato chips onto them from a bag. ". . . is gourmet group. That's twice a year—because they hop around to everyone else's house, too. That's good for chilled cucumber soup, chicken Kiev, baklava, chocolate mousse—left over, of course. Us servants have to wait until the guests have eaten."

"Your parents do all that?"

"Sure." He investigates the refrigerator shelves, retrieves a bowl of dip and hands her a plate. *"Gandhi*'s on HBO, but it goes 'til eleven fifteen. Want to watch?"

"I'd like to see it."

They head for the sun porch.

"Here's a step. Be careful." He thumps his plate onto the coffee table in the darkened room and twists the TV knob. Fuzzy pictures appear and instantly resolve, casting rays into a cloud around the screen.

They accidentally sit too close to each other, she on the side of his leg. As she inches away, he unexpectedly presses his lips to hers. The kiss is minty and tentative—her first. She clings to him in gratitude and stark loneliness. His body is responsive; he cradles her until she pulls away. Parting, they bump noses. He laughs, unperturbed, running his fingertips lightly across her cheek.

She wore a garland of coral rosebuds and baby's breath in her hair, coral lipstick, an ivory bridal gown, coral nail polish, ivory satin shoes. She carried a spray of coral roses: an armful, twenty-three to be exact, one for each year of her age. The five bridesmaids, in pale coral gowns and coral shoes, were crowned with ivory rosebud garlands. Their bouquets were ivory, their lipstick and nail polish coral. Ivory roses and coral ribbons adorned the ends of the pews. A flower girl spread coral petals in her path, a ring bearer held an ivory satin pillow.

The newspaper write-up was not adequate to describe the wedding's elegance; in its society-page description, the colors seemed gaudy and monotonous after the second paragraph but the event definitely was not. It was the culmination of a lifelong dream, executed in such high style that many who were in attendance still mentioned it to her when she went home. Every item was of her choosing, from the mothers' dresses to the bridesmaids' stockings. Hues were precisely matched, no shade too garish, no corsage or boutonniere too large, no gait too casual, no hymn too usual. She walked down the aisle to "Morning Has Broken" rather than "Here Comes the Bride." She chose a gothic private chapel rather than her father's church because of its interior splendor: thirty-three-foot vertical Tiffany windows depicting the life of Christ, a series of awesome, peaked stone arches overhead, a pipe organ imported from France.

Her parents thought it unseemly—such a large wedding for a divorced man—but she shrugged off their comments. To her, wedding day perfection would herald a perfect marriage. She had been superstitious, relentless, in her pursuit of the details. She thought of the wedding as the stunning and satisfying finale of a movie about her early life: an odd, ignored girl, at last rightfully claimed by Prince Charming in front of envious witnesses. All future years were assigned to the "happily ever after" category. She had spent her entire savings account on the "joining of Katherine Lee Vogel to Mr. Michael Richard Stockman." Love seemed sufficient for any eventuality.

What did she know.

This evening has been spent appeasing him, helping him write a preliminary outline letter to the Reynolds Bank Group, listening to periodic rages about Rick's increased absences. He roams in front of the living room window now, waiting for Lee, his jaw growing slack with moody impatience.

She has given up her promise not to talk to him; too much is at stake here. Landing this account would sustain his finances if she left him.

She's been reconsidering that action, though. If she moved out, she would have no right to proceeds from their mutual property. A judge could term her act "abandonment" and strip her of means. She has invested eighteen hard years in him. What they own together is all she's got.

"Where *is* Lee?" he fumes. "I want her to type this. There's a midnight mail pick-up at the post office. Reynolds could get it Monday morning."

"She'll be here in a minute." She, too, longs for the comfort of her daughter's presence. It always calms him.

This is intolerable. His daughter is flouting the rules. She understands very well that she's supposed to be home by eleven thirty; the clock is climbing toward twenty to twelve. He can't make the midnight mail now, can he? It is imperative that Reynolds receive his outline promptly. Imperative. Imperative.

Imperative.

In his legs are long rivers of electrical current that keep him from sitting down. He's been trying to walk it off, around the couch, his knees and hips centers of energy that must be spent. The drive to motion is a maddening itch; his brain pulses, propelled by a single vision: the flawless, even-margined Reynolds letter lying at the bottom of the mailbox on the stroke of midnight. To rid himself of the spur, to rest, he must accomplish his goal.

His legs are hurrying on their own now, dragging the rest of his body with them.

Her father will be slumbering on the couch, kicking fitfully in his dreams, her mother dozing propped up in bed, a magazine spread across her breasts. There is still a moment to linger, her ear to Jason's heart, feeling the wind whip her hair and pleasured by the silver undersides of leaves flashing in darkened yards. The smell of impending rain seems to rise out of the concrete as they stroll the last half block toward her house. Her father is waiting on the shadowy stoop, his arms folded in that queer fussy expression of annoyance she has known since childhood, shoulders raised in a prolonged shrug, fingers pinching his biceps. Jason's back straightens; his pressure on her hand intensifies.

She is afraid.

As they approach her dad, he uncrosses his arms and reaches for her. "I was very worried about you." He seizes her at the elbow and snatches her away from Jason.

"But you knew where we were."

His eyes widen in rage. "Get in the house!"

"It was my fault," Jason says. His stance is humble but direct. He looks at her father squarely; his strength strengthens her, his devotion a refuge.

Her father turns his head until a single eye is fixed on Jason.

Precognition darts through her. Before she can speak, her father has drawn his fist back. Reflexively, Jason jumps sideways, his demeanor transformed from wariness to alarm.

Her father takes two quick menacing steps off the stoop; Jason stumbles at an angle, beginning to run.

His figure blends into the night. As he races through the

street's tunnel of trees, all she can see of him are the diminishing white soles of his shoes.

The insane streak of fury in her would welcome the impact of his fist upon her lips and teeth. She wants to be destroyed or to destroy, the struggle made physical, decided forever.

He pushes her inside. In the dim foyer, the outline of her mother shimmers against a blazing background of living room lamps. *Was she watching?* Reassurance seeps through Lee, but she finds her own agitation mirrored in her mother's shallow breathing and silence. They are like prisoners communicating wordlessly under his suspicious gaze, their pact absolute. Her mother's strange placating of him and cautious siding with him suddenly make sense. They are fashioned from her fear.

"Dad needs you to type a short letter," her mother says.

"Now?"

"Yes. You can do it faster and neater than we can."

"I want to get it in the midnight mail." Her father anxiously rolls paper into the typewriter. "We've got fourteen minutes."

Her mother folds her hands in supplication.

Trembling, she goes to the typewriter and sits before it, anchored by the secret knowledge of their leaving.

It is her mother who rushes to the car with the letter. Her father, exhausted, sleeps.

══ 29 ══

She is in the hall waiting for him when Jason emerges from his last-period classroom, flanked by five or six boys. He gives her a blank gaze and focuses his attention on Dave Koenig, who is winding into a joke. The group churns toward the staircase.

This really worries her, Lee's decline—eight days now. All of it over a little boy.

She crouches next to the bed. "Sweetheart?"

"What?" A whisper in darkness.

"Won't you get up and have some dinner?"

"I'm not hungry."

"But you have to eat."

A convulsive shuddering; her daughter is weeping again. "Is this still because of . . . Jason?"

"Yes."

"Have you talked to him?"

"He ignores me."

She'd love to shake him. Kids can be so cruel. "You deserve someone better," she says gently.

Was it something her husband did outside, the night Lee came home late? She didn't see what went on. She should have stayed right next to Mike—but she had been in her robe.

Should she ask? Oh, God, she doesn't want to know. He probably created a rift. If so, how could she possibly mend it? She wouldn't even try at this point—he's doing so much better since he's been on the Reynolds proposal. He's finally on his way up.

White smoke rises from the chimney and fades against a rare white California sky. Lee stands across the street from Jason's house, envying its precise beauty, the glossy Wedgwood colors, the topiary trim of the trees. A crayoned cluster of paper shamrocks left over from St. Patrick's Day decorates the front window.

Her exile has rendered the scene flat, with no more possibility than the photograph on a greeting card. Nostalgia and jealousy grip her. *People are happy here.* In spite of its interior chaos, the house is tightly prideful, secure. Under an intentional neglect rests the deliberate knit of contentment.

She crosses the road and passes into the yard. Should she ring the bell? No one uses the front door; it is always barricaded from inside by a card table with a thousand-piece puzzle on it or by a bike or stacks of magazines. She presses the button; grave metal tones seep back to her. Behind the door, items are being shifted. Mrs. Gates smiles into the daylight.

"Hello . . . Lee. What can I do for you?"

"I'd like to speak with Jason."

"I'll see."

She understands, from not being invited in, that he has told his mother of their parting.

After a moment, he appears, his pose defiant. She wants to fall on her knees, to beg. Instead, she says the two short sentences she has rehearsed. "I apologize for my father. I'm sorry."

His posture remains unchanged. "Why doesn't *he* apologize?"

Has she ever seen him apologize? Her father simply begins again. "He . . . doesn't know he did anything."

"Well, he should, shouldn't he?"

This is like asking why grass isn't purple. It isn't. It never will be.

Jason shoves his hands into the pockets of his jeans. "Shouldn't he?"

"I guess."

"Then why don't you tell him to come over and apologize to me?"

"I can't." Tears squeeze off her words.

"Why not?"

She shakes her head.

"I think he's crazy," Jason says seriously, shivering in the wind, elbows tight against his ribs. He steps farther inside. "I think you're all crazy."

"Why?"

He grasps the doorknob, and she realizes she is about to be shut out.

"Wait! *Why?*"

He swings the door toward her. "For putting up with it."

"You know what you could do?" her mother asks, stopping to sit next to her on the couch and stroke her hair. "Have a party. I'll help you plan it. Would you like that? You could invite friends from school."

"No."

"Maybe . . . we could all take a vacation—a weekender, to the desert or north along the coast. There's much of

California we haven't seen. That would be good for Dad, too, getting out of here for a while. Would you like that?"
"No."

When they leave him. She and her mother and brother will drive east without a decided destination, ordering lunch in a mountain town café with plank floors and red gingham tablecloths. They will sit eating kraut dogs and potato chips from plastic baskets lined with waxed paper, relax in a sunny cubicle next to the sidewalk of Main Street, sizing up the populace by their plaid flannel shirts, their beards and cowboy hats, the handmade sweaters and primly stockinged legs of the older women, the satisfied, casual greetings, the low prices posted neatly on panes in shop doors, the shining green symmetry of plants in the open-air nursery opposite the restaurant.

They will linger, paying the check at an antique cash register, watching fat pies slipped from the kitchen onto a gold-speckled Formica ledge: banana cream, apple crumb. In the time-weathered entry, they will discover a bulletin board they had overlooked and, among curling pages and yellowed business cards, the crisp new ad for a house.

Their house. Fifty years old and whitewashed gray, nestled into a piney curve that school buses take with a whistle of brakes and a thunking of gears; a rambling bargain home undesired by others because of a rocky backyard gully and sheer stripped slope on the other side.

They will raise goats for the fun of it, buy very little furniture for the mammoth square rooms, preferring to leave wide, fire-lit spaces in which packs of friends can dance and sit cross-legged in circles. It will have a European style: sparse and earthy, wrought from trees and stone, made cozy by constant large gatherings and heavy baking and a few simple decorations like calico herb bags

strung in rows, a hearth broom bound with dried flowers,
a single round piece of colored glass suspended in a win-
dow.

Couples get back together at dances. It happened to Amy
and David. It happened to Tracy and Steve. It can happen
to her.

She leans across the basin in the school lavatory and
looks at herself critically. She spent four hours getting
ready and has been waiting an hour and a half for Jason
to arrive. She has let Aaron Lowe dance with her over
and over again, hoping to appear popular and confident
when Jason enters the gym. Her arm is tired from Aaron's pumping her around the room. Pumping, that's what
it was. As though he expected water to gush out of her
ear.

Will Jason show up? She applies a fresh coat of lipstick
and purses her lips. The elastic line of her bra is damp
beneath her breasts; her hair has wilted on one side from
Aaron's breathing.

She sidles into the gym, managing to avoid Aaron, who
is scarfing cookies at the refreshment table. A cloud of
humidity envelops her, the sickly warmth of several
hundred bodies in strenuous exercise. As she glides into
the safety of a sideline throng, she spies Jason at an entrance with Alison McKenna, his hand possessively on the
back of her neck, under her black hair. They pause to talk
with each other, Alison saying something first; she is an
awkward contact-lens-wearer and her eyes are as fixed and
unblinking as a doll's when she stares up at Jason. A grin
eases across his expression; he touches his nose to hers
affectionately.

Dizzy with humiliation, Lee shoulders through the
crowd, away from him. He mustn't see her. If he does,
she will have to stay, letting Aaron push her around the

floor with the bone of his cheek hard against her forehead, steering it. She can predict the evening: her theatrics in vain, Alison and Jason gliding comfortably past her countless times, her own practiced smile enticing no one but Aaron.

She is nearly running now, startling people in her path; they draw their cups of red punch toward their chests and give her arrogant, chin-in frowns. And then she is outside with the music fading behind her as she descends the maze of steps and passages into the parking lot. She turns back and studies her path in the dim chill. If this were a movie, he would find her, he would have followed her. They would not speak, merely embrace.

The stars seem brightest along the ridge behind the school. She concentrates on them, listening for his approach.

He does not come.

"Daddy?"

Is she inside the telephone? It's that little baby voice that used to cry at him from the dark. *I had a bad dream.*

"Dad?"

The bedroom takes shape. "Yuh."

"I don't want to stay here."

"Where?"

"At the dance. I don't want to wait for Becky's mother. Can I walk?"

It must be nighttime. Why else would she ask permission? "Hold on." He pulls himself up, away from the pillow, his brains sliding down a whirlpool in his throat. In the far corner, a lamp is burning: Victorian, painted with swirls of roses, fluted and globed, the one that reminds him of the body of a lady in a bustled dress.

His brains come back up. He snatches the receiver from the mattress. "I'll get you. At the school?"

"Yes. Out front."

He knows that quiet fragmenting of her words. "Are you ill?"

"No." She begins to sob. "Daddy . . . I just want to come home."

"Okay. Of course, you can. I'll be right there, sugar."

"Bye."

He cannot decide what to do. He'll need a coat. Where are his keys? She's at the junior high school. That's on . . . Foothill? Different from Rick's school. Rick is older.

Regardless of how cold it is or how much she has to go to the bathroom, she'd better stay here on the curb. The minute she reenters the building, her father will arrive and become confused or irate because of her absence; he will imagine her kidnapping and mutilation, will be breathless and out of sorts when she climbs into the car.

Twenty-five minutes. Should she call again? Is he sleeping? *Don't go inside.* Numbly, she continues to screen the shapes of cars traveling toward her on the boulevard. How many hours of her life have been left on school lawns, under department store clocks and outside doctors' offices? Still she believes each time that he will arrive promptly. Foolish. She should understand by now: the price of a ride is a wait.

Oh, for evermore! This can't be right either! So damned weird, as if someone's taken entire streets away and filled the spaces in with houses. His night vision's never been good and seems worse without a moon. But this stretch is familiar—he bought Lee's birthday necklace here, in one of these fancy shops. He's too far west. Dang it.

No reason to panic. He knows a shortcut, at the next avenue.

Where the roads converge, an island of brilliance at the curb splashes light in his eyes. Police car.

He sure as hell doesn't need any more points against his license. He consults his speedometer. *Thirty.* No one could argue with that.

The officer, standing at the side of his vehicle, gestures at Mike; patches on his cap and uniform pop brightly like flashbulbs.

He cruises past, haunted by the face: stern. Could he have meant . . . him? He consults the rearview mirror: the policeman is getting into his car. A brief siren splits the air. He'd better stop just in case. The steering wheel seems stiff; a lot of curb goes by before he can connect with it. The flashing lights are . . . attached to his bumper?

"If you weren't sick, why couldn't you have waited for Becky's parents?"

She gazes down at her mother who is stretched out on a lawn chair by the pool; the eyes are closed, the brown-tinged skin under them stressed with vertical indentations. "I'm sorry."

"I thought we had agreed! I never just go to work, do you know that? I plan everything for you and Rick and Dad first. But I need you to help me, not foul me up."

She is silent; Katy, shading her eyes, looks at her with remorse. "Oh, honey. It's not your fault. I remember how it used to feel to be in love and have nothing come of it. It hurts."

She kneels next to her mother, who caresses her arm and whispers, "I guess I'm rattled. Royally. I don't know what's next. I'm so tired. He won't cooperate in any way. When I try to talk to him about it, he gets . . . violent.''

"When are we going to leave?" It is scarcely audible.

Her mother looks at her incredulously. "We can't. The man has no job. And now he's got no driver's license. How would he get along?"

=== 30 ===

"Poetic justice, that's what I call it."

"Rick!"

He fingers the smooth plastic surface of his driver's license, still hot from the laminating machine, and smiles at Eva. "Tell me it isn't."

"You've got to feel sorry for him."

"Boo-hoo." They reach the car; he swings the door open for her. "I'll drive."

"You're on."

He playfully pets the steering wheel of the Metsingers' BMW and jams the key into the ignition, remembering his mother's solicitous approach.

You have three hundred dollars for auto insurance, is that right?

Yes.

Where did you get it?

Borrowed it.

From whom?

From . . . Eva.

We need to use it. We need for you to get your driver's license. Tell her you'll pay her as soon as you can.

"Pride goeth before a fall," Eva says.

"It sure does." He has them right where he wants them. He inches the car out into traffic.

She pinches his earlobe. "Big man, huh?"

"I'll be breaking hearts all over L.A. And I'll start with yours."

"Oooh!" She laughs delightedly. "Let's see those muscles."

He puffs out his chest like a weightlifter, which he knows is ludicrous because he seldom lifts anything heavier than textbooks.

"Good. Now arrange the rest, lady-killer. Knock off that wimpy grin. Sensuality, that's what we want to see. And a whole lot of self-centered aloofness."

He contorts his face into an exaggerated sneer.

She squeals. "Bulging beefcake!"

They are creeping along in a bumper-to-bumper line of cars. "You think I can't attract other women? Here comes one now. Check this out." He has spotted a lone female drifting toward them in a Monte Carlo. As she begins to pull alongside, he fixes her directly with a macho stare, pushing his chest toward his chin, raising his eyebrows at her suggestively.

The woman does a double take. She is gray-haired and full-cheeked; her corkscrew curls flounce gently as she— her window now even with his—tries to understand his meaning. The curls hit the headrest with force, the hood on the Monte Carlo flies up suddenly and he realizes she has struck the car in front of her.

"My God!" he gasps as the BMW slips past her. "Oh, my G—" He is in the left lane and would have to cross two lanes of traffic on his right in order to park and go to her; at his left, three oncoming lanes of cars, densely packed together, dissuade him from turning around. He is stuck, being nudged homeward. It will be miles before he could take any action.

Forget it.

He looks quickly at Eva. Her lower lip trembles; she begins to shriek with laughter.

He tosses her a haughty over-the-shoulder glance. "I told you what I do to women."

Ready for the Metsingers' party, Rick considers leaving his room through the glass door so he won't have to walk past his father. Is he sacked out on the couch? His dad can get him started on nine things when he's ready to go out and insist he accomplish every one of them before he can leave.

What the hell. He's probably dead to the world. All his father does is sleep since he lost his license. Makes it a lot easier to come and go, a lot easier to be around home. His dad's oblivious most of the time, snoring through meals and TV programs. The times he does sit up in their midst, it's like someone's thrown a grenade into the room: they clear out. No one wants to hassle with him.

He locks the sliding glass and walks through the hall to the family room. His father is sitting, dazed, on the sofa.

"Will you take me to the store?" he says.

"I can't do it right now, Pop."

"You can't?"

Wants to get booze. What else? He can put his thumb down on his dad's drinking, stop the son of a bitch.

"Please, buddy." The arms are sticks, holding him up on the edge of the sofa. "It won't take very long."

"Tomorrow."

His father hangs his head docilely. The pose is wrenching. Why did he think he wanted the upper hand? His father is nothing, nothing at all, and the man knows it.

There's no satisfaction in this.

How could one family have so darned many friends? The Metsingers' party is a bash, a continuing comic strip

of people trying to tap a keg, eating asparagus with their
fingers, making the dog beg for Fritos, demonstrating yoga
positions, setting up a telescope on the balcony to view the
rings of Saturn. He's the uninitiated, backed into a corner
and groping for conversation starters.

"I'm Don Irons." A young man next to him pokes out
his hand, which he shakes.

"Rick Stockman."

"Glad to know you."

"Same." What now?

Don seems to be assessing the shape of his skull, his
hairline. "Say, there was a Stockman who worked with me
last summer." It is said with reservation bordering on distaste. "Michael. He any relation to you?"

"No."

"That's good. He was a real so-and-so. Famous in the
ranks."

"Where was that?"

"An ad agency. Adams-Wenborn. Ever hear of it?"

"No."

"I was their mail boy for the summer. I'm at USC.
Business Administration. What are you in?"

"High school."

"Umm." He dips a stalk of celery into the shrimp paste
and crunches it.

"What . . . do you mean, famous in the ranks?"

"A hot dog."

"Like what? What did he do?"

Don finishes the celery and sucks a finger, shrugging.
"Just had a reputation for raising hell with people. They
finally booted him out. Everybody thought he had a
screw loose." He tenses. "This *is* a relative of yours,
isn't it?"

He nods.

"Not your *father?*"

"My father's cousin."

"Hey, I shouldn't have said anything."

"That's okay. I don't get along with him either."

He locates Eva in the game room and pulls her away from the crowd, hunting for a private alcove.

"Where are we going? Rick?"

No one in sight. He guides her into the bathroom, shutting the door; it's black as the inside of a cow around them.

She giggles, but hushes when he embraces her, sensing the seriousness of his mood.

"I believe you—what you said about my dad insulting you at the brunch. I've never told you that. I believe you."

"I've already forgotten about it. You don't have to apologize for him."

"I'm not. I'm apologizing for me."

"You don't have to do that either."

"Yes I do."

This is the real world, sitting on the back steps of Eva's house with her, in hooded sweatshirts, as the moon climbs through tree branches. At last, he understands. Pleasure is not rare in the real world but is its heartbeat.

He deserves the permanent peace that others have and, listening to the soft strumming strength of his own pulse, knows he is capable of creating it for himself, in a separate place; knows that tranquillity is an individual's choice and that he cannot carry it home like a lantern. Knows he must leave his family behind.

The act of pushing his key into the lock of his front door takes all his courage. It shouldn't. He shouldn't have to be afraid to come home. The lulls here are as threatening as the storms; he stays clenched.

When he hears the bolt snap back, his plan steels him: it is turning April and he will go in June.

His parents are in the family room, sharing tea. His mother smiles at him. "How was the party?"

Guilt stirs. "Nice."

"That's good. Want some tea?"

His father regards him with a certain gentleness. "C'mon and sit with us."

"Did you remember that tomorrow is Dad's interview with the Reynolds Group?" his mother says cheerily. "They liked his proposal."

It is hope that he sees rising in his father; she has a way of reviving him, coaching his anticipation.

"On a Saturday?"

"The big cheese, Alex Villanueva, travels to Canada a lot and gets back Friday nights. We have a breakfast meeting," his dad answers.

"Well, good luck." He makes it as sincere as he can. Not to encourage his father would be to change the direction of the wind instantly. He has to keep him buoyed. "Did you need me to drive you there?"

His parents look at him with gratitude.

"Thank you, but I'll do it," his mother responds.

"You could take me on a dry run."

He scrutinizes his father. "When?"

"Tonight."

"It's one o'clock."

"I want to know how long it takes to get to the restaurant. So I won't be late."

"Where is it?"

"Beverly Hills."

"That's an hour and a half round trip." He appeals to his mother. "Why don't you go extra early in the morning?"

She stares back at him. "We could."

263

"I'd like to have a rehearsal."

Should he do it and avoid a scene? *Enough.* "No, Pop."

A whip-quick anger reddens his father's eyes.

"Maybe . . ." his mother starts.

"No!" he says to her. "Good night." He goes to his room, sensing that she is in his wake.

She closes herself in with him. "Why can't you do this for Dad?"

"Because it isn't logical. I'm not going to waste my time on any more stuff that isn't logical."

"You *brat,*" she says.

"Why don't you take him?"

Her face hardens. "I'm dead on my feet from working all evening. I'm the only person who's bringing money into this house. Can you imagine what that feels like?"

"It's the middle of the night. And *I'm* tired, too. I have the right to go to sleep."

"You were at a party, and you're tired! You don't care about us since you have Eva. You ignore us."

He sits on the bed and begins to remove his shoes. "I'm not going to do it." His voice is surprisingly calm.

"You've never supported him. Do you know what effect that can have on a man?"

"It isn't me, Ma. I used to think it was."

"Put your shoes on."

"No." He feels a swish of air as her hand flashes toward his cheek. He ducks away from the intended slap and stands up. "Do you really think it's going to make a *difference?* Do you? Do you think that if I take him on a dry run, he'll get the job? Do you think that by pacifying him and pacifying him we're going to make him better? Do you think that if he got the job he could *keep* it? You think that if he gets this job he'll be happy and stop drinking, don't you? *Don't you?*"

He has reduced her to tears. "Please help me."

"Not that way. Not anymore."

* * *

He's damned well not going to be afraid to wake up, either. They've messed with his brain long enough. He always hits the first instant of waking like a swooping bird smashed in flight by a plate-glass window. Including this morning. He's not going to slink around trying to figure out the mood of the house before he shows his face. When he thinks of the years given over to their nonsense, it burns his ass. He's going to stand toe to toe with them, twenty-four hours a day. If they punch him, he'll punch back.

Groggy, he zips himself into his jeans and takes a long, slow leak in the bathroom, brushes his teeth.

Passing his sister's doorway, he sees her motionless in the rocker.

"Hey, Lee, Mum and Dad go?"

"Yes."

The word is so flat that he asks, "What are you doing?"

"Nothing." She is dressed in a white blouse and slacks, with bare feet. Every part of her looks white, even the lips.

"I heard you last night," she says. The comment and the way it is delivered are unusual. They never verbally acknowledge the other's battles. Is she going to try to twist the screws, too? Miss Goody-Goody. Forever doing what she's told.

"So?"

In the queer stillness, she moves her left elbow slightly. *"So?"*

"Could I talk to you?"

He is uncomfortable with this. They exist in separate compartments. Her room is as alien to him as a museum display roped off to visitors. They never enter each other's space or thoughts.

"Come out to the patio," he says.

They sit on the cold metal bench at the table; he busies

himself dumping Wheaties into a bowl and pouring on milk, mashing the flakes with his spoon. Her blouse and slacks seem like a fat lady's. "What?" he asks her, deliberately making it a challenge. She squints toward the family room and he realizes how strange it is for them to have a conversation without the chance of being overheard by their parents.

Now she will tell him to shape up and support this idiocy.

"Do you get . . . do you . . . feel it isn't any use?"

His spoon disappears into the swamp of milk-sogged cereal. He cannot look at her. A taboo is being broken; their communication has set up a magnetic field; his ears perceive a fine crackling, the hairs on his arms rise slowly with a tightening of pores. "Yes."

She gulps loudly, a whimsical sound, but he is riveted in stark attention. "I do, too."

The sorrow is unbearable; she is touching all of him, every memory, every emotion. No one else can know what they know from the well of their mutual experience. He must cut this off. He cannot relent, even with her. She will pull him back into it and his mind is made up. "I'm getting out of here as soon as I can."

"In June?"

"After graduation."

Her reply is an arid stiffness.

=31=

The quail resists being tucked into Jason's mailbox; it spreads its wings and pecks at her, struggling, scolding in a gravel-throated warble. She firmly thrusts it to the back of the box and slams the lid. Then, fetching a piece of string from her pocket, she uses the padlock holes to tie the door partially open so the quail can breathe. His beak pokes up through the slender slot; could he catch his head in the opening and choke? She waits a moment to see. He tries to escape repeatedly, but retreats. She mounts her bike again.

At the edge of the subdivision, where the road takes a sweeping upturn and becomes rougher beside tall houses stacked against the hillside, she pauses. Even with her ten-speed, it will take a couple of hours to reach the summit. Midday sun warms her scalp like a cap. Vehicles stream by: faded motor homes, vans bearing big dogs and roof luggage, rusting cars full of sweat-shirted college students. She waits for a truck, sticks out her thumb. On the first try, a pickup halts a few yards beyond her; two boys in the back lift her and the bike to a spot among their bedrolls and tent gear.

As they lumber in zigzags up the mountain, the panorama of Los Angeles unfolds, blanketed in haze and sprinkled with the tops of spindly palms jutting out of the smog into clear air. The breeze renews her; she faces the mammoth ripple of peaks. The boys do not try to commune with her. They tip their cowboy hats over their eyes and doze. The truck passes by a reservoir entrance: a declining dirt drive barred by chain-link gates. The lanes grow narrower, the gouged overhanging rock more craggy. They are entering a vertical crease in the earth; she has to look straight up to see the sky above the mauve-dappled crests.

As they round a blind curve, a crowded plateau parking lot fans out—behind it, a crouching series of cement ranger barracks. The area is not as she had imagined. There are too many people.

She leaves her bike beside the ranger station and walks to the center of a weather-cracked helicopter pad at a precipice, disappointed to find no sheer drop but a steep, stubbled slope. She follows the guardrail along the outer edge of the parking lot and down the road a brief distance. There is no place to jump here; the slant is too gradual, the turf spiked with shrubbery.

She hikes to higher ground through a section of trees, discovering a woodland path from which she can view men with backpacks on the other side of a plunging valley. Hurrying, she searches for the place where the angle will sharpen, but it remains oblique, littered with the compost of dead leaves and rotting branches. A swinging bridge, secured by thick guy wires and enclosed in mesh, offers no possibilities. Barbed wire flags all the places that a person could climb. It must have been tried before.

She goes out onto the swaying span and stares through the mesh. This would do it. She is incredibly high over a river of foliage and boulders. She wants to feel her body break. The simple release of cutting veins or swallowing pills would be no match for the hopeless spiteful anger and shaming guilt that feed upon each other. Dying isn't enough. She needs to be dashed, dashed to pieces to make the hurting stop.

She inches back across the bridge and lies, defeated, at the edge of the path, gazing downhill with her cheek against her outstretched arm. Heavy boots trudge by, baby strollers with squeaking wheels, crying children, adult pairs whose slow steps are so in unison that they must be lovers holding one another; no one disturbs her. The shadow under her hand changes color and slides into different shapes. Footsteps become less frequent; a throaty roaring fills the valley, shaking the bridge. She sits up, causing the furious power to course through her again. She can never lose it, this vengeance intertwined with longing. It has a future that will outlast her strength.

She moves down the path to the lot; most of the cars are gone. Her bike has been set inside the garage of the ranger station next to a tractor mower. She retrieves it and stands, thinking. Her parents will be worried by now. Should she call for someone to get her? It is perilous to ride her bike down the mountain at dusk.

She remembers the reservoir. The vision engages her. She glides toward it, squeezing the brakes rhythmically, dodging the several cars that rush at her from behind and overtake the bike as she hugs the bank at the side of the road.

A swift left brings her into the reservoir area; she stops at the gate, assessing the barrier. It appears to be tied to an alarm mechanism: a square gray metal box, obviously part of the electrical system.

Across the city, gold pinpoints glisten. She does not want to go home.

There will be opportunity on the way down. Not every curveside cliff will be graded. She pedals into the road, steering the bike gingerly along a series of hairpin corners, gauging the outfall beyond the guardrail.

Halfway to the bottom, she understands: there will be no mistake in design. The entire run was fashioned for safety.

Descending cars net her with their headlights, barely missing her. One honks, starting a spurt of molten liquid through her limbs. Another car swerves by. A woman rolls down the window on the passenger side and shoves her curl-framed face out, yelling, *"Bitch!"*

An unsteadiness possesses her. The front tire weaves; she straightens it, decisively clutching the hand brakes.

But hate has hold of her. She wants to kill. Like a soaring bird, she can see her house, fabricated under the accurate eye of her mind. She is hovering over it, determined not to be put inside again.

The intent grumble of a car approaches from below. Faint yellow splashes the pavement. She veers to the middle line—a ribbon in darkness—releasing the brakes, feeling a backlash of wind. Is she traveling fast enough? The car appears.

As they connect, the bike crumbles away from her. In a split-second of disillusionment, she fears she will not achieve sufficient impact. But the windshield flies toward her and the million splinters of glass along her length precisely answer the million splinters of bone.

She is inside the car, in the front seat, the window beside her open just a crack. Through that slash is the world: the action of bodies at play, merchants selling rainbow candy, dandelions sprouting between sections of sidewalk. She rises to the slender band of light and, effortlessly, slips out.

=== 32 ===

She will be dead, is already dead. They want you to be at the hospital when they tell you.

His mother pulls the car beneath the overhang of the emergency entrance and waves the keys at the security guard. "My daughter's been in an accident! Can you park this for me?"

"Yes, ma'am."

They jump out. He realizes that his dad, in the backseat, is fumbling for the door handle. His father stares helplessly through the glass; Rick releases him from the car and takes his arm.

Inside, they're shown to a small waiting room beyond the public one. The shielded silence speaks clearly to him. He braces himself against the tense but optimistic expectation on his parents' faces.

An elderly man enters; he is wearing a suit. Was he looking for the restroom and picked the wrong door? It is the doctor—he sees it in the dutiful bearing. Death itself, this figure: the lowered gaze, the straightened shoulders. Ice grips Rick.

"Mr. and Mrs. Stockman?"

His mother nods, the kind of good-girl nod that begs for leniency.

"I'm Dr. Habersham. They're still working on your daughter. She's badly hurt. She—"

"I want to see the head man." His father stands up, with his hands on his hips.

"The administrator?"

"Whoever."

"Sir, I don't think he's here."

"Well, call him."

"May I ask the reason?"

"You may not!"

"Mike . . ." His mother gets to her feet unsteadily.

"We've got to make them do everything they can! We can't leave it to chance."

"We *are* doing everything, I assure you."

"Pop—"

"What kind of a hospital is this? Don't you have a trauma center?"

"Of course."

"I want the head man!" The whites of his eyes are enormous, the pupils as unseeing as marbles.

Sufficiently intimidated, the doctor retreats. "I'll ask the chaplain to come in."

"I don't want the chaplain. I want the administrator! Send him in here! You . . ." His fists are clenched, but his stooped body shows he is already beaten, the reality of the situation seeping through to him.

"Please, Mr. Stockman—sit down. I understand how you feel. I'll see what I can do."

Alone, they weep. His parents turn to each other. He is left outside their circle, crying into the sleeve of his jacket.

"Here she is," the nurse says, leading them into a dark room and fumbling with a lamp on the other side of the bed; the railing bars glow silver. The light comes on, a harsh floor lamp with no shade.

"That's too bright," his mother says.

"She won't wake up."

The burst of raw cuts on his sister's face leaps at him. Her nose is taped, surrounded by gouged bruises.

No accident. She centered herself on this attempt. Her hair is damp where they must have rinsed blood from it; her chin is tilted up, mouth open, lips blue around a gap where two teeth are missing.

Let it be morning again, with her beside him! Why did he say that to her? He's a jerk. A damned stupid jerk. He caused this.

"A man resuscitated her." The nurse checks the IV. "She had mud in her mouth. He took it out. She wasn't breathing."

"The driver?" his mother asks.

"No, a hiker. They charged the driver with being on the wrong side of the road."

"I'll sue the pants off him," his father says.

Lee stirs; his mother leans into the sun's lemony rays that illuminate Lee's hospital bed and spill onto the glossy floor in rivulets. They have waited two days for her to reach consciousness. He and his father rise from their chairs and move closer. Lee seems to become aware of them one by one, her trepidation intensifying. She flicks the lashes shut under purple lids.

"We love you," his mother says.

As they gather around Lee, he senses her flight from them.

His mother hunkers down until she is looking through the rail. "Is there anything you want?"

"No." The sound elongates through the space in her teeth.

"A car hit you. Do you remember it?"

"Uh."

"A woman is in a lot of trouble over it. She may have to go to jail. They say she was on the wrong side of the road. Was she?"

The lashes twitch. "Nooo."

"She wasn't?"

"No."

Lee's skin is shiny and bloated like a water balloon; the answers squeeze from her.

"You were?"

The only response is a shift of Lee's head.

"Did you want to do that?"

They wait in vain.

"Why?" his mother whispers.

Without opening her eyes, she points at his father.

Him?

"Because of Daddy?" his wife says.

"Yesssss."

"What does she mean?" he asks Katy. She stares at him with disillusionment.

"Lee, baby, what . . ."

Katy puts a finger to her lips.

He glances at his son, hardly recognizing him. They have assumed the air of strangers—Rick and Katy—the unfamiliar indifference of people who brush by on the street. They do not belong to him; in a single parched second, they have removed themselves. He understands without doubt the shocking permanence of his new condition. He feels his mouth opening in surprise.

In the elevator, his wife concentrates on the flashing numbers above the door; his son gazes at the black-buttoned control panel.

They walk swiftly ahead of him down the corridor; he has a sense that if he does not keep up, he will be left behind when they drive away. He begins to run, overtaking them as they glide out the electronic doors.

"What did she mean?" he pleads, dancing sideways to stay abreast of them. He never meant harm to anyone, least of all them, her, the little girl he wanted, always wanted.

Ignoring him, they shoulder and slam into the front of the car; he still has a foot on the ground, climbing into the backseat, when his wife pulls away. The pavement slips past, trying to draw him with it. He tucks his shoe inside and forces the door closed.

"Hey, I won't put up with this. I'm not going home with you if you won't talk to me." Silly threat, but he has to reverse this, has to use whatever wedge he can find.

His wife stops the car at the perimeter of the lot; waits, without looking back.

A person doesn't lose his family. They've invested too many years in each other, too much love. The children are the sacred issue of their bodies. It can't be unbound. He has to break the moment or it will not heal. He opens the door and steps out.

His wife drives away.

"What did you say the number is again?" The cabbie's eyes find him in the rearview mirror.

Mike squints down at the page he tore from the bar's telephone book but cannot read it in the dark. The taxi halts. He hands the driver the sheet.

A light goes on, at the dashboard. "You read it." The man passes it back to him.

"I'll get out now. It's in this block. How much do I owe you?"

"You can't see the meter?"

Even cab drivers don't like him. He must have a garbage

personality. People can tell in five minutes that he's not worth fooling with. He fingers the pad of money in the pocket of his wallet, shoves the billfold forward. "You pick it out for me."

The man hesitates, then selects two pieces of paper. Mike cannot see what they are but, as he receives the wallet, he is saluted with a courteous, almost jovial, "Thank you. Have a good evening."

He is left along a series of street lamp circles, studying houses. After a few false starts, he discovers the white L-shaped ranch with the picture-window addition on the back. Walking gingerly into the driveway, he glimpses Monica working at the kitchen sink. Her hair and face match perfectly; they are the same blond color, the same sleek silky texture, the same skinny shape, the same length. She suddenly comes to the glass and peers out as though she knows he is there, but he can tell by the way she moves off that she has seen nothing.

As he approaches the side door, he becomes suspicious of a shadow beside the garage. He inches past it, watching. From the deep gloom, truth leaps at him like a wolf. *She did. He was. He is.* He begins to wail to keep the memories away.

He drifts awake, knowing instantly where he is: his brother's den, on the sofa bed. Through the window screens come night pleasures, the leisurely sighing of leaves, the pure breeze of wee hours saturated with mist.

He would never leave a window open overnight at home, but Ted's presence secures the house; if Mike were in charge, things could go wrong. Seeing the dim outline of books precisely arranged on their shelves, he is touched by assurance. Ted pays the bills here, makes the decisions, stands guard. He can let go for once. Sleep.

* * *

The aroma of bacon and coffee coaxes him up into sunlight. The quilt spread across his legs is a merry flower patch. He is safe. Still safe.

Rising eagerly, he begins to tremble. One quick jolt would do him for the day. But Ted stores his liquor in the kitchen and Monica is cooking. He dons his trousers and rinses his face in the powder room, Lee's gashes shimmering along the wallpaper. A salty metallic taste floods his tongue, reminiscent of blood. She has butchered herself. *Because of him.*

It's all a mistake. He's not to blame. Lee must have been delirious. She will tell them so today. Shame on Katy for her disloyalty. He hopes she is good and worried about him.

He takes the kitchen slowly; if he does not startle Monica, she will not frown at him. He needs her acceptance. Seeing him, she brightens. "Morning, Mike."

"Hello." The panic in him settles as he confronts her radiance.

"Coffee?"

"Yes, please." Perhaps she will leave the room and he can zip a shot into it.

"Breakfast is ready."

"Where are . . . the kids?"

"At school." She pours the coffee and sets the mug on the counter. "Ted's outside. Puttering in his garden. He skipped work today to be with you."

Isn't that it, after all? *Home is the place where, when you have to go there, they have to take you in. Robert Frost.* His brother has seen Mike's entire history, knows the factors which shaped him, knows he is worthy.

Ted bumps past the back door, greeting him with special tenderness, washing his stained hands at the steel sink.

They eat in a huddle around the small table, Ted and Monica smiling at him occasionally. He hugs his coffee cup, draining it twice, relying on a kick from the caffeine to nudge the hour along. If he can't get a sip from Ted's supply by ten o'clock, he'll go out on some pretext. The food is mildly tasty to him; it's more the idea of closeness, their companionship, that he is enjoying. Near the end of the meal, the bottom drops out of his stomach.

"Feeling rocky?" Ted says with concern.

He realizes that he has begun to sweat profusely. "If I could . . . lie down." He pushes his chair back and, nauseated, plods to the den. Monica rushes to pull the blinds as he stretches out on the bed.

His brother stands over him. "How 'bout a cold rag?"

"No. Thanks." He covers his eyes. "It's nice of you to let me stay here. It won't be for long. I'll be getting a job and I'll straighten out the problem with Katy."

"You can't stay here."

He scrutinizes Ted. "Just a while."

"No." His brother's voice is gentle, his manner incongruous with what he is saying.

"Why?"

"You're an alcoholic, Mike. I have to put you into treatment."

"I'm not an alcoholic."

"Do you recall what happened last night, how upset you were?"

He does not want to remember. The crying. Crying on the carpet . . . not being able to get up.

"Your life seemed terrible, didn't it?"

"Yes. But I'm better now."

"That was *reality.*" Ted kneels beside him. "Your life *is* terrible. Because you're an alcoholic. That's the reason. The only reason."

"I drink because my life is a mess."

"Your life is a mess because you drink."

Is it? "No." He begins to weep.

"Look—if I saw someone trying to kill you, I'd stop him, wouldn't I? Alcohol's trying to kill you. I'm going to put you into treatment." His brother grips his hand. "It'll be okay."

He was talked to like this once before, through a haze of absolute pain. They wanted to cut out his appendix when he was twenty, but he was determined not to be dragged to sleep in that fearful tiled room. In the end, he had to give up and let them do it because of the agony. He couldn't stand it anymore.

=== 33 ===

Dear Katy,

You told Ted you weren't interested in participating in my treatment but I'd like to ask you to reconsider. Even if we don't get back together, I wish you would explain to me what's been going on in my life. It is increasingly clear that there is much I don't remember and I'm afraid of what is in those gaps.

I've only been here a week and I'm ready to say I've got the problem. Alcoholism. I've had the bends trying to come up out of it. That makes all of you right and me wrong.

I'm still in a bunch of trouble and I honestly wonder if I can pull this off—the getting well. I've hurt you in every way possible, but I hope you'll come and talk.

Love (believe me),
Mike

"Where's Daddy?"

Her daughter seems more alert today. Katy leans over the railing of the hospital bed to kiss her. "He couldn't come."

"But he hasn't been here for a long time."

Should she tell her the truth? "He's gone into an alcoholism center."

Lee's face registers amazement. "Is he doing all right?"

"I don't know. I don't go to see him."

Her daughter's gaze follows her as she lowers the railing and rolls the table and lunch tray within reach. "Well, when is he coming home?"

Should she get into all this? "Ahhh, the soup looks good today," she says, lifting the lid on a black bowl. "Chicken noodle."

"I should write to him, or call him."

"Let's leave well enough alone. Honey . . . he's not coming back. I don't want to be with him anymore. This will be best."

"For him? Or for you?" She pushes the tray to one side.

"For all of us."

"But this is what we've been trying to get him to do! And now that he's doing it, we act like we don't care. He won't think it's worth it. He won't make it without us."

This is turning into a scene. "Don't get excited."

"You should have told me before!" Lee turns to stare at the wall.

"If we were going to encourage him through his treatment, we would have to be prepared to forgive him."

"I do, I *do* forgive him," her daughter says angrily. "Don't you?"

"No."

She closes her eyes to escape her mother. She cannot explain how she feels about him. Hitting the car took it all

out of her—all the spite—and left a terrible loneliness for
him, her real father, the one she misses so much. This
might be her only chance to find him. *"Please,* Mama."

"I can't."

The alcoholism counselor's office is about as big as a
large walk-in closet, with peach walls and an aqua rug.
They seat themselves, separated by a desk. She is aware
of the relaxing ambiance. They are trying to control her
mood with the upbeat interior design. And with their
friendly style.

"My name's Annette," the woman says. She is fiftyish,
with red hair and freckles, prominent front teeth. "I admire
both you and your husband for doing this."

Is she being patronized?

Annette's green eyes convey a softness. "You may not
think it can work, but people get well all the time."

She nods.

"The hardest thing after getting the alcoholic to agree to
treatment is getting the family to agree to be treated. People don't understand that *everyone* in the family is affected
by the drug. Their lives have been revolving around it. So,
even though they may not drink themselves, they are considered co-alcoholics."

She nods again, unable to speak.

"I'll bet you felt as though you were going to have a
nervous breakdown. Nothing you did helped. You felt that
somehow it was your fault and that if you did just a little
more, he would stop." Annette slides a box of tissues in
her direction. "Nobody makes anybody else drink. That's
an individual's choice."

She will not show weakness in front of this woman.
"Yes."

"But there are ways you and the children can make it
easier for your husband to decide to stay sober. That's why

the best success comes when the whole family participates in recovery. Each one of them needs to recover, too. Each has a separate set of problems. Is your daughter doing better?''

"Pretty well. She'll be home in another week or two. We've been keeping the hospitals busy this year."

Annette leaves her chair, and goes to lean against the windowsill. "When you start getting a lot of medical bills and hospitalizations, it can be a signal for help. Like when you start moving a lot."

"What does that have to do with it?"

"The family runs away from the problems the alcohol has caused. Starts over. Again and again. We call it the 'geographic cure.' "

"We *have* moved quite a bit." Because of Mike's drinking? She hadn't thought of it that way.

"Would your daughter be willing to participate in Mike's treatment?"

"That's why I'm here. She insisted. I don't want to upset her."

"And your son?"

"I'm not sure."

"And you? Are you committed to this?" Annette asks with the nonjudgment of a waitress taking an order.

Is she here only for Lee, or is she still married to Mike in spirit? She is . . . married to one of his personalities, the old one; the other belongs to the devil. "If I can win."

"There are no guarantees."

Katy shrugs. "What do I have to do?"

"Communicate with him—in the sessions—about his past behavior, and allow your children to do the same. It has to be done in a totally honest but caring way." Annette comes to sit beside her. "And you have to handle him differently when he rejoins the family. You've learned to cope with his drinking by working around him, by doing more than your share and by keeping aggravations away from him. I would guess that you apologize for him fairly frequently, and that you manage the money by yourself. You have frustration with people for not giving your husband a fair shake in business, when alcohol's actually been in the picture and they were responding to that. And I would guess that your children don't talk to him directly, but go through you.''

How can she know all this?

"These are enabling behaviors, behaviors that enable your husband to continue drinking." She touches the arm of Katy's chair; Katy draws back. "It's an odd effect, but by creating an ideal climate for the alcoholic, we make him believe there are no consequences for his actions. You've been taking all the consequences *for* him. No wonder you're tired. The family has to detach from what he does and learn to act in their own interest. Let him sink or swim."

"But it would be a hopeless tangle! You don't know what you're asking! Is this one of those theories they're going to change in five years and say, 'Oh, sorry about all of you who used that method—it doesn't work'?''

"It works. Active alcoholism is a cooperative effort between at least two people: one who drinks and one who helps by protecting him."

"I don't help him! I've *never* helped him! Why are you accusing *me?* He's the alcoholic!" She jumps up.

"Stay a while," Annette says kindly. "I know how you feel."

Mike's drinking is *not* a cooperative effort. She's driven herself wild trying to make him quit. Now she's trying to help again and she's being *blamed.* "How could you possibly know that?"

"I'm married to an alcoholic."

His mother is sitting at the dining room table waiting for him, as he comes in from school. He recognizes her intent immediately: a powwow, critical, unpleasant. News has to be revealed. He won't like it. He equates these conferences with a court convened for a judge's sentencing. Why can't one of these occasions be for the purpose of telling him she's won a lottery, she's signed them up for a cruise, she's decided to redecorate his room and he can pick the colors?

"Dad didn't get the Reynolds account," she announces bitterly as he seats himself opposite her. "It's just as well. He's going to be in treatment at least a month. We won't . . . be able to send you to college," she says, her words faltering. "We have to use that money . . . to live."

He doesn't want their money, doesn't want that on his conscience.

"I'm sorry," she offers.

The apology moves him.

"It's just . . . out of control." She chews her lower lip thoughtfully. "I don't know what to do."

He tries to imagine his parents as a young couple, eager. They have come so far. Down so many roads. Wrong roads? How in the world did they all get here?

"Dad's counselor told me that the whole family has to participate in his treatment."

"Why?"

"There are things we should say to each other."

Being honest only leads to more trouble. This is some social worker's idea of kiss-and-make-up.

"And there are ways we've been helping Dad to continue drinking."

A *lie*. If he lets himself in for this, they'll tell him *he's* at fault. "I don't want to participate."

"Yes, you do." The tone is shaming.

"He's screwed us up enough! This is *his* problem. He put the booze first, ahead of us."

"Yes. He did. I brought pamphlets for us to look at. Please—read them."

"I'm not going to spend one more minute on this dumb-ass drinking stuff! I'm tired of fooling with him. That's all we do. That *is* our life. It takes up our whole life!"

Her expression shifts from sympathy to superiority. "Now wait a minute."

"It *does!* Can't you see it? I hate him."

"No, you don't," she says.

The woman has freckles and red hair. She seems friendly, but he isn't deceived. She intends to whip him into shape. Well, he's here to tell her off. With delight.

"I'd like you to come into one of the sessions and explain to your dad how you feel," she says.

"I already have."

"He couldn't hear you then. The alcohol was in the way."

"Can he hear me now?"

"Yes."

"He'll forget it later."

"If he drinks, he might. But I think he's through with that."

"You know what I am?"

"What?"

"Do you read the comic strip *Peanuts?*"

"Yes."

"I'm Charlie Brown and my dad is Lucy. Charlie doesn't learn. He thinks she'll hold that football for him. Do you know what happens, every time? He runs as fast as he can and kicks and, at the last minute, she pulls it away and he falls flat on his back. That's me. I believe him every goddamned time."

"He doesn't mean to do that."

"I think he kind of gets a kick out of it—pardon the pun."

She grins. "I like your sense of humor, Rick."

This is a counselor's ploy, to get him on her side. He

isn't flattered by it, or by the cozy first-name, no-last-name bit. *Annette. How cute.*

"I'm as concerned about you as I am about your dad. Did you know that alcoholism seems to be passed from generation to generation?"

"I'll never be like him!"

"It's not just a physical disease, it has psychological aspects. It can stem from a childhood of living with an alcoholic. That happened to your father."

"*Who* was an alcoholic?"

"His father."

He has not heard of this, but it makes sense; Grandpa Stockman was alternately hilarious and a terror.

"Fifty percent of alcoholics are children of alcoholics. You have to safeguard your future by unloading that rage. This is a good place to do it. In other words, *break the chain*, Rick."

"I already have. Annette."

Pull out the big guns. This time they've got the head of the Chemical Dependency Unit to talk to him.

"I wanted to meet you," the man says.

"Is this about my dad?"

"About you. About your recovery."

"I'm not sick."

He is being sized up. This guy looks like a construction worker rather than a doctor. An Italian construction worker.

"Living with an alcoholic makes everyone sick. Each person in the family needs therapy—it's very important. But he's got the main problem, I'll grant you that. You have a million reasons to be angry. I understand."

"Do you understand that he's crazy?"

"A good definition of alcoholism is intermittent insanity."

"Intermittent?" He smiles cynically. "How about incessant?"

The director takes it in stride. "As the disease progresses, there are fewer and fewer lucid moments."

"How can you tell?"

A pause. "You've been having conversations with his *disease*."

"It's not a disease."

"Why not?"

"Because a disease is something you didn't deserve. He drank, didn't he?"

"He drank because he was in mental pain. Researchers believe that potential alcoholics have a different brain chemistry than the rest of us. They are missing some endorphins, which are the body's natural painkillers. They can't relax—they're constantly agitated. Alcohol calms them. There has to be sufficient intake before the disease can affect you, that's true. And then you're stuck. Whenever your dad tried to stop, he became physically ill—that's what alcohol does. You feel worse when you try to stop than you do when you're drinking. But listen—tell me— why won't you help him? He needs to know that you want him to get well."

He lowers his eyelids at the man, who squirms slightly. "Are you the child of an alcoholic?"

"No."

"You've *read* about it, then. At college."

He expects a backlash but is met with attention.

"And counseled many people. Describe it to me, the way you see it."

"It can't be described."

"Try."

The walls grow white-hot. He finds a single leaf on a tree outside the window. "It's always there. Even when you look like you're at a movie or at school or on a date, you're involved with it. It never goes away. Basically, it's being mentally tortured over your lifetime. And when you give me that 'recovery' crap, what you're really saying is that people can do anything they *please* to you, and suddenly they're sorry and you're supposed to be gracious about it."

The man seems stunned by the description; he regards Rick silently for a moment. "It is abuse. I agree with you. But if we could ease your anger, shouldn't we?"

"I'd like to hang on to it."

"What about your mother? Could you do this for her?"

"She's worse than he is."

"How so?"

"My father had an excuse! He was blitzed most of the time. What's *her* excuse? She knew what was right—and she didn't do it. She made us kowtow to him. She *knew* he was wrong—all those years—and she did nothing!"

"She felt she was doing the best she could. She didn't have a perspective on it. She was as addicted to his needs as he was to the alcohol. This is *usual* behavior in a chemically dependent family. That's one reason why it's so hard to break the cycle. Son . . . I know it's a long way back from here."

He stands up. "You don't get back from where I am."

The doctor stays seated, gazing at him with tremendous empathy. "Your own recovery will begin. I can't tell you when or how, but you'll feel it. And you'll start to forgive."

34

"God, grant me the serenity to accept the things I cannot change, the courage to change the things I can, and the wisdom to know the difference." As the group prays in unison, he eyes his sister, her face a mass of discolorations and stitches, her ankle bound in a calf-high cast.

He is welded to his chair with resentment as Annette passes out white sheets of paper to the small gathering. The room looks like part of a model home, pale orange and turquoise. *Cheery-cheery chipper. Let's all get happy.*

He stares at the stapled papers in his hands and sees that they illustrate a series of circles. Each circle is labeled: The Chemically Dependent Person, The Chief Enabler, The Family Hero, The Scapegoat, The Mascot, The Lost Child. He is struck by the accurate description of his father under "The Chemically Dependent Person": manipulation, anger, charm, rigidity, perfectionism, righteousness, aggression, grandiosity, irresponsibility. These characteristics are marked "Wall of Defenses." The inner circle on this chart shows hidden feelings of pain, shame, hurt, guilt, fear. Doubtful. His father is a dyed-in-the-wool blowhard. He inflicts pain and fear on others.

"Before we start, I'd like for us to introduce ourselves.

I'm Annette. I'm the child of an alcoholic. Also . . . my husband is an alcoholic who went through treatment and is not drinking.'' She glances at Lee.

"I'm Lee. My father is a patient here, trying to get well from his alcoholism, and . . . I know he can do it.''

Seven other teenagers give their first names and explain that their parents are or were alcoholism patients. When it is his turn, he grunts his name and gives no explanation. It's none of their damned business. He wouldn't be subjecting himself to this if his sister hadn't begged him.

"An important thing to remember is that nobody wanted it to be this way,'' Annette says to the group. "When we begin to think of our parents as victims themselves, we begin our journey toward forgiveness. Our topic tonight is family roles. Every person in a chemically dependent family assumes at least one of these roles. The spouse of the alcoholic is usually the Chief Enabler. The children each take one or a combination of the other roles. These are from a booklet called *The Family Trap* by Sharon Wegscheider-Cruse. I'd like you to read the descriptions and share with us which one you think you play. By being aware of the role you took to survive in an alcoholic household, you can begin to free yourself from the confines of that role.''

He doesn't want to read this. He's not a *type*.

"Rick, can you find your role on there?''

He folds the paper and glares at Annette: the wife of an alcoholic. This is his mother, leading the group. He won't give her satisfaction.

"Is it hard to identify which one is you?''

He answers with a frown. Lee puts a hand over her mouth, gazing at him.

"Would someone else like to talk about a role?'' Annette asks.

"I think I'm the Mascot,'' a fat girl volunteers.

This is kindergarten. Show and tell. He gets up and walks toward the hall. No one acknowledges his departure.

He waits for Lee in the parking lot, which is slick with rain; he is lost in loud music from the car radio when she hobbles out into the glassed entryway of the center. She uses the crutches laboriously, as though harboring a hundred hidden aches. He leaps from the car to help her.

"Why didn't you stay in the meeting?" Her question is directed at the door as she heaves against it, trying to maneuver her way outside.

He grabs it and holds it for her. "Because it's theory. It doesn't mean anything. In the real world."

"It does so."

One of her crutches skids in a puddle; he catches her under the arm to restore her balance.

"Rick, are you going to be mad forever?"

"I hope so."

"Why did you come at all?"

"You asked me to."

"You don't have to do stuff because I ask you to." It is slow going; she takes tiny steps and bends forward with each one. "Do you feel like you have to appease me?"

Yes, sweetheart. The last time I was direct with you, you tried to smash your skull against the front of a car. "Sort of."

"You're mad at me, isn't that right?"

He opens the car door and lowers her slowly onto the seat.

"Why *are* you?"

Lobbing her crutches into the back, he shuts the door.

"Because you'll try to kill yourself again, that's why," he says, getting in beside her. "That's the answer to the appeasement question. Because you tried in the first place: that's the answer to the *mad* question. What was I supposed

292

to do after you blew yourself to pieces? You were willing to leave *me,* too, weren't you? All you wanted was *out.*"

"You wanted out," she says quietly.

"That's . . . different!"

"Not to me."

"I'm the one who should have gone and done it. They're sick of me. You've been great, all along. What makes you qualified to *kill* yourself?"

She unzips her purse and, reaching into it, flings a sheaf of papers at him. "If you'd read these, you'd know!" They smack him in the chest, scattering onto the floor. "We had roles! It's a *pattern.* A proven pattern. You *did* get a raw deal—you were the Scapegoat. But I was the Family Hero. There's pressure in that. The most. Read it," she sighs. "Read it."

Tears glisten in the irregular terrain of her facial cuts and bruises. Looking at her injuries makes him weak. He takes her hand and presses it to his lips.

"If you could see him," she whispers, "you'd change your mind. He sits there crying while we tell him what he did. Mother cries. I cry." She rolls down the window and gazes into the screen of bright drops starting in still air.

His father is a con artist of the first order who is probably relishing the attention. "We don't know what's inside his head," he says, releasing her.

"I do."

"No, you don't."

They stare at each other in silence.

"I can't live with him again, Lee Ann. I want to go."

"Go."

"What will *you* do?"

She meditates for a moment. "Love you anyway."

The sailboat creaks and rocks. Eva is drowsing next to him on the deck, in The Orange Bikini. The firmness of her body reassures him; it is like her mind, assertive. He is struggling after that decisiveness, intrigued by it. She has no second thoughts that he can see; crews the sloop alone, feasts on strawberries and kiwi fruit, prepares for final exams, all with the same competently adventurous tilt.

"Marry me," he says.

"Nope."

"I didn't think so."

"I want to go to college. What do you want?"

"I'd better not want that."

"You'll find the money. Apply for a scholarship."

"Yeah."

She rubs her nose against his, humorously squinting into one of his eyes as though peering through a telescope. "I can see the future from here and you are very happy."

"Yuh."

"Don't you have any faith?"

"As in 'Amen'?"

"No, as in 'Gotcha.' What do you want to *be?*"

"Left alone."

This piques her. She sits up. "That can be arranged."

"I didn't mean you. What am I supposed to do?"

"Steer." She says it without malice.

"My life is grass."

"Fertilize it." She starts down the stairs, into the cabin.

He gets up quickly; seized by a leg cramp, he hops after her, shouting, "That's easy for you! My father's in a damned funny farm and my mother's on my case every minute to go see him. Here's my future: my father's going to show up at the door in ten days, expecting me to shake his hand. I don't even like my parents."

"I've noticed something," she says, perched on the bottom step, speaking softly up the stairwell. "You give them too much power over your emotions. They're just *people.*"

Just people. What a stupid comment.

April 25

Dear Rick,

I didn't put my return address on the outside of this envelope because I was afraid you would rip it up. Please give me a chance to be heard. Nothing I did can be excused, on any terms. But one of the twelve steps of AA says that I must make amends. In other words, apologize, whether the apology is accepted or not.

I do apologize to you. I'm sure I don't know half the things I did to you and your mother and sister, but the ones I remember and the ones they've described are enough to make me stay in here for good.

I can't promise anybody anything at this point because I am suspicious of myself. The whole business might sneak up on me again. I suppose Mother and Lee have told you about their meetings with me and the counselor. I wish you had been in on them, but I understand why you weren't.

I'll be home on the 10th of May. I'm looking forward to seeing you.

> *Love,*
> *Dad*

Manipulative. *Feel sorry for me. Feel sorry for me.* That's what his dad is saying. Apology, my foot.

He's supposed to rush a letter back to him. *Dad! Don't be so hard on yourself!* Even the loops and curls of his father's handwriting are false, showy. Grandiose: that's on target. Grandiose and manipulative.

If he were not related to his father, he wouldn't know

295

him. Peculiar, to end up related to people you wouldn't choose as friends.

I do apologize to you. Ha. Rule One concerning his father: never let yourself feel cherished. The higher you get, the farther you'll have to fall.

"We'll give him a brand-new start when he gets home," his mother says, weeding clothes out of his dad's side of the closet. "I'll buy a couple of new sports shirts and slacks for him, maybe deck shoes."

As he waits, she hedges about suits with too-wide lapels, shirts with long pointy collars. She repeatedly offers him sweaters and jackets his dad seldom wears. He declines, uncomfortable with the idea of his father's belongings against his flesh. He is in the midst of refusing a blue bathrobe when she perceives the message. Her animation evaporates; she flushes as though he has struck her but says nothing, merely fixes him with those golden-brown eyes. She folds the bathrobe with swift angular motions and places it atop a pile of clothing on the bed.

"Well, then, we'll give them all away. How about boxing them for me? Check the pockets." She goes to her bathroom, closing herself in with a deliberate *crack*.

A numbness takes over. His body is wrapped in cotton. He fetches the boxes and fills them rapidly, each item a tangible memory of his dad, loads them in the trunk *dangerous cargo*, drives them to a collection station in a shopping center where a limping man chases him to try to give him a receipt. He has daydreamed past six intersections when he realizes he forgot to go through the pockets.

The hell with it.

They've had this conversation before: Your dad's coming home tomorrow and I'm counting on you to welcome him.

"I won't be here," he says to her.

"Oh, now, Rick." She continues to dole coffee into the pot with a tablespoon, making sure each scoop is level.

"If he's in, I'm out."

"Don't be silly." Her eyes widen as she sees that he means it. "Dad's changed."

"In a month? Five weeks?"

"It's like college. They teach you how, then you practice it."

"You're forgetting about one thing. Access."

"I'm not forgetting. I've cleaned it all out. But he's not a puppet. He'll do what he wants to do."

"I'm not going to watch while he decides, either."

"Where will you go?" It is delivered lightly, like a joke.

"To Eva's. Until I can get my own place. I'll line up a job for after graduation."

She aims her massive disappointment at him. But she cannot bully him with it anymore.

Who does he look like, this son, dark curls and chocolate-brown eyes? He has always been a visitor, assessing them with long glances. People have told her that he looks like her, but she doesn't see it. Not at all.

Is he going, then? What can anyone *do*? He is a man, no longer able to be stopped by a word, lifted up, brought back. He lives in his own beliefs and has his own resource: himself.

He takes his time leaving the kitchen. He has the rest of his life. The room is empty. She pours water into the top of the percolator and, plugging it in, waits.

She has failed. At her most important task.

She can try to make it right. They may be friends someday. But she cannot erase these eighteen years. They are stored in his head, jumbled and stark. He may come to understand them, but he will never lose them. She did that. She and Mike.

The percolator's popping burble begins, covering the sound of her weeping.

The moon wakes him, peeking through shutter slats. He finds his gym bag under the bed and puts a single change of clothes in it; slips into his jeans and T-shirt, sneakers; slings the bag over his shoulder.

Reaching the back door, he inches it toward him. A column of breeze licks at his face. *He is supposed to wait here. His dad will be along.* He listens for him, then pushes a shoulder into the windy crack and slides out.

= 35 =

Commencement. A sea of caps and gowns: navy blue for boys, white for girls. The students are lining up alphabetically for the procession into the stadium, among scattered laughter and a crush of visitors. He leaves Eva at the M's and steps in behind Marla Stitt. Mr. and Mrs. Metsinger have been hovering over him all morning. Betty straightens his cap, and Carl, smiling, takes his photograph from three angles. Whatever they have worked out with his parents, he has—mercifully—been spared the details, simply been given the guest room and plenty of freedom. He's managed to get his head together in the last four weeks, slept soundly under their roof, enjoyed whole evenings watching situation comedies. Time has seemed larger, longer; he can move around in it. He and his mother and sister spent untold hours compensating for his father's inabilities and adjusting to his demands. He sees that now. It filled all the gaps where leisure was supposed to be.

A box of boutonnieres and corsages is passed down the line; he pins a yellow rosebud to his robe. The students begin to march toward the rows of folding chairs clustered about a stage in the middle of the football field. It is five o'clock on a windy afternoon. Glorious. Let it be written that his father could not keep him from his own graduation. He looks at Marla's blond braid as he walks. His family might be there. He has not seen them since he left home.

As he approaches his chair, he glimpses Eva. She is a cameo, her nearly black hair and pinkish cheeks startling against the snowy mortarboard and gown.

For a couple of agonizing minutes, he stands with the others facing the seniors who are still filing in. He watches only them, certain that he can feel his parents' attention riveted on him. Is Lee there? The music ends; they all turn toward the stage for "The Star-Spangled Banner," and then are seated. Two hundred sixty-one names are printed on the program, with adjoining stars for scholastic, sports and other achievements. There are no stars next to his.

His parents will look odd and small to him, the way they did the first time he came home from camp. He was like a stranger viewing them, surprised to find his mother a little overweight and his father shorter than he had thought.

What will he say to them? Will they speak? He doesn't want to wait around for that.

He strains to comprehend the words of the valedictorian, Ross Dwyer. Much of the year's recounting is hearsay to Rick: baseball games and dances, writing the school paper, the candy drive for band uniforms, a visiting choir from an Atlanta high school. Was all that going on? It will be words in a yearbook.

They move slowly up to the stage to receive their diplomas. As he descends, he catches sight of the Good One with his arm around Lee, his mother with the camera to her eye. The flash blots them out. He sits down quickly, shaken. Embarrassment is heavy on the back of his tongue, like food he is being forced to swallow.

Power. Eva had it figured out—they have incredible power over him. He *gives* them power. How else could they have so much now that he is grown? He needs to care less, not be so wounded by them. If he cares less, he may be able to give them some latitude, let it all shake down.

His uncle reaches him first in the crowd of shouting seniors at the end of graduation. Unexpectedly, Ted seizes him in an emotional embrace. He surrenders to it, sensing a genuine undercurrent of kinship, which comforts him.

"Congratulations," Ted growls into his ear. "Good luck at UCLA."

"I'm not going to college. I have a job."

His uncle is taken aback by this. "A financial decision?"

He hesitates. No need to be secretive anymore; they can't control him. "Yes."

"We'll see about that," he says affectionately.

Aunt Monica and his cousins and the Metsingers mob him with giggles and thumps. He allows himself a tiny feeling of pride.

His sister reaches his side and, without his consent, hugs him breathless. Whether it is the costume of cap, gown and diploma that gives him courage or a slight inching up of his faith, he is able to accept his mother's kiss.

His father is not with her. "Where's Dad?"

"He was uneasy. We have to respect that."

=== 36 ===

"I'm going to look at sandals. I'll be right back." Eva lets
go of his hand and crosses the mall, heading for the shoe
store; he is left facing a card shop decked with banners:
FATHER'S DAY IS JUNE 17TH.

Not this year. This year, the calendar is blank where
Father's Day should be. He does not have to respond.

It used to be a struggle anyway. He moves into the card
shop, surveying the splashy assortment: it is seven racks
wide and ten rows high.

Dad, You're the Greatest.

To a Terrific Dad.

What Is a Father? That one will contain a mushy poem.
He always tried to find a neutral cover and hope it had a
distanced message inside. He had the same problem on his
dad's birthday, but he could cheat, bypass the Father section and go to the general ones: *Have a Wonderful Day.*
Father's Day was impossible. Even the cards for fathers
and children who have had their differences read, *Although
I seldom tell you of my love, you know it's there.*

The gift was the easy part. On his annual card hunt, he
would spend twenty-five minutes and—frustrated—buy one
he was lukewarm about. If it had been up to him, he would

302

have given the present without a card, but his mother would have been riled. Gifts and cards go together like salt and pepper. A gift without a card is a poor offering.

She will be especially riled this time, with no gift arriving. No card. There will be a lot of blame attached to this act.

What does he care? He hasn't been in touch with them since graduation.

He used to be ashamed of himself for picking over the cards to locate a bland one. But his father hadn't earned praise. He was not about to reward him. If he thought his son were nuts about him regardless of what he did, there'd be no incentive to change.

You're the Best Father in the World. He hasn't given a card like this since he was very young. He remembers choosing that style at age seven or eight, hoping that his father, pumped up by it, would make it come true.

He zeroes in on a cover showing cornstalks against a mountain dawn. *His father's big shoes are next to him as he hunkers in his very own little-boy garden, planting gold kernels in holes he's poked in the earth with a stick. Each time he runs out, his father places more in his palm. There is an endless supply; the man is a source of wealth. Generous, generous. Gold. And sun. They meld until he is hot with triumph and fatigue. His father carries him into the shade; they wait for a deer they have seen on other days test the salt lick down by the pond. His head is dizzy against his father's chest but gradually grows clearer with the reassuring whoosh-slosh-whoosh-slosh of the grownup heart beneath his ear. He and his father are one being, as far as he knows.*

How old was he? Two?

He feels the afternoon fever break, the coolness settle over him.

Buy the card. The man needs a few strokes.

The back of his neck begins to prickle. He walks out of the shop, walks back in, confused.

He can buy one, he doesn't have to send it. His to decide. Later.

He selects *For Father*, thumbs to the inside: *May your special day be just right from beginning to end.* Tossing it onto the counter, he digs out three quarters.

The Finest Women Writers Are Published by Pocket Books

Spitbrook Exit 1
1st L ~~st~~ after a/it
(under bridge)

2 or 3 lights (no main
intersect)
1st main intersec
R on DW Highway
~~Marshall~~
¼ mile on L.